To Sophie

Nothing to Lose

ALSO BY TANIA KINDERSLEY

Goodbye, Johnny Thunders

Don't Ask me Why

Elvis has left the Building

TANIA KINDERSLEY

Nothing to Lose

SCEPTRE

Copyright © 2002 by Tania Kindersley

First published in Great Britain in 2002
by Hodder and Stoughton
A division of Hodder Headline

The right of Tania Kindersley to be identified as the Author
of the Work has been asserted by her in accordance with
the Copyright, Designs and Patents Act 1988.

A Sceptre book

10 9 8 7 6 5 4 3 2 1

A CIP catalogue record for this title
is available from the British Library

ISBN 0 340 68588 3

Typeset in Sabon by Hewer Text Ltd, Edinburgh
Printed and bound in Great Britain by
Mackays of Chatham plc, Chatham, Kent

Hodder and Stoughton
A division of Hodder Headline
338 Euston Road
London NW1 3BH

1

When Maude Strong was twenty-five years old, she killed a child.

It sounds ugly and stark written like that: bald and grotesque. But what other way is there to say it? Ugly, and true.

Maude once read that every life has at its central core one sentence, the distillation of all the contingency and chaos and randomness that lives are made of; all the hopes and fears and years of striving and failing, the moments of glad grace and the pedestrian routine.

Maude knew her life was no good because at its core was that one ineluctable sentence.

When she was twenty-five she had driven down an unremarkable street in north London on an unremarkable afternoon, and a child ran out from between two parked cars and Maude didn't brake in time.

People say that life-changing events happen in slow motion – it's a movie conceit, a cheap dramatic device – the drowning man with his life flashing before his eyes.

It wasn't like that. It was so fast it took her breath away. She felt the air being punched out of her solar plexus as if someone had hit her there with a curled fist. Playing it back in her head afterwards, playing the reel over and over so she couldn't believe it didn't wear out from use, she remembered: street, heat, motion, a revolting and inappropriately subdued bump (there wasn't much flesh to hit, she thought afterwards, when she was torturing herself with it). It was strange: the sound came before the visuals – she seemed to *see* the child after she heard the connecting noise – then violent braking, a clichéd tyre squeal, a feeling in her stomach of flinging vertigo. Then nothing.

The street was still and unremarkable again for a moment; a trapped moment between her old life and the new one, which would always be scarred by this event, this inescapable fact, this death.

And then, in the new life, in which nothing would ever be the same, the hard fact of the mother running out to her son, her distorted face, her unearthly and somehow familiar screaming (the keening of the violently bereaved which we know from what? twenty-four-hour global news, old black and white footage, earnest films about war and death).

Maude saw the collapsed heap of clothes on the tarmac and knew, as good helpful people came out of their square houses to see what the noise was, as one solid and excited man took out his telephone to call for an ambulance, that there was no point. She watched the crowd grow as other cars stopped and a traffic jam developed and a passing policeman came to take charge, and she knew that there was no point because that small undefended head had hit the ground too hard and there was nothing left.

She remembered standing to one side of the crowd, apart from it, dislocated in those first moments from the reality of what was happening (a voice in her head saying no no no no, as if it could undo all this by sheer weight of repetition; no, it said, this isn't real, this didn't happen to you). She remembered standing in a still suspension, as if she was watching some other person, dispassionate and apart, thinking, This is what they mean (what *they?*), this is what they mean, by that fine line, that thin line, between love and hate, between order and chaos, between life and death. One moment, animate and running and full of potential, the spool of future unravelling into the horizon – adulthood, friendship, marriage, children, a fine career, who knew? a golden prince perhaps, sent to cure cancer or invent world peace – the next, nothing at all, all possibility rubbed out, a still empty body, a *corpse*, a vacant space.

It happens all the time. Every year 600,000 people die in Britain, young and old, undeserving and wicked – but to see it there in the street, so immediate and inescapable – from living to dead: *this*, Maude thought, as the crowd grew about her, this is what they mean.

Then it was as if something shattered inside her and she heard a voice, flying into the day, over the gathered and concerned heads. The voice said: It's my fault, *it's my fault*.

After a moment, she realised it was her own.

There was a court case. The police and the Crown Prosecution Service were reluctant: Maude had not drunk anything or exceeded the speed limit, her licence was clean. There was a picture of her on a CCTV camera driving at twenty-eight miles an hour a block before the accident happened. (A sedate twenty-eight miles an hour in a built-up area was all it took to kill a child: not illegal but all the same fatal.)

But for all that, the insistence of the mother's lawyers, Maude's own determined protests of culpability (it's my fault, it's *my* fault) led to a day in court. The prosecuting barrister was tired and distracted: you could see from the start that his heart wasn't in it. Maude was young, educated, clean-looking, not an unrepentant felon or a serial offender; it was a horrible and regrettable accident but what were you going to do? This kind of thing happened every day. He clearly wanted to get on to the crack dealers and the pimps, the burglars and the Rolex muggers; this pale quiet girl with her palpable guilt and weight of self-recrimination was a victim, standing there, wanting to be punished. He had seen it before, a thousand times; he knew he couldn't do anything to her that she hadn't already done to herself.

Maude's counsel was sharp and over-qualified and without finer feelings. Maude's parents were dead but she had an uncle who looked out for her, when he had the time. He knew people, his job was to know people; he was a fixer and mover, he introduced people for a living, making connections and living off the ten per cent. He knew, of course, the people to go to, the top chambers, the specialists, the pros. So she had the best defence.

Her lawyer, faced with a small and mundane and uninteresting case, made a meal of it, as if to keep himself amused. He put the mother on the stand, and by the time he had finished with her it seemed as if it was her fault, as if Maude and the car had been an irrelevance. He brought out reams of damning accusations – the mother let her child run wild, she had an unhappy marriage, her babysitting arrangements were erratic, her child was an habitual truant. By the time this fat educated barrister finished with her, it seemed as if the mother had pushed her son out into the traffic herself.

So Maude left the courthouse the winner, free, unpunished, and her lawyer congratulated her as if she really had won something, a lottery or a competition or a prize, and she wanted to spit at him. She wanted to say, I have to be punished, I killed a child, I need to be made to pay for what I did.

'What now?' she said.

Her counsel smiled his yellow smile at her and said, 'That's it, you can go, you have your life back.'

Maude thought that showed he knew absolutely nothing.

The mother walked down the steps with her head down to hide her face, swollen from crying, and Maude looked away.

The barrister said, 'Don't worry, there is insurance, there will be money.' As if that was an end to it, as if a cheque and a day in court fixed everything right and tight.

Maude wanted to say, What's the going rate, for a dead child? But she didn't. She nodded and avoided his outstretched hand, and she walked away into the afternoon, and she didn't know where she would go.

That was over ten years ago. The world had changed, slightly, seamlessly. Maude thought that ten years sounded like a long time but it went past faster than she could believe. She thought everything was the same and then she caught a glimpse of something from ten years ago, a newspaper story, a fashion spread, a television movie, and she realised that no matter how much they said that everything came round again, was reinvented, became fashionable one more time, it was all different.

Maude felt the same but knew that, possibly, she was different.

She had a job now, she had a flat, she had, in some way, a life. She had invented a life for herself. It wasn't what she had started out after. When she was working for her degree in the clever university where everyone went on to become a mistress of the universe, she didn't dream that she would end up like this, in a dark basement flat, seeing no one for days on end, inhabiting a small contained world that just had her and her guilt in it. But then perhaps our lives never turn out the way we plan them; perhaps that is why people walk the streets of big cities with that perplexed and resentful look on their faces, as if to say, Who would have thought this would happen to *me*? All the ballet dancers who ended up as civil servants, the fire-fighters who became personnel managers, the mountain climbers who manned call centres, the dress designers and opera singers and acoustic guitarists and matinée idols and downtown divas who finished up ground down by the corporate mill. That's what those looks are about: how did I come to *this*?

So Maude thought perhaps it wasn't just her. She had grown skilled at rationalising; she did it daily, to keep insanity at bay.

She had a job, a different job from the one she started in. She was a ghost-writer. Most people who do this job regard it as slightly shameful, with its uncomfortable echoes of selling out and deceit – it's something done on the side, not a proper job, bread and butter only, to pay the rent, supplementing the scant cash that comes in from *real* writing.

She had started by chance; sometimes she looked back and thought it might never have happened if her parents had not died.

She had left university with her good English degree and no direction or ambition; the world opened up in front of her like a map, a hundred roads and all of them possible. While she was making up her mind, considering various patterns, imagined futures, a friend of her father's, fired perhaps by pity and worthy outdated ideas of philanthropy, looking out for the poor orphan, offered her a job in publishing and it didn't occur to her to say no. She didn't know if it was her life dream (when would that dream arrive, she wondered, young and hopeful enough to allow it to take its time; she knew revelations had to be waited for, they wouldn't be hurried) but it would do for the time being. She needed something to pay the rent, to get her off the streets; she felt in some nebulous way that she needed to do what other people did – work, eat, go to Soho at the weekend.

She was hired as an editor's assistant, working the telephone, recording lunch appointments and publishing deadlines, intercepting temperamental authors, occasionally reading atrocious and astonishingly misspelt manuscripts from the slush pile.

During this time, she found herself dealing with a furious and demanding celebrity author – an actress of uncertain age who had had a small success with a large and luridly illustrated book of beauty tips ('rest on a *chaise-longue* for an hour each afternoon with the feet a little higher than the head').

The old diva, whose face was lifted to the seventeenth floor and who had been forty-five for the last ten years, was in negotiations about her autobiography. This involved calling her editor at least eight times a day. It became Maude's job to protect her boss from these calls –

'So sorry, Miss Lane, she's in a meeting, at lunch, left for the day, gone to the South Seas.'

Rita Lane, twitchy, lonely, fearful for her fading looks, started talking to Maude instead. By the time the deal was struck, she insisted that Maude ghost-write the thing for her. 'She understands me, unlike the rest of you philistines,' the old screen siren said. 'You never thought I would have time to write it *myself*?'

For six months, Maude sat in a dim, airless apartment in Hans Crescent, listening to the actress's fears and fantasies, surprisingly good jokes, rash outbursts of candour, and occasional unexpected slivers of universal wisdom.

Maude had no experience of writing for publication but the fierce discipline of her two essays a week lingered in her; she was still young enough to believe that anything was possible. She found that she liked Rita Lane, and she started prolonging the afternoons, searching for more stories, more characters, another glimpse into a lost age, when they did things differently (Rita seemed stranded in the modern world like a western tourist in a third-world country, baffled by a foreign language and rudimentary toilet facilities; she truly didn't understand how the end of the century *worked*).

Maude started to feel angry at the knockers and the cynics, the system that said after the age of thirty-five an actress had to start playing the mother, the arcane rules that kept them on insane diets, lifted and tucked and peroxided and painted, until the looks went. 'After forty,' said Rita, as if it were a known fact, nothing strange, a law of the universe, 'a woman no longer exists as a sexual object.'

Maude, who by now was in love with Rita, with her

dogged survivor's humour, her theatrical history, her pretend courage, ended up writing the book with all the energy and fury of a polemic. Because she didn't know what she was doing she had nothing to fear and no rules to break; she wrote it fast and furious and with a passion she didn't know she had. She wrote it in four months flat and sent it off to the publishers, who gave it over to copy-editors and proof-readers for pulling and polishing, and two weeks later Maude drove along that north London street and her life changed for ever and those afternoons with Rita Lane seemed as distant and lost to her as something from another age.

The book was a success. Right after it was published, Rita Lane made a Norma Desmond screen renaissance. An ironic post-modern film director, from the Lower East Side by way of Kansas City, who had been raised on junk TV and video games and was the new wonderkid *du jour*, put her in his breakthrough movie, because he had once seen her late night on cable when his girlfriend had broken up with him. He watched Rita playing down-at-heel and alcoholic, trailing lost dignity, which was what she did best, and she was all the lonely people, and the jilted director cried in the night as he watched her and he never forgot it. Also she was cheap and out of date, and she would do anything. She gave the campest funniest filthiest turn and she sent herself up and she was shameless; the film went to Sundance and Berlin and Telluride and won prizes and garlands and suddenly you were nobody if you were shooting a picture without Rita Lane in it.

So Rita got famous again and everyone wanted to read her book. The publisher stepped up the print run, and

Maude was on a quiet percentage and she could afford to buy herself a place of her own. She had been living in a white rented room looking over treetops north of Regent's Park. It was too high, too light, too open; after the accident, Maude knew that she had to hide. She bought the darkest basement she could find. It was cheap because no one else wanted to live there, and she thought that was appropriate. She didn't ask any questions and she closed the deal fast, because she couldn't bear much human contact; such mundane things as dealing with surveyors were beyond her, too terrifying to contemplate. When it turned out that she had dry rot eating up the skirting, she thought with bitter satisfaction that it was nothing more than she deserved.

She sat in her basement, and the cheques rolled in as the book sold in twenty-seven different countries, and she felt that it was happening to someone else, someone she had never met.

Sometimes, she wanted to give the money back. When she was so filled with recrimination and loathing that she could barely stand it, she wanted to throw the blue notes out of the window into the street. She wished instead of a bank balance with close black figures there was a pile of cash sewn into the mattress that she could pull out and fling away. The tearing sense of dislocation after the accident led her to yearn for some grand grotesque gesture; normality seemed entirely wrong and out of step; going through the motions of everyday life was jarring and obscene.

For the first time, she started to understand why people cut themselves, why young girls sit in their bedrooms and carve delicate razor lines in their smooth arms, why they have to watch themselves bleed. She couldn't put it into words, but she understood it: it was something to do with physically seeing the pain, something to do with blood-letting in the old-fashioned sense; something also to do with punishment and branding – *see what I did, see what I deserve.*

She didn't throw away the money, although after-wards she looked back and thought that during those first months after the accident she was almost unhinged, deranged enough to do anything. She took the cash and found a good shrink in north London (was there any-where else, for shrinks to live? Maude had once heard rumours of one near the Elephant and Castle, but that sounded so improbable as to be an urban myth). The concerned uncle, who called from time to time, knew a man who knew a man who had been to someone; Maude, submissive and exhausted with guilt and grief, drove north on Fridays and sat on a couch and tried to make sense of it all.

The shrink, who was surprisingly young and liked the short stories of Raymond Carver, said that Maude should forgive herself. Maude looked at her in rank incomprehension and said how exactly did she think that would be possible.

'That's what we're here for,' said the shrink, looking at her watch. 'Same time next week,' she said.

Maude went for years, like a dutiful child. She didn't seem to get much nearer to forgiving herself.

'I don't want to forgive myself,' she said, one time. 'Don't you see? That's the point. If I forgive myself then the whole thing might never have happened. It's like remembrance. It's restitution. It's right. It's an eye for an eye.'

'And then the whole world is blind,' said the shrink.

'Who do you think it will help,' she said, another week, 'if you insist on punishing yourself like this?'

'The mother,' said Maude. 'The mother of the child I killed.'

'It was an accident,' said the shrink. 'You do know that? It was an accident; it was one of those bad things that happen to good people.'

'You don't know I'm good,' said Maude. 'How do you know I'm good?'

'How do you know the mother would want you to suffer like this?' said the shrink, who had been trained to answer a question with a question.

'Because that's what they want, the mothers of dead children,' said Maude. 'I heard one talking once, a woman whose child was killed by Ian Brady on the moors, thirty years ago. Thirty years on, and she still wanted him to hurt. He demanded the right to starve himself to death and the woman came on the radio and said they must force-feed him, they must make him eat, because if he dies then he's out of it, and she wanted him to suffer. She said it like it was a crusade.'

'That's one mother,' said the shrink. 'That was a murder. It was evil and premeditated and nothing like the thing that happened to you. One woman on the radio, and you extrapolate all that.'

'But,' said Maude, 'there are some things in life, you hear them, and you know they are true. You don't need twenty people to tell them to you, you only need one.'

When, after ten years, she decided that her time was up, she apologised.

'I'm sorry,' she said. 'I must be your worst patient. I never really got better, did I?'

The shrink smiled and looked mildly enigmatic.

'You perhaps got better than you thought,' she said.

Afterwards, Maude thought that was the kind of thing that shrinks have to say when they have failed because otherwise you might ask for your money back.

It was ten years on, and punishing herself took up most of her time (not in an active way, not in pain and flagellation; it was more in the things she didn't allow herself to do, which was pretty much everything). She had written six more books with other people's names on the spine; she lived a silent life in a dark basement room.

She read novels and, curiously, books about love; she listened to records and watched films; this was most of the human contact she had. She learnt everything she knew about life from one remove, filtered through someone else's eyes. Sometimes she wondered if that meant she knew more or less than other people, who were in the world, living it. She wondered whether they were so busy making their own mistakes that they had no time to learn from them; she wondered about the gap between theory and practice. She had, mostly, too much time to think.

Later, when she looked back, she wondered whether everything would have changed anyway, whether that was the way life worked. She wondered if the catalyst was actual or imagined; whether what happened afterwards would have rolled on, without any outside agency.

But it did seem that there was a series of before-and-afters – before and after the accident, before and after Sadie.

Whatever the truth was, there were ten blank empty years; (funny how time slips away, was what Willie

Nelson sang, most nights, in Maude's dim basement, and she wondered about time, how half an hour can seem like a lifetime and then ten years have gone and it seems like nothing at all, as if you stopped paying attention for a moment and that time spiralled away, and you didn't know where it had gone); and then there was Sadie, and everything was different.

2

It was the end of the summer. The weather was heavy with dust and heat, as if the city was worn out from the pressure of air and expectation; it was ready now for autumn, for cold winds and sweeping rain to wash away the grime. The street where Maude lived was more grimy than most: the Talgarth Road, that wide curving highway that cuts into London from the west. There was little to redeem the Talgarth Road; its sides were flanked with high anonymous office buildings, seventies monstrosities and ambitious nineties white elephants, advertising hoardings and petrol stations and gaping wastelands giving on to fading Edwardian terraces, filthy with years of car exhaust and neglect.

Then, unexpected as a shooting star, just beyond the Hammersmith flyover, there was a short stretch of beauty: seven studios in leaning dark red brick, with high arched windows. They were used as houses now, divided into flats, and it was here that Maude had her basement. Baron's Court station was round the corner; she was sandwiched between the road and the railway; dust and rattle came in all day long, had done for so long that she didn't notice the noise any more. It suited her because the road was too wide and anonymous for there to be any neighbourhood spirit, there were no invitations at Christmas or moments of casual conversation in the street. The houses were marooned, as if on an island, cut off at high tide.

The body of the house, a ground floor with its double-height studio above, was shared by three or four people, Maude was never quite sure. She had seen them from a distance, one man and two or three women; sometimes at night she heard them walking on their wooden floor, she heard them laughing and talking. Once she heard fighting: shouting and crying and the sound of objects being thrown, a crash of breaking china, slamming doors and running footsteps. She wasn't sure how it worked, who was friends with whom, who was sleeping with whom. She wondered sometimes if it was a *ménage*. Maude might have cut herself out of the world, as a child cuts a figure out of a piece of paper, leaving only a space behind, but it didn't mean that she didn't know things. She was, in a paradoxical way, quite worldly; she read too much not to be.

She avoided her upstairs neighbours as successfully as she avoided everyone else in that short stranded stretch of street; she listened and watched, she managed to leave her flat when no one else was around. If, occasionally, she ran into someone on the pavement, she looked distracted and walked quickly past. It wasn't strange enough to be remarkable. London wasn't a neighbourly city, not much, not any more.

People watched soaps on the television and thought that they were missing something, not living in a square where everyone knew everyone and met in the pub and helped each other out when times were hard; but this was some kind of pre-war dream, when there were neighbourhoods, tight urban enclaves, and everyone left their doors open and the kids played in the street and when the wives wanted to see their lovers they left a packet of Omo in the window, which meant Old Man Out. Or perhaps that was a dream too, and people had always kept to themselves in cities, packed too close together, afraid that if they gave an inch they would lose a mile, furiously protecting their small patch from invasion. It's only in the country, where there are acres and acres for everyone, that people get frightened by the wild space and uncontained scenery and huddle together in villages and gossip and commune and know each other's business, so they can feel safe.

That day in early September, with the city hot and airless from a late blooming summer (it rained all through May and most of June, Wimbledon was a washout, the taxi drivers could talk about nothing else), Maude went for a meeting with her editor. Her editor was an easy woman in her mid-thirties, the same age as Maude, a million miles apart in every other way. Her name was Joan Bellow, and she was good at her job and contented in her home life; she was married with two children and she complained genially about the pressures of work and family and how her husband thought he did all the housework when in fact he acted as if he deserved the Nobel prize every time he took the rubbish out. This kind laughing woman, with her mild ambition and her distracted maternal nature, was like an alien to Maude. She seemed so comfortable in the world; she seemed to know all the expected responses.

She was also incurious, which was a great advantage in their working relationship. She never asked any awkward questions. She liked Maude because she delivered on time and she was reliable like a Swiss watch, but she didn't look at Maude's shut face and tight forehead and shadowed eyes and imagine what all that was about; she didn't wonder about the exaggerated pallor and the flat black eyes and the way that Maude walked quickly and defensively, with her head down and a frown on her face as if to deny anyone who might attempt to talk to her. Perhaps it was like the neighbour defence; perhaps there were too many people and too much to worry about and too much to ponder. Someone once said that no one would be paranoid about what was said about them if they realised how little time people spent thinking about other people. Everyone is interested in themselves, and their immediate dependants, and after that, it's every man for himself.

Maude had read this somewhere and didn't believe it. She thought people thought about other people all the time because they were far too frightened to think about themselves. She had read the books, she followed, at a discreet distance, the prevailing winds; she knew all about denial, which was what everyone was in, just now. But she also thought that some people were more curious by nature than others: Joan clearly had no searching need to know about other people's lives, and Maude was glad of that, because she couldn't have explained any of it to anyone, if they had bothered to ask. She barely understood it herself. She knew that she had to stay apart, and she had her bitter scarring secret, and she would never amount to anything, and that was all.

This time, this lunch, this meeting, Joan wanted her to start a new project: an explorer, famous for tramping over Antarctic wastes and coming home with half his hand off from frostbite and a salty old sea-dog beard and blue eyes shining out of his pickled face with blinding intensity.

Joan said it was a sure money-spinner because everyone was obsessed with Shackleton all over again and it wouldn't take more than six months.

Maude, surprising herself, said no. 'I have something else, just now,' she said. 'There is something else I have to do.'

Joan ate her green salad and didn't ask what it was. 'Ring me up,' she said, 'if you change your mind.'

Maude went home on the underground, looking at the unhappy displaced rocking people who rode the tube trains in the middle of the day. She got out at Baron's Court and walked the twenty yards to her flat, and as she went down the steps and put the key in the lock, she heard a voice behind her say, 'Oh, thank goodness. Can I come in with you?'

She turned round and found an unknown woman standing in front of her, and the strange thing was that for a moment, just a fleeting subconscious moment, Maude thought she was looking at herself.

It was only for a moment. Maude had a long diamond-shaped face, with black hair that stopped at her ears and a straight nose and clouded grey eyes that sometimes looked black, set deep in the sockets, with heavy lids that gave her a melancholy cast. It was an uncompromising face, with the thick white skin that sometimes goes with dark hair. Anglo-Saxon skin can be pocked and discoloured, dappled with living and weather; it can age fast, collapsing under junk food and fag smoke, veins rising and pores opening like flowers in springtime. Maude had dense flat skin, without a mark on it. Sometimes she hated that, as if she wanted a sign, a stigmata; this pure surface hid the truth. But the reality was more prosaic: she didn't drink, she didn't smoke, she didn't go out; there were no expressions to line her face, no reminders of days in the sun and afternoons of wine and laughter. Her face was a straight blank thing because she had spent the last ten years underground, blaming herself and not speaking.

The woman opposite her had been out in the world, she could see that at second look. It was only in that first fleeting moment that Maude thought there was a resemblance. In the distance, in a crowd, you might think they were the same, but close up there was nothing the same at all. This woman had marks on her face from living and laughing, lines around her mouth from smiling, thin traces fanning out from her eyes from happiness or squinting into the sun. Her eyes were more green than grey and she had thick dark hair cut into points that fell against her face and there was a slight flush in her cheeks, Maude couldn't tell whether it was animation or Max Factor.

'Can I come in?' said the woman, as if that was what was meant to happen.

Maude was so surprised, the door half open, that she just walked in, and the strange woman followed.

'Nice,' said the woman, looking around. 'My name is Sadie,' she said. 'I'm visiting upstairs and they're not there and the battery's gone on my mobile and I'm bored of sitting on the step. So when I saw you I thought I could come in and have a cup of tea or something. Is that very forward?'

Maude said, for some reason, 'I don't have a mobile telephone.'

Sadie shook her head and smiled and said, 'Oh well, you see, there we are already, sisters under the skin.'

Maude hadn't met very many people in her life; a few students at university, a few publishing people, some of her parents' colleagues, members of the legal profession when she was in court, her scant ghost writees, her editor, and Mr Seth, the irredeemably pessimistic owner of her corner store. She had never, ever, met anyone who took her aback like this woman Sadie did. She felt entirely unmanned, as if all her defences were crumbling. She was so used to her flat white face and her reticence keeping people at a distance; it didn't take much to discourage people, everyone was sensitive to rejection, to saying the wrong thing, to crossing invisible lines. But Sadie didn't seem to have any of that. She blew into Maude's dim basement room like a hot foreign wind, and asked for tea, and there was nothing Maude could do about it.

'Nice,' Sadie said again. She stretched her neck and blinked slowly, as if getting used to the pale light. 'It's not like other places. It's like a swimming bath from the turn of the century; it's like something out of the world.'

The door opened into a wide hallway, paved in black and white tiles, and it was true there was something Edwardian about them, something outdated. They had been there when Maude moved in and she saw no reason to change them. The walls were white and there was a thick deco cornice at the top, which had been painted green many years before Maude had arrived. The paint was flaking a little, and when the sun came in through the glass in the front door the green lit up and started to glow. The light played on the ceiling in mysterious patterns, as if it was trying to tell them something.

'So,' said Sadie, as if questioning herself for the first time. 'Can I really come in?'

They stood in the tiled hall, looking at each other, looking for clues. Maude felt as if something had come along that was stronger than she; it was as if something fundamental had shifted and she wasn't sure what it was.

She shook her head. She was feeling this way because she had turned down a project and it wasn't what she planned and it was going out on a limb when really she belonged in her hidden room, writing other people's words, and there had been a long journey back on the underground and now there was a strange woman in her hall and she wanted to be left alone and she didn't know how to ask.

'I can go back to the step,' said Sadie, as if she saw some of this running through Maude's mind like tick-ertape. 'I can, you know. I don't want to intrude.'

'The kitchen is this way,' said Maude, surprising herself again, but in a removed second-hand way: as if she felt she should be surprised, but wasn't.

'There's tea,' she said. 'Or coffee. I have beans. I have a machine that grinds.'

Sadie laughed for no reason and said, 'Coffee, then. Let's go wild and have caffeine in the afternoon. That's like doing drugs, these days.'

'Why?' said Maude, who never asked questions.

'Because you have to have camomile tea and cleanse your liver and get decent sleep and not play fast and loose with your lymphatic system,' said Sadie. 'You know the drill. You can't be wild any more because then you look like hell when you're forty and no one wants to go to bed with you any more.'

'All that,' said Maude, 'from one cup of coffee.'

The kitchen was square and formal: laminated units that looked like a poster for the fifties (keep your home sparkling with *DAZZLE!*), the same black and white tiles from the hall. There was a scratched Formica table and a fat green fridge and a silver toaster and a gas cooker and nothing out of place. It was as tidy as if someone didn't really live there.

Sadie looked at it and laughed. 'I wish someone would come and make my place look like this,' she said.

Maude took out the coffee beans and ground them up and put the dense powder into a heavy steel pot that went on the stove. She wondered why she was making coffee for a strange woman at three in the afternoon. Sadie sat at the table and watched her, a friendly and engaged expression on her face. She wasn't to know that in the ten years Maude had lived here she had never had another person in the flat.

The sun came in from the kitchen window. There was a door that led out into a small dark green garden, trees and shrubs and bushes jostling together in not enough space; there were some ageing stone slabs instead of grass and a bench to sit on.

'We could go in the garden,' said Sadie. 'Then I can look up at the windows and shout when they come in.'

'You'll hear them,' said Maude, surprising herself one more time. 'You can hear the footsteps.'

She poured out the coffee and it smelt strong and unfamiliar, a small sudden intimation of the exotic; for some reason she found it exciting. She felt as if she had been let off classes a day early.

Sadie took her coffee and drank it and said, 'That's good.'

She smiled up at Maude with her open, questioning face. 'Can I look around?' she said. 'I love other people's houses. You know that thing when you secretly think that everyone is like you, because you forget that everyone is different. And then you get little glimpses into other people's lives and you realise how different they truly are and it gives you a shock every time?'

Maude didn't know. She hadn't seen the inside of someone else's house for years. But then she thought again, and she realised that something in that sentiment hit a chord in her, something remembered. It was the feeling she got when she walked through the streets around her flat, on her way home from somewhere, or just out for a walk, because you can't sit your whole life in a dark basement room even if you are wearing a hair shirt for the duration. There was something about a certain time of day, when the dusk was falling and the street lamps were coming on and people hadn't closed their curtains yet; the neat squares of light and warmth bloomed out into the street and you got flashes, snapshots, of people's lives – someone reading or watching television or cooking or practising scales, a cat asleep or a child crying, small potent domestic moments. Maude did think those people were different from her, but then she thought (*knew*) that everyone was different from her. She couldn't imagine ever thinking that anyone might be the same. She was different and other and must keep herself separate, in case she contaminated anyone.

'This is the sitting room,' said Sadie, from the next

room. She had just got up and walked into it, without being asked. 'You have a lot of books,' she said.

Maude walked in behind her. The room was dark, as it always was, a diffused half-light coming in between the slats of the Venetian blinds. It reminded her of a film like *Chinatown*, where everything is murky and mysterious and nothing is as it seems and everyone is playing a part and there are more twists than in a rattlesnake's tail.

'I have a lot of books,' she said. 'I read a lot.'

'Yes, you do,' said Sadie. She walked along the bookshelves which covered the whole of the far wall, floor to ceiling; she bent her head to one side as she walked so she could read the titles.

Then she stopped, as if she had run into an invisible barrier.

'Alexander Dent,' she said. 'You have a whole shelf of him.'

She looked at Maude as if this was some kind of subversion.

'I like him best,' said Maude, because that was the truth. She thought that Alexander Dent wrote about loneliness and alienation and despair better than anyone else; when she read his books she felt that she wasn't the only one.

The part she couldn't tell Sadie was that there was some sinister symmetry in their lives, because Alexander Dent was not just famous for being one of the great literary voices of the last fifty years, but for the fact that he had killed his wife.

He was backing out of a driveway and she walked behind the car and it was on a slope and he pushed her with the bumper, not seeing her. She fell and knocked her head on the concrete and that was it, because the human head is not protected much and all it takes is one hit in the right place.

Maude sometimes thought human beings died more easily than they did anything else.

It was like Sylvia Plath all over again, except that Claudette Dent wasn't a poet. She was a siren, and she dripped sex and beauty and neurosis over everything, she blinded people with it. She had slavish followers and people lining up to paint her and take her photograph and claim her for their muse. She was mercurial like a high wind and she had no moral compass; she would do anything and say anything, without limits. People said they were a perfect couple, because Alexander Dent was measured and quiet and thoughtful, and Claudette was wild like a bronco out on a desert plain. Mostly she threw sand in people's eyes because beauty does that; beauty doesn't have to do anything else except be. It's so rare, the real kind. There are many kinds of attractiveness, prettiness, handsomeness; there are fine eyes, and expressive mouths, and sexy little noses, but real beauty, the true kind that chimes instantly like a tuning fork the moment you see it, that's rare as hen's teeth, and it stops people short and all bets are off.

Claudette Dent's beauty was so blatant and outrageous, it was hard to see past that: sometimes people would come away from a half-hour conversation with her and not have a single memory of any word she had spoken; they were standing dazzled by the light.

So maybe she got wild because she was sick of people standing and staring like she was some kind of public monument or freak of nature, and maybe that was just the way she was, and maybe her desire for other men came from need or foolhardiness or defiance, but it seemed all of a piece, and when she died so young, so needlessly, so grotesquely, with that exquisite head hitting the mundane concrete slope, people were shocked and saddened but no one was surprised.

The thing that linked all this to Maude, that started her searching fascination with Alexander Dent, was that he ran over his wife on the exact same day that she hit the child with her car in the further reaches of north London. So that was it, for her; they were joined in some indissoluble bond, and she read all his books and his essays and the scant interviews he gave, she read the memoirs about him and Claudette, the conspiracy-theorist monographs about how he thwarted his wife's talent and drove her to throw herself under his car, the magazine articles running old blurred fake-happy photographs from the late sixties, when everyone was happy because it was the law. She knew every single thing ever written about him, but now Sadie, this strange woman who had invited herself in and stayed for coffee and looked around without permission, was asking questions and Maude couldn't tell her any of that.

'I like his books,' she said, 'because they make me feel . . .' She was going to say: they make me feel as if I'm less alone, but then she didn't. She stopped and cleared her throat and started again.

'They make me feel,' she said, 'as if there is some hope, for things.'

Sadie looked startled and stared hard at the shelf of books and frowned as if there was something she wanted to say. Then she brought her head up and smiled a lightening smile and said, 'As opposed to no fucking hope at all, which is how it does feel most days.'

She put her head back and laughed as if she had said something funny, and Maude wondered, looking at her, how someone so alive and vivid could know anything about there being no fucking hope.

3

Sadie became Maude's friend. Maude didn't want a friend; that wasn't in the script. She sometimes looked back on her life, the life she had before the accident, and tried to remember what friendship was like. She wondered if she had ever known.

She had been a silent child: there was only her, no brothers or sisters to tease or laugh or fight with, and her parents, who were academics, were always talking, and had no time for children. Children, to them, were potentially interesting, a promise of an adult that might be of use, might have a good mind, a sharp incisive brain, which was how they judged people. Her mother was a serious, certain woman, unsuited to motherhood or domestic activity. She got help with Maude, and the child was kept out of the way, brought out occasionally to wander among the grown-ups, who were too preoccupied with talk to pay much attention to her, occasionally patting her on the head and asking her what she wanted to be when she grew up. She never knew the answer to that question.

Maude was a silent child because no one ever asked what she was thinking and it didn't occur to her to say it without invitation. At school, there were girls she played with and swapped stickers with and ran skipping games with. At school, in her uniform, with her hair done in pigtails, which was the craze just then, she didn't look

like a misfit, something unwanted and uninteresting: she
looked like everyone else. But even then she kept something of herself back because she didn't want anyone to
find out that she had these inexplicable creatures for
parents. She didn't want them to find out that her parents
didn't do a normal job, that they read and wrote
and argued all day long and meals were never on time
and they did unsettling things like eat soup for breakfast
and leave cigarettes smouldering in a dozen ashtrays all
over the house and wear the same clothes three days in a
row because there wasn't anything else that was laundered.

Maude, like most children who don't have it, longed
for order, hankered for the ordinary. So she had people
she knew, but she never had a friend. A real friend might
ask questions, and Maude didn't think she had any of the
answers. At university, even after her parents were dead,
killed instantly when their aeroplane crashed straight
into a mountain in India in perfectly fine weather, and
she had learnt enough of the world to see that no one had
normal parents, that the ones who pretended to be
normal turned out to be the most twisted of all, skeletons
trooping out of their closets like children on their way to
a Christmas party, the habit persisted, of putting herself
to one side.

'I don't have a talent for intimacy,' she said, to the first
boy she ever slept with.

She wanted to offer him something at such a momentous moment (not that it felt entirely momentous, they
had trouble with the condom, it got rucked up and hurt
inside her, and she was tense as a pole and shut her eyes
tight and thought that everyone said it was painful the
first time and she should at least pretend to have a good
time, for his sake). She didn't know what there was to

offer, so she told him this secret, and he laughed a low rolling laugh from his belly and said, 'You don't have to be a Ph.D. in pure maths to see that.'

He seemed to realise that it might have sounded a little harsh, considering they had just been having sex and there was still a smell of rubber and salt in the room so he looked at her and smiled and said, 'But you have great tits.'

Then there was the accident and she put herself away from the world, and there were no friends, there was no one.

So when Sadie started coming by, dropping in, Maude didn't know what to do. She felt a baffling mix of emotions: exhilaration, resentment, terror, some kind of disconcerted anxiety – this wasn't right, this wasn't what was supposed to happen.

She had put herself in a box and although it was lonely and painful, that was the point. But also it was known, it was in her control: there were no intrusions, nothing unexpected or unimagined. There was a bitter satisfaction to this; she understood, from the films she watched and the books she read, that other people lived life like unsteady surfers, riding the high rollers, while she knew what each day would bring her. She knew also that this was a waste, she could see that this was how people became stuck and atrophied and frittered away all their promise and all their hope; but that also was the *point*. She couldn't allow herself to go out and live in the world because she should be in a jail cell right now, looking at the little square of blue that prisoners call the sky, and knowing that it was what she deserved.

And then, after all these years of knowing the drill,

something started to shift. She refused a commission because there was something else she wanted to do; on the same day Sadie turned up, and now she wouldn't go away.

For some reason she wouldn't examine too closely, Maude found she couldn't turn round and say, Leave me alone, I don't want you. But then, she thought, as she lay in bed at night, not sleeping, because she didn't sleep much, she could easily have said that. Sadie would have been hurt and puzzled, or perhaps sarcastic or just – what? – not that interested anyway. And she would have gone away and that would have been an end to it.

Maude wondered why she didn't say it. It was as if there were two people in her, talking all the time. She wondered if it was true that when you started hearing voices you really were losing your reason (she loved that word *reason*: for sense, for sanity, for the opposite of madness). She heard voices like a radio tuned in to three stations at once, broken up by static and bad reception. She wondered if this was the same for everyone, if other people walked the streets with radios in their heads, never daring to admit it for fear someone would misunderstand and come and take them away, to the nuthouse, which wasn't called that any more, because it wasn't politically correct, even though nuts was still what they were, the people who went there.

One voice was saying: Tell her to go, you know that's what you must do.

It wasn't only that she didn't allow herself intimates because that might be too much like pleasure or relief or normal living: it was that intimacy would mean sharing secrets, telling tales, because that's what intimates did, that's what *girls* did, and Maude knew with one look at

Sadie that she was a girl at heart. (Girl to Maude had nothing to do with pejorative pigtails and gymslips reduction: it meant opposite of male; it meant talking and secrets and whispers late at night and frivolity and laughing at nothing much and understanding things without having to be told.)

She knew that Sadie would ask questions, unlike Joan Bellow, who wasn't a girl at all, for all her heels and skirts and two children – proof of femininity, proof of a fully functioning womb; all those women in the streets wearing their children like a badge – *Look* what I made. Joan Bellow wasn't curious and she didn't ask questions because that wasn't her thing. But Sadie was bursting with it, curiosity running alongside her like a faithful dog.

The other voice, the second voice, more muted than the first, was saying, Yes, yes, *please*, be known, let your secrets spill into the street, ten years is long enough, it's long enough to hold everything so tight and hard against you, so that you think you will break with it.

Just lately, the second voice had been saying: Enough. Just lately, the second voice, which hadn't ever got much of a hearing, had been growing strident. Enough is enough, it said; it's stupid, it's futile, this punishing, this hiding, it doesn't bring back the dead. This guilt, this regret, there's no point to it, it's self-indulgent, soft, the easy way out. Get out in the world and do something, make some small thing better, add some tiny iota to the sum of human happiness, instead of sitting in your lonely room castigating yourself for something that is irreparable and cannot be undone. The second voice said: Get the hell out and use the time you're given because you only get it once and you're a long time dead.

And then Sadie appeared, like a sign, a portent, and the second voice, full of its moment in the sun, said See, *see*? and that was why Maude couldn't turn round and tell her to go away.

September got hotter. Maude sat in her room and thought about her project, the secret project that had been burning in her for months and for which she had turned down a commission with money guaranteed. She felt as if things were slipping away from her. She felt displaced and dislocated and she wished that someone would come along and tell her what to do.

There was a knocking at the door. Maude knew it was Sadie. There was a perfectly good doorbell, but Sadie always knocked, rapping at the glass with her hand, impatient to be in.

'You're here,' said Sadie, as if it were a surprise, as if it were an achievement, something to be celebrated.

She was wearing purple sunglasses and she had put green streaks in her hair; she looked like something out of a film about people without day jobs in downtown Manhattan. She made documentaries about uncomfortable subjects and had to fight to get even the BBC to take them and she had that look of people who don't work regular hours, something a little loose and undressed about them, as if they have more important things to think about than power suiting.

'I brought coffee,' said Sadie. She held out two polystyrene cups. 'I brought it all the way from Soho.'

Sadie had a tic about the best: the best coffee, the best American novel, the best place to eat fish, the best train journey. She said the best coffee was made at a hole in the wall near Old Compton Street, and she bought it there and then took it half-way across the city and sat down and drank it and closed her eyes in pleasure, because it was the best coffee in London. Maude wondered how she could tell.

They drank the coffee and Sadie looked pleased and lit up a cigarette. 'I know,' she said, 'I am giving up, but I'm having problems with my relationship.'

Sadie was always having problems with her relationship, but it didn't seem to bother her that much. 'Serves me right for falling for the world's most commitment-phobic man,' she said, as if she had learnt it by rote.

Maude sometimes wondered what she was in it for, but she didn't ask. She knew about love from books only: seeing it before her, she realised that the gap between life and print was sometimes too wide to bridge.

Sadie sat smiling in Maude's kitchen and talked about love as if it were a person she knew from way back. 'Sometimes,' she said, 'I want to kill him with my own hands because he makes me so angry and I don't know where to put it, it's like a sickness or a fever. I feel it raging in me and I have to leave the room, and most of the time he doesn't even notice. He thinks I've left the stove on, or something.

'Other times,' she said, 'I want to kiss him all over his face and still that isn't enough; I want to kiss him until he wears out and I feel childish and sunk in love and I don't care, even though there is something in the back of my head that says, This isn't seemly, you should know better than this.'

Maude wanted to ask questions but she didn't know how. Revelation frightened her. Sadie didn't seem to mind that it was one-sided. She sat in Maude's kitchen smiling and laughing at her own jokes and drinking the best coffee in London and talking about love, and Maude thought she had never seen anyone who was on such close and easy terms with pleasure.

'You should meet my friends upstairs,' Sadie said, another afternoon. There was no coffee that day because she was coming in from the west; she had been meeting with some adopted children in Swindon for a programme she wanted to make. She was wan and transparent with tiredness. Maude was surprised: she had never seen Sadie anything except vivid and animate. She was reminded of the part in *Peter Pan* when Tinkerbell is dying, her light fading and fading, and Peter turns to the children in the audience and asks them to clap their hands if they believe in fairies.

She wanted to say to Sadie: I believe.

She made some tea, instead. Tea was supposed to be a great restorative, everyone knew that.

'I don't know,' said Maude.

'They are normal people,' said Sadie, 'just like me. They don't do anything alarming.'

She smiled and her smile was bare and thin today and it shocked Maude a little. She realised that she had started to invest something in Sadie, in these visits; her mind veered away, not liking it, the first voice shouting instructions in her head like a drill sergeant.

'I'm sure they are very nice,' said Maude. 'I don't go out much, that's all.'

'I know,' said Sadie. 'You keep yourself to yourself and you are a nice quiet young woman, and when they come and dig up the twenty bodies in paper bags under the patio everyone will be highly surprised.'

Maude smiled against her will. Then she stopped

trying not to smile and told the first voice to shut up and sod off and she laughed, because there was something funny about the blood-drenched paper parcels, and even if it was black gallows humour, that was the kind she felt most at home in.

'You are a sceptic,' said Sadie, putting her head on one side, considering. 'Or a cynic. Or a misanthrope. Perhaps all three. Everyone is supposed to be loving and giving these days, everyone is out there, rowing away, desperately trading on their charm. And you don't give a damn. I like that in a woman.'

'I don't see what's likeable about it,' said Maude. She put her elbows on the table and looked at Sadie, at her tired face and her muddled hair and her thick black spectacles that looked like the ones Michael Caine wore in the sixties.

'That's the point,' said Sadie. 'In my business, everyone wants to be loved; everyone is out there, networking like crazy, talking horseshit until their throats are sore from it, trying to make everyone love them, and you, you don't care. In fact, you don't want to be liked at all.'

There was a pause, and she smiled in it. She drank her tea, and made an appreciative noise, a quiet sigh of recognition, the way people did when they had a nice cup of tea, and then she looked at Maude and frowned, and said, 'Why is that?'

'Come once,' she said, the next day. 'Just for lunch. They're only neighbours, they don't have strange growths or anti-social habits. You'd like it.'

How did Sadie know, Maude wondered, what she would like? She had read an article once that rubbished the seductive late-twentieth-century idea of empathy, the notion that you could feel someone else's emotions as you could feel your own; this was all so much rabid liberal nonsense, said the article (Maude looked back at the name, a man called Roland Hand, clearly aching for the return of Victorian values). No one, said Roland, with dyspeptic authority, can ever know what anyone else thinks or feels, it's not the way the brain works.

Maude, who listened to a lot of music in the long nights when she didn't sleep, had heard Nanci Griffith sing about the same thing. Nanci Griffith had a small poignant face and eyes like pools and a sweet singing voice and a fat acoustic guitar; she played with an ensemble called the Blue Moon Orchestra, and every year she came to the Albert Hall and sang songs about people from Texas who worked in five-and-dime stores. Nobody, she sang once, ever knows the heart of anyone else.

Maude wondered if this was true.

'I know you never go out,' said Sadie, who was eating a biscuit. 'And there's nothing worse than people telling people what to do. But you should all the same, it would be fun.'

In the end, out of excuses, Maude said yes. Sadie seemed pleased.

'Sunday lunch,' she said. 'That's what we'll do.'

That Sunday the heatwave was still shimmering over the city. Maude's basement stayed cool throughout the hottest summers, because of the tiles and the dim light; sometimes she went out wearing a coat and got a shock when a blast of eighty-degree heat hit her like a wall.

That hot Sunday, she got up early as usual and put on a pair of jeans and a T-shirt that said JUST SAY NO on the front (she had bought it in aid of some charity, some drug-rehab or lung cancer thing, she couldn't remember; she gave indiscriminately to charities, out of penance; sometimes she came home with seven copies of the *Big Issue* tucked into her bag) and went to get the papers. The newsagent was round the corner, two blocks away, in a short parade of shops – a greengrocer, a florist, a launderette, a sandwich bar and, incongruously, in this unfashionable backwater of west London, a small bookshop, with enticing piles of Penguin Modern Classics in the window, as if nothing worth reading had been published since Scott Fitzgerald's poor abused heart gave out on a warm Hollywood morning among the palm trees and the Hispano-Suizas and the flint eyes of ambition.

Maude always wondered how the bookshop survived. She had been shopping there for ten years, but she was barely on nodding terms with the woman who ran it. The bookshop woman was in her sixties, maybe older, very straight and proper, astonishingly clean; she was entirely correct and punctilious and never exchanged more than a word of greeting, never remarked on the weather or the pleasures of reading; she said hello and good morning and please and thank you, rang up the total on her old-fashioned till that chimed like a bell when the cash drawer came out, took the money and offered a receipt and said goodbye.

Maude could have understood this place surviving if it was run by a great character, one of those London legends, fondly remembered by generation after generation, but the bookshop woman wasn't like that. She wasn't a lush or a nymphomaniac, she wasn't a crackerbarrel philosopher or an agony aunt; you would never come in and tell her your problems, how your husband was sticking it to his secretary and your children never came home any more and the dog died and the cat ate the goldfish and sometimes you felt that the whole world was a spinning vortex pulling you down with it.

Maude kept shopping there stubbornly, even though she knew she would get more smiles and welcome in one of the fat shiny chains, because it was something that was dying, and also, in the reticence and silence of the gaunt bookshop woman, she recognised something of herself. She wondered if that was how she would end up, thin and white and silent, barely able to manage even the most rudimentary social conventions. She wondered if that was what happened, in the end, if you didn't get out much.

Next door was the newsagent – or, at least, a shop that sold newspapers and magazines. It also sold many other wonderful and entirely unrelated objects: tins of chick peas rubbing shoulders with pots of Tiger balm, boxes of basmati rice up against squat brown bottles of citronella oil for keeping the flies off in summer.

Maude had seen this shop every day for ten years; she walked in like clockwork, each morning; it was part of her regime, the thin black and white life that she allowed herself. Sometimes she wondered why she hadn't let herself go, the way that wounded people sometimes did, why she didn't just sit on a stained floor in unwashed clothes surrounded by empty pizza cartons and smeared bottles of rancid milk. This was the picture she had seen, in the films she watched; she knew that was what people did when they gave up hope, when their lives were worth nothing any more. In these films, about the smashed-up people, the men stopped shaving and the women let their hair get stringy and filthy, beds were left unmade and the sink was jammed with dirty plates and unopened letters piled up against the door, so that it was wedged shut with the weight of neglected mail. Maude had seen that, she knew that was the movie version of degradation. But she also knew, somehow, that this was how people got saved; someone noticed in the end, and came along and cleaned up the mess, and then there was redemption and the promise of a happy ending.

The punishment she had devised for herself was more subtle and twisted than that: she couldn't just take to the bottle and block the world out, she had to remember, every day, what she had done. So she stayed sharp and present, she forced herself to work, to keep clean, to eat, even though the food she chose was the barest sustenance, bony sardines on dry toast mostly, so unadorned that sometimes she choked as she tried to get it down. She punished herself by giving herself glimpses of the ordinary world in which people lived their lives, and pulling herself away from it. She didn't know why she had chosen to do it that way, but it seemed right to her, to have some correctness to it, so she lived in her monochrome universe, knowing that there was no way out.

But since Sadie had arrived it was as if someone had turned on a light, switched the black and white into singing colour, and it was that, perhaps, that was frightening Maude. She saw it, this shimmering Sunday, as she looked round the newsagent and saw properly, for the first time, the blaze of colour in the shop, all the things she had never noticed before. It was like a treasure trove, some chaotic Aladdin's cave. There seemed to be no theme or plan, no common thread running through the assortment of items offered for sale, or their arrangement. Here you could buy Mexican prayer candles and Spanish rosary beads carved out of black wood, shining like ebony; there, you could find Moroccan slippers and red lacquered Chinese boxes and thin glass perfume jars with twisted stoppers that came all the way from Cairo. And on the same shelf, you could get washing powder and black dustbin bags and Brasso and beeswax (was there anyone left in London who actually used beeswax? When there was Mr Sheen in his easy-to-use spray tin?) and red and blue boxes of Brillo pads and yellow Marigold gloves and mop heads and dusters and every kind of useful household object.

You could find plugs and fuses and ten different kinds of battery, and turn round and pick up a bag of Guatemalan worry people or a box of sandalwood incense or a packet of saffron strands, picked out of the crocuses that grew in the high plains of La Mancha.

Maude never bought more than a newspaper and sometimes a bottle of water or a bag of bitter coffee (fair traded, all the way from the Dominican Republic) but for the first time, on this hot morning, she realised that she liked knowing that all the other things were there, waiting for her, or for someone else more deserving, all those disassociated objects, chosen for what? – happy memories, or future hopes, or whim, or chance. Did the Tiger balm salesman come round, she wondered, on a sunny day, when Mr Seth was in a buying mood and what the hell?

Mr Seth, who presided over this curious assembly, was as unexpected as his shop. He had been born in Amritsar, where the golden temple was (Maude only knew about it because of the massacre there years before, and Mr Seth agreed mournfully that that was what people did remember and why shouldn't they?). He had been educated in Scotland and Paris – 'Scotland is a wonderful country,' he said, 'but a very mysterious people.' He claimed to understand the Parisians better: 'Still furious about the occupation,' he said. 'They don't know which way to look, collaborators or Gaullists, either way they have the shame of being wrong or being defeated; imagine the humiliation of having to be helped out by their old enemies. They don't forget Agincourt, you know,' he said, looking accusingly at Maude as if she had suggested they had.

Mr Seth had pale brown eyes set into a sculpted face, high cheekbones and uncompromising eyebrows and a nose with a hook in it, and a perfect Cupid's bow mouth that pulled down at the corners as he considered the ills of the world. He had read a great deal of Schopenhauer when he was younger and it had stayed with him. 'I forget nothing,' he said, frowning with his iron grey eyebrows; they came low over his eyes and gave him a sinister forbidding look.

Maude knew that Mr Seth had, like all the best patrician characters, a heart soft as butter underneath all the gloom and despond; she had seen him on Sunday mornings giving out food and cigarettes and yesterday's papers to the three neighbourhood bums. Every week he told them that this was one time only, that they should get a job, in this land of opportunity, this first-world place of milk and honey. He told them that they were slackers and idlers and he had no sympathy with them, that they only had themselves to blame and this was never happening again, but every Sunday morning he handed them a fiver and a little parcel of goods, and he scolded them like naughty children, and they blinked and laughed at him out of grimy desperate faces and promised that they would give up the drink and get on the straight and narrow, and they never did.

'With some people,' he had once said to Maude, when she walked into the shop and heard him talking to one of the dossers, who was called Gerald and had a hopeless methadone habit, 'it's not a question of choice: something gets broken, and then there's no going back. Some people go too far and it's too late and you can only watch.'

Mr Seth voted Green out of fury at all political parties and said that zero tolerance was the work of the devil.

This Sunday morning, the sun was shining brightly, like it had every day that week, every day since anyone could remember. Heat like this had a curious effect on the British, it was so rare (although there were those who still talked of the blinding summer of '76) that it brought out a kind of magical thinking, as if the national psyche was suspended for a moment; the phlegmatic mustn't-grumble ironic detachment fell away, leaving something naked and childish; people smiled at each other in the streets and men in suits laughed gently to themselves on the buses for no reason.

It was hot: everyone was drunk with it, believing in it, accustomed to it, thinking that it would never end.

Mr Seth hated the heat. He had come three thousand miles to get away from heat and dust and he took each unseasonal day as if it were personally aimed at him.

Maude bought two newspapers and a bottle of water.

'Global warming, Missy,' said Mr Seth.

Maude had never told him her name. He had never asked. She knew that he was called Mr Seth, and that was what she called him. He called her Missy. In anyone else it might have sounded patronising, but from Mr Seth it sounded like a badge of honour.

'The ice caps are melting in the Antarctic,' he said.

He looked at her gravely with his hawk eyes; sometimes Maude thought he had the most perfect face she had ever seen.

'Soon,' said Mr Seth, 'Kent will be gone. There is no hope for the Maldives. In the South Pacific, there will be thousands of people floating around in the sea, like Noah and the ark all over again.'

Mr Seth shook his head.

'Of course,' he said, 'the government won't do anything about it. They long for Kent to fall into the sea, because it's where the last twenty Conservative voters live. So that's why the deputy prime minister has two Jaguar cars: he is trying to get rid of Kent with his bare hands.'

Maude looked at him solemnly. She was used by now to Mr Seth's theories: she sometimes wondered whether he went home and surfed the Net at night, looking for the newest conspiracy, but then he was old enough to remember Watergate, and the Bay of Pigs, and the Iran-Contra business, and another half a dozen improbable things that the CIA did before breakfast.

She handed over her money. Mr Seth gave her a fleeting smile. She sometimes thought that he could see right into her soul, that he guessed every single thing that had ever happened to her, that he knew her life better than she knew it herself. She knew this was fanciful; but all the same, he didn't smile that way at anyone else. Perhaps, she thought, he recognised a kindred spirit. In these days of optimism and affirmation, when everyone was believing in angels (suddenly the height of fashion, especially to have your own guardian one, the magazines were full of it) and the general beneficence of the universe and that all things are meant to be for the greater good (many small books selling this idea grew on bookstore counters like fat black mushrooms), there weren't many pessimists left. It seemed to Maude that Mr Seth thought she was on his side. She thought he was right.

She took the papers home and sat in her kitchen and read them. She thought about going out for lunch. She hadn't been out for lunch in a social way for ten years. She had seen people for business at lunchtime, but that was all. She had no idea what she would say, she could barely remember how to act among normal people.

No, she thought, that was not true. She was not quite as desiccated as that. You have to live to eighty, like a hermit, without seeing a soul, for all the social reflexes to dry up completely. It's like riding a bicycle or swimming breast-stroke or playing the piano; it comes back, your body remembers better than you do.

But all the same, Maude was nervous. She felt things were changing without her volition, as if some current of time or history or event had started flowing and was sweeping her along with it. She was used to being in control, policing her own punishment, and she wasn't sure she liked this sudden involuntary shift.

The two voices were chattering in her head. The first voice said: What are you *thinking*? This isn't allowed, said the first voice, in the tones of a prison warder; this isn't part of the deal.

The second voice said: Go to lunch and drink a glass of

wine and sit in the sun and eat food and talk to people you've never met before, and it's not going to kill anyone.

The second voice sometimes had a twisted sense of humour.

4

The first thing Maude noticed when she walked in was that someone was playing 'The Ballad of John and Yoko' very loud. Maude always got a shiver when she heard that song: John Lennon, syncopated and tongue-in-cheek, saying the ways things were going, they were going to crucify him. He didn't mean shot dead in the street like a dog by some nutcase who already had his autograph; Maude was sure he didn't mean that at all. But all the same, it was the kind of thing that could get you spooked, if you thought about it long enough. It was such an upbeat song, with some wild swirling piano going on, and a swooning seductive chorus. Eating chocolate cake in a bag: what did he mean by that? Maybe it was a drugs thing.

Sadie tapped her foot and smiled. Maude wondered that her mouth just didn't get tired of it and take the day off, she smiled so much. Maude wondered whether she knew she did, if she had read somewhere that it was the way to make friends and influence people; a smile costs nothing, after all, and how many things in life are free? But she couldn't imagine Sadie doing anything she read in a book; she wasn't a dime-store guru kind of woman.

'Stop it,' said Sadie. 'It's just lunch.'

Maude looked at her and wondered if Sadie could have any conception what this was like: like jumping into the deep end of a swimming pool with no armbands and no lifeguards and no clue how to swim.

John and Yoko gave way to Janis Joplin and 'Me and Bobby McGee'. Maude felt a thin tugging bond of sympathy with Janis Joplin. She felt like she went in the same box: the hopeless cases, the social misfits, the lost and the lonely. Janis did it in public, all that clawing for position: let me belong somewhere, like a normal person, just for five minutes. Janis did it by drinking and doping and fucking men who didn't love her very much. But it was the same in the end. All those songs were the same in the end.

'They'll be upstairs,' said Sadie, leading the way along a narrow hallway with three doors off the right side of it.

'They just leave the door on the latch like that?' said Maude.

Sadie laughed. 'Nothing to steal,' she said. 'One crappy stereo no self-respecting burglar would be seen dead with, and the telly gets hidden in a box. Anyway,' she said, 'they knew we were coming.'

Maude thought this sounded slightly sinister.

Upstairs the building opened up into a square studio room, dominated by a long arched window that looked out into the street. It was too high to see the cars and the trucks and the furious white vans that clogged the Talgarth Road; instead there was a misleading and fantastic view of verdant treetops, as if they were in the middle of some bucolic idyll.

The walls were painted a bright shining green, like a joke, like a tree full of apples. The light came in thick and hot and gilded from the big window, and the expanse of floor was covered in bare boards, smooth and white with use, and it seemed as if it wasn't quite real, something about the quality of the light giving it an air of suspension, as if it was distorted slightly, coming at you from one remove.

There wasn't much furniture: a long sofa and three fat armchairs in worn red leather, the kind of thing you might see in a pool hall or a lost bar in the middle of some dusty French one-horse town where tourists never went, and a long low table covered in books and magazines and a collection of haphazard unrelated objects: three blue paper packets of American cigarettes, a carved jade lion, a silver paperknife, a pot of vermilion tulips packed together like passengers on a commuter train in rush-hour, a heap of discarded jewellery, a bottle-opener, two packs of cards, a miniature ship in a bottle.

At one end there was a rudimentary kitchen with a long table with a zinc top, crowded with china and glass and candles and vases and bowls, and all around the walls were covered in photographs, in black and white and sudden bursts of technicolour, framed in flat black frames, as if someone had gone out with a camera and got all human life and brought it back and put it on the wall.

There were three people in the room: two women lying on the sofa, and a man sitting in one of the fat red chairs reading a three-day-old newspaper, with his legs stretched out in front of him. The women were painting each other's toenails.

Maude wanted to turn and run away.

'Here we are,' said Sadie. She stood at the top of the stairs and looked into the room, planting her feet square, like a traveller arriving for the first time on a foreign strand.

'This is Maude,' she said.

The women looked up and smiled and the man lowered his newspaper and put a pair of spectacles on and squinted a little and brought his eyes into focus.

'You're the neighbour,' he said. 'We never even saw you before. One time I heard you playing Willie Nelson very late at night when I was lying in bed trying to sleep. My heart was broken and you were playing "Always On My Mind" and I cried all night long.'

Maude felt breathless at this sudden revelation. Was this what people who went out for lunch did?

'He's in touch with his female side,' said one of the women, pulling her feet away from her friend and swinging them on to the floor. She walked towards Maude, balancing on her heels so as not to smudge the scarlet paint on her tiny toenails.

'That's why we love him so,' the woman said, holding out her hand. Maude paused, not sure what was expected of her. She smiled and nodded as if someone had asked her a question and held out her own hand and the woman took it. As she did so, she pulled Maude gently towards her and kissed her on both cheeks.

'I'm Ruby,' she said.

She smelt warm; some faint odour of citrus came off her, something clean and nostalgic, some tang of lime or lemon, one of those scents that used to go into eau-de-Cologne in the fifties, when people wore that kind of thing. Her cheek was soft and firm against Maude's. Maude, who hadn't had human contact since she could remember, felt overwhelmed. This woman had the same ease and confidence as Sadie did. Maude wondered where it came from, whether it was learnt or born, whether it was just a question of luck.

Ruby was in some ways a similar type to Sadie altogether. They both had a rangy, lean kind of body, an adventurous body, with long strong legs and arms set squarely on to straight shoulders; capable bodies, practical more than beautiful, everything in the right place, functioning at full capacity.

By contrast Maude felt insubstantial and small; but then she felt like that most days, as if she were half a person, while everyone else walked the streets in three full dimensions.

Ruby had brown hair cut into feathers so it moved and shimmered when she walked; she had pale walnut eyes with short lashes and thick eyebrows and a straight nose and a mouth that was wide and went down on the right-hand side, so she looked like a *commedia dell'arte* mask, half smiling, half frowning. There was something plastic and mobile about her face, as if she used it a lot.

'Have a drink,' she said. 'We made bullshots in a jug. It's a terrible thing.'

Maude had no idea what a bullshot was; she said yes because she didn't know what else to say.

'And those,' said Ruby, gesturing over her shoulder as she walked towards the kitchen, 'are Pearl and Dean.'

'It's true,' said Sadie, laughing. 'It really is true.'

'I'm Pearl,' said the other woman. 'It's all right, I'm used to it by now.'

She had a pretty face to go with her pretty name; a tilted nose and round lollipop eyes the colour of cornflowers and a curving mouth and dark blonde hair that fell thick and straight down her back.

'I'm Dean,' said the man, standing up and shaking hands. He had small bright eyes behind his glasses, optimism shining out of them like starlight. He didn't kiss Maude like Ruby had, but he held her hand for a moment, like he meant it.

Oh, these people, she thought, where did they get invented? They were too real to be true.

'My parents,' said Dean, smiling a friendly reassuring smile, 'had a drink once with Colin MacInnes, so that's where my name came from. Don't ask Pearl about hers.'

'It's not so bad,' said Pearl, as if this was an old joke. 'It could be Ethel or Mavis or Araminta. It could be Delaware or Lula-Mae.'

'You're just making it up now,' said Ruby, coming back with glasses and ice and a jug on a tray. 'Sit down,' she said to Maude.

Maude wondered when she was going to say Welcome to the family.

They ate chicken cooked with olives and thyme, and new potatoes baked in their skins, and tomatoes with basil, and to Maude everything tasted like it was in some other dimension of food: the chickenest chicken, the most tomatoey tomato. The sun came washing in from the high window and the air was thick with the end of the summer and the refracted green colour from the walls.

Maude sat and listened as the others talked. They didn't stop talking for a single moment; they were full of talk, and they let it spool into the afternoon as if they knew it would never run out. Maude found herself mesmerised by the strangeness of it, by their ease and fluency, and, as the bullshots worked inside her, insidious with vodka, by their beauty. Watching their talking heads round the table, the glimmering green light of the room playing on their skin, she thought they were the most beautiful people she had ever seen.

They talked and talked; they laughed and shifted and used their hands to make a point. They exaggerated and sketched stories in the air and used modish buzz-words with a palpable air of irony, as if they knew better. Maude, not used to drinking, found herself sitting back and watching, as they melded into each other, indistinguishable.

They talked about love; it seemed something with which they were intimate, in all its twisting variety. They teased Sadie about her relationship – they all called it this, rather than affair or any other word: they said, Oh, your relationship, your *relationship*, with the most commitment-phobic man in the world. 'It's started you smoking again,' said Ruby, with a falling air of sorrow. 'You know that can't be a good sign.'

Sadie laughed, unrepentant.

'It's angst,' she said, 'because he can't commit. And he's partial to the odd gasper or thirty himself; I can't beat 'em so watch me join 'em.'

'I don't think,' said Dean, who was eating a chicken leg with gentle precision, 'that you really want him to commit. I think you just wanted an excuse to start smoking again.'

'Cigarettes are more reliable than love,' said Sadie, as if she was enjoying herself. 'You know that's true.'

'Nothing is reliable,' said Pearl, with some gravity at odds with her blonde hair and ostentatious prettiness. 'And everything kills you in the end.'

'She auditioned for a Pinter play last week,' said Ruby, 'so that's what *that* is.'

'I don't see why I can't be the pessimist for once,' said Pearl. 'I don't see why that's against the law.'

'You have to dye your hair, if you're going to do it properly,' said Dean.

'It's prejudice,' said Pearl. 'It's terrible outdated animus against anyone with blonde hair.'

'Everything is prejudice, in the end,' said Sadie. 'Because we all think that we are right and everyone else is wrong and we just get to dress it up in compliance because we want to get laid.'

'That's entirely untrue,' said Dean. 'And you've used that line before.'

'I don't know anything at all,' said Sadie, holding up the palms of her hands. 'I'm just shooting in the dark.'

Maude thought it was like some secret language she couldn't decipher. She wondered if they talked that way all the time, or whether it was for her benefit, whether they were posturing a little, showing off for their guest.

They didn't ask her anything. She wondered whether Sadie had warned them, told them she was different, strange, private; all those things that people weren't supposed to be. She wondered whether it was just a graceful diplomacy. They had grace, she thought, hazy from drink; they had some kind of good grace. For a moment, in this hot green room, with its high ceilings and its curving window, she forgot that she wasn't allowed this kind of thing, that it was reserved for other people, who hadn't committed her ineradicable crime; she forgot that she was tight in the box of her own recrimination.

For a moment, she felt something so unfamiliar that she couldn't put a name to it; she suddenly realised, with a starting shock, that it was pleasure.

Monday morning, and Mr Seth gave Maude a sorrowful look and said that there was a meteor heading towards Earth and that the government had set up a task force.

'I read it in the paper,' he said, with a small spur of triumph, as if he had been right all along.

When Maude was going to Hampstead every Friday,

she read many books about the soul and the psyche and the ideas of Jung and Adler, as if somewhere, like a code in all that dense black print, she might find the answer to everything. She had time on her hands, anyway. Where other people had friends and family and social obligations, she had a void, the dark crawl space of her loneliness.

She never found the answer ('Perhaps,' said the shrink, shining with reason, 'you are not asking the right question') but she learnt a great deal about world thought, for all the good that did her. The enlightened writers she read talked about the wisdom of the East; that philosophical view of life and death that Indians knew. She sometimes wondered how it was that the gleaming light of optimism had passed Mr Seth by. If she had been another kind of woman altogether, she might have asked him.

'You see,' he said, handing over her change. 'We are all toast, now.' He had picked up unexpected slices of argot from his education in Scotland; or perhaps it was from his Sunday-morning conversations with Gerald and his brother bums.

Maude walked along to the bookshop, where the book woman was frowning over her till. There was a pile of new books, just arrived and not yet arranged on the tables that lined the front of the shop. Right on top, there was a shiny new hardback by Alexander Dent: *Without a Trace*. Maude wondered whether it was a sign. All she had been thinking of for the last two weeks was Alexander Dent, and now here was his new novel.

She picked it up and the bookshop woman stared at her without interest and took her money and Maude thanked her and carried the book away to her basement room.

Sadie came round the next day, in the early evening. She was on her way upstairs.

'How did you like lunch?' she said, walking in and settling herself down at the kitchen table. She was tall and vital in the evening light, which was dense and evocative and tinged with melancholy and the end of the summer. Maude watched her, as always in curiosity and some kind of awe; this ease Sadie held, this idea that she was welcome anywhere, was entirely alien to Maude. It seemed like something that happened in fiction and she wondered at how easily Sadie translated it to life.

'Did you enjoy yourself?' said Sadie. 'They liked you.'

Maude wondered how they knew that, when she had barely opened her mouth the entire day.

'I liked them,' she said, which was true. She felt it was a betrayal of all her principles, of the hair-shirt life she had so ruthlessly constructed for herself. The mother of the child she had killed wouldn't be going out with people to talk to, she wouldn't enjoy Sunday lunch, because how could she ever forget that gaping space where her son should be? Maude knew (the first strident voice told her, many times a day) that she shouldn't enjoy anything either, for the same reason. She didn't deserve careless good times as other people had; she was branded by what she had done.

'Come up with me,' said Sadie, as if it were all arranged, as if it was the thing that was expected to happen next. 'Come and have supper.'

Maude tried to say no, but in the end there was no excuse. The second voice, sensing an ally, basking in its moment in the sun, was yelling at her to say yes, so in the end she said it.

This time, when they got upstairs, 'Wish You Were Here' was playing, on vinyl, 33 r.p.m., with lisps and scratches and some kind of atmospheric yearning, the way it used to sound.

'I brought Maude,' said Sadie, as they came into the high studio room. The others were arranged much as before, Ruby and Pearl lying on the sofa, Dean in his red armchair. They looked up and smiled when they saw Maude standing there, and she wondered how they could have decided that she was someone they wanted to know, when she had nothing to offer them except the blank walls of her secret.

'That's good,' said Ruby. She got up in an abrupt movement and came over to Maude and did the same kissing ritual as before, and Maude looked for a moment into her wide brown eyes and saw some shadow of sympathy and understanding there, like a phantom; and then Ruby went over to the kitchen table and got a bottle of red wine and poured out two more glasses.

'We're drinking,' she said, 'because Dean got his heart broken. Just in case he hadn't got the point the first time round.'

'Oh, Dean,' said Sadie. She went over to him and leant down and stroked his hair with a tender hand, as if he were a lost child. 'I know how *that* feels.'

'We all know how that feels,' said Pearl. For some reason this shocked Maude; looking at that pretty fair face, she couldn't imagine it ever getting rejected, not wanted, put aside for someone else. Pearl looked like the kind of girl who ran across cornfields stained with poppies, in advertisements about perfect lives.

'But still,' she said, with some composed wisdom, 'we don't know how to make it better for him. So we're drinking red wine instead.'

Ruby guided Maude into the second armchair and went back to the sofa. Sadie sat down on the arm of Dean's chair, and kept her hand in his hair, as if to anchor him, as if the touch of human flesh would keep the worst of the night fears at bay.

He smiled a twisted smile and said, 'I loved her like hell and I did all the things a man is supposed to do, I listened to her problems and I didn't go into my cave and I did my best to be sensitive and kind, and then she left. I don't,' he said, 'understand anything any more.'

'No,' said Ruby, 'that's what happens. Sometimes there isn't anything to understand. Sometimes shit happens, and there is no sense or sensibility.'

'Maybe,' said Dean, taking out a crumpled pack of Chesterfield cigarettes and lighting one, 'I was too *fin-de-siècle*. Maybe she wanted me to be butch and macho and uncommunicative.'

'I don't *think* so,' said Pearl. 'I don't think anyone wants that, these days.'

'The man she left me for deals in futures,' said Dean, inhaling like a condemned man with his last smoke before the chair.

'You didn't tell us that,' said Ruby, looking affronted. Maude couldn't tell if it was because he had withheld the information or because of the idea of a man with his fingers dirty from financial speculation.

'I don't understand,' said Pearl. 'She could have had lovely artistic sensitive you, and she ran off with an insane free marketeer.'

'Some people like that kind of thing,' said Sadie, as if it wasn't really their fault.

'Maybe it's us,' said Ruby. 'All this time you've lived with me and Pearl, and we taught you everything we knew about what women really want, and then you found one who didn't want any of that at all. If you see what I mean.'

'We all choose badly,' said Sadie. 'And I should know.'

'Yes, you should,' said Ruby, starting to laugh. 'Oh, Lord, you should know. And it's not just you.'

Later, Ruby and Pearl made a pot of spaghetti with clams and a dish of cucumbers with mint and olive oil, as if it were nothing (Maude watched them with fascination as they cooked; she ate nothing that didn't come out of a tin). They sat round the long wooden table and opened another bottle of wine, for Dean's poor broken heart, and kept right on talking.

'So what do I do now?' he said, staring dolefully at all that food. 'I feel like someone kicked my insides out and now there's an empty space.'

'Oh,' said Maude, who hadn't meant to say anything at all, 'I know what that is like.'

They all turned and stared at her. Sadie shot a pleased look across the table, as if to say, I told you so. There was a new record on the machine; Pearl said it was a girl called Lucy Kaplansky who only ten people outside Austin, Texas, knew about. She had a voice grave as rocks and velvet, and she played her guitar like it was the end of the world, and she sang sad songs about selling out, and lonely hearts, and never getting what you wanted.

'So you got your heart broken too?' said Ruby, leaning her elbows on the table, looking right at Maude, as if she wanted to know.

Maude, with the wine warm inside her, entirely un-accustomed to having anyone show an interest in her life, found herself answering before she knew what she was doing.

'I got my heart broken,' she said, 'so hard that it feels like there are a million shattered pieces of it out there in the street and no way to put them back together.'

There was a small silence; instantly, Maude wished she hadn't spoken. For all that these were people who dealt in intimacy as surely as a dealer in Vegas shuffling cards for the blackjack table, she was new here, and there was a raw passion in what she said that had brought them up short. She was the spectre at the feast, the stranger at the table; she wasn't supposed to do this.

But then Ruby started laughing her wide open laugh, and she leant her shoulder against Dean and said, 'See? This is what happens to everyone. This is what happens when you are over twenty-one, the moment you are legal. You get your heart smashed up, sooner or later, and you can't work out how to put it together again.'

'There must be something I can do,' said Dean. 'There must be a book I can read or a theory I can follow.'

'I don't know,' said Pearl, looking over at Sadie. 'I don't.'

Sadie, taking her cue, put her head on one side, as if this was her territory. They all looked at her, waiting for answers. Maude wondered why; Sadie seemed so sure in the world, so full of life and promise, and yet they all seemed to think that this was the kind of thing she knew about.

'There is no book,' she said. 'There are no answers. There's no short-cut for any of this. You hurt like hell, and you get confused and furious, and you think this can't go on, this is too bad; you watch other people running around like it all makes sense and you think Can't I have some of that? You just have to let it settle, and time comes along and does its thing, and one day it gets better, even though you thought it never would. There's a moment when the clouds roll away, and you see the sun come out, and you think, That's it, *that's it*. The world comes back to you in a rush, and you wonder where it went, through all those dark lonely months, and you do something entirely uncharacteristic like going to the seaside or taking a train ride, and you know the corner is turned, and it might not be completely fine, but something tells you that it will be all right, in the end.'

At the weekend, Maude was walking back from the newsagent and she ran into Ruby on the doorstep, and Ruby said Come in and have tea, there's no one else at home, and Maude found herself sitting in the wide high room at the top of the house and she did something she never thought she would do again: she asked a question.

'I don't understand,' she said, 'about Sadie. She seems like the most assured person I ever met, and then there was all that stuff she said the other night, and I wondered how that was.'

Ruby looked at Maude with her unflinching eyes and hesitated for a moment, as if wondering how to put it, and then she said, 'Well, you see, Sadie's mother died when Sadie was seventeen, in a horrible senseless accident, so she knows all about grotesque things happening when you least expect them.'

Maude felt as if she were pinned to her seat with shock:

it was the last thing she would have expected. She didn't know what to say. She looked around the room, casting about for something. She looked at the photographs, all over the walls, all those still caught images. 'They're such beautiful pictures,' she said. 'I never saw such beautiful pictures.'

'Thank you,' said Ruby. 'They're mine. That's what I do.' She smiled at Maude, with the generous smile Maude knew she didn't deserve, and they talked of other things.

Afterwards, when she went back downstairs to her empty Saturday night, just her and an unread book open on the table and Whispering Bob Harris playing obscure tunes on the radio, Maude thought that perhaps she had got everything wrong. She knew, in the part of her mind that was still rational, that terrible things happened to good people, because the shrink had told her over and over; she had read enough newspaper stories and listened to enough country-and-western music and watched enough indie films in darkened afternoon movie houses to see that this was clearly the case. But she realised now, still shaken with Ruby's revelation, that she had started to believe that it had only happened to her. In her irrational mind, which grew stronger and more insistent with every solitary year, she thought that she was the only one, that she must keep herself separate from all the other good, normal people, with their sensible, everyday lives, in case she should infect them.

She thought that perhaps it was time to face up to the fact that the world wasn't the way she had skewed it.

She felt that this made some fundamental difference to everything, but she wasn't sure what it was.

She felt paralysed with terror suddenly, as if all the

things she had taken for granted for so long were being shifted from under her. There was a cruel bleakness to the life she had built so carefully for herself, but she knew how it worked. And now there were these new people, and they were showing her something else, and she felt as if her careful construction was starting to sway on its foundations, and she didn't know what happened next.

5

The next day, Maude woke early as always and walked from her bed, her bare feet cool and new against the tiled floor, to the kitchen, and put the kettle on. She had a steel kettle that you set on the stove to boil, and it took a while to get going, and she looked out into the dark green tangled garden, where the sun was just starting to touch the top of the hedge that kept the trains at bay.

I don't know, she thought, what is happening. Something is happening, but I don't know what it is.

She sat at her table and thought about all the people all over this wide city getting up and going to work and making breakfast and arguing over the toast and marmalade; all those people she would never know, going about their business with small, careful steps. Maude wondered sometimes how people managed to live these ordinary clean and decent lives, without stopping one day in the street and screaming out loud.

She got dressed and walked up to get her paper. She always read the news, although it seemed distant and removed, as if the outside world had nothing to do with her at all. She looked at the pictures of the politicians and dictators, the serial rapists and the sporting heroes, the union leaders and the soap starlets; she read the columnists with their strident daily opinions, she traced the tortured debates about asylum seekers and equal pay and the crumbling health service and vigilante justice; she read about war zones and ethnic cleansing, about factories closing and interest rates rising. Sometimes she thought that every day it was the same, and only the names were changed.

'Forget the meteor,' said Mr Seth. 'Today we are all going to die from Aids because the charlatans who run the multi-national pharmaceuticals won't make the medication cheap enough for the third world. A tide of sickness will rise up from the poor countries and swamp us all, in the end.'

Maude nodded silently, because she was never sure what to say to these doomy pronouncements.

'You see,' said Mr Seth. 'You see? Schopenhauer was right. Human existence must be some kind of error, that was what he said. He said: It is bad, and every day it gets worse, until the worst thing of all happens.'

Maude went home and read the paper and drank another cup of coffee. The light was moving round, pushing its way into the room. She liked this light, she realised; she liked sitting at her plain table and watching the light move. She liked the bitter taste of the coffee and the smell of it, that evocative smell which conjured hot afternoons in Italy, although she had never been there. These small pleasures were things that she hardly dared admit.

She finished the paper and thought about work; work was normally what she did now. But she had turned down the hoary explorer, she had no commission to fill, no deadline to meet. There was just the vicarious idea of her private project: vicarious because, sitting now, in the still morning, while the city went on outside, it felt as if it had been thought up by someone else. And also it was improbable; what she wanted to do had been attempted by other people, writers and intellectuals with more qualifications than she. She wondered at her presumption. She should call up Joan Bellow and tell her she would take the frost-bitten hero, and do a good job of it, and pay the mortgage for another year.

She looked at the telephone, that silent machine which never rang, not in her house, and she couldn't bring herself to pick it up.

There was a sudden banging at the door. Sadie, thought Maude, all at once blessing the intrusion, so she could put off the telephone for another hour.

It was Dean.

'I'm sorry,' he said. 'The others are out, and it's lonely upstairs. Do you mind?'

Do you mind? Wasn't that what Sadie had said too, at the beginning? Maude stood and looked at him and he looked so white and sad in the wide sun-filled day that she couldn't say no.

'Come in,' she said. She gave a shot at a smile. She thought that it would be nice, for once, if she could act like a normal person, if she could offer sympathy, and tea. It wasn't in the agenda, but how could she explain that to this poor heartbroken man? He wore his misery like a badge on his sleeve; for all that he must have been into his thirties, he looked like a six-year-old who had been ostracised by his schoolfellows, standing in the corner of the playground with no friends and nowhere to go. Maude knew what that felt like, at least. She knew all about that.

'Of course, come in,' she said, stepping back and letting him into the hall.

Dean gave her a look of ineffable gratitude and she felt like the worst kind of fraud.

They sat down and she made him a pot of tea. She found a box of biscuits and gave him those as well because she wanted to offer him something and she wasn't sure of any other way to do it.

'I'm sorry,' he said again. 'That room is just too big, when you are empty inside.'

Maude nodded. She understood that. That was why she had chosen her low dim basement; it made the emptiness easier to live with. When there is terror inside you, space is the hardest thing to bear.

'You understand this,' said Dean, 'don't you?'

Maude didn't see how he could know that. She didn't know what to say to it, so she said nothing.

'But you do,' said Dean, as if she had spoken. 'I can see that.'

Maude occasionally wondered whether she wore her loneliness and her shame and her broken self like a brand on her forehead; sometimes that was the way it felt. Now she saw that perhaps it was true.

'That's why I came down here,' Dean said, still looking at her. He had a grave and serious regard, straight as a die. Maude thought, suddenly, shockingly, that in another lifetime, another place, if she were another person, she would fall in love with him and never let him go.

He wasn't obviously beautiful or handsome even: he had freckles and ordinary brown hair and a nose that was too short for today's ideals. But he had some patent air of goodness shining out of him like the sun on a good day, and when he smiled his eyes lit and his mouth opened up, as if offering something more than this.

But Maude knew that she was out of the loop, there was no place for her here. She could listen for a while, and he would go back upstairs, and she would subside into her blank life, where she belonged.

'I did love her,' he said, as if Maude had questioned it. 'I loved her more than any woman I had ever met. It was so fine, in the beginning. And then the warning signs started, I think she was trying to drive me away, caution me, something, and I ignored it all, like a fool. I thought if I wanted it enough it would happen, the way I dreamed it.'

Maude knew the time had come for her to say something, but she wasn't practised in this, not like those women upstairs, who always knew what to say.

'I don't know,' she said. 'I don't know how any of this works.'

Dean gave her another of those grateful looks, and she felt again that she didn't deserve it.

'People think,' he said, 'that men are different. Men are supposed to be able to put things in compartments and retreat into their boxes when the going gets tough. I can't seem to do that,' he said. 'I was meant to be working, and all I could think of was Leonie and what happened with us and where did I go wrong.'

Maude realised that she didn't know what he did.

'What do you do, for work?' she said.

He smiled, fast and unexpected, and she saw that there was a part of him that was not killed stone dead, however bruised his trusting heart was.

'I'm a choreographer,' he said, and there was a discernible note of pride in his voice.

Maude recognised it and thought he deserved it. She smiled at him, thinking of the spectacles he could create, and she said, 'Well, there you are, that's something, that's really something, and no woman and no broken heart and no messed-up relationship can take that away.'

Dean looked at her, as if that was not what he expected, and he started to laugh, almost against his will.

'Ruby and Pearl say that's why I'm in touch with my female side,' he said. 'They say I'm just a gay man trapped inside a straight body.'

Then it was Maude's turn to laugh, even though she didn't do that any more. They sat there together, and laughed into the beginning of the afternoon.

After he had gone, Maude thought that for the first time she understood what they meant about the comfort of strangers.

The strangers upstairs turned into something else, over the next couple of weeks; not friends exactly, but something, something more than people glimpsed from a distance, through a veil.

Mr Seth was preoccupied with a civil war raging somewhere in Africa and viruses circling the Internet and global conspiracy theories; he had decided that the whole world was in fact run from an anonymous office block somewhere in Washington, D.C., a building that didn't have a number or a name or a postal address.

Maude saw him every morning, and she wondered, as he told her about the imminent demise of the civilised world, whether he could see that her own small world was changing, whatever she tried to do about it.

Dean had taken to coming down for tea in the mornings, and telling her about his life. She listened and gave him biscuits to eat and he thanked her, as if she had performed some extraordinary service, and the tight knot that lived inside her started to loosen a little, from the bare fact of human contact.

Sadie dropped in whenever she was in the neighbourhood, and she took Maude upstairs for supper and the women talked their fluent talk, and Maude watched them, and wondered why, when it seemed that they had the world at their feet, they would want her.

She read the new book by Alexander Dent and the more she read, the more obsessively she thought about her project. She started to take notes, read old material and collate it, give it shape. Each day the pile of notes grew, and she wondered what the hell she was doing it for.

One day, a Tuesday at the end of September, when the weather was still holding and it was hot as July, Maude forgot to lock the door, and Sadie, instead of banging up a storm, turned the handle and let herself in before Maude realised what had happened.

'Hey,' said Sadie, coming into the kitchen fast as always, like a sirocco blowing through a dusty north African town. 'What's all this?'

She looked at the papers and books piled on the kitchen table, the dense pages packed with Maude's tight black script.

'You must be the only person left in London who doesn't use a computer,' Sadie said merrily. 'It's like stumbling on Henry James.'

Maude tried to cover up what she was doing, but it was all spread out for anyone to read.

Sadie picked up some of the books and looked at the titles. 'This is all about Alexander Dent,' she said; the same curious look crossed her face as it had the very first time she had been here, walking along the bookshelves and coming along a whole line of Dent's work. 'What is this? Are you doing a Ph.D.?'

'It's just something,' said Maude, who was still not sure what it was.

'I suddenly realised,' said Sadie, sitting down abruptly and putting her chin in her hands and looking at Maude with the air of complicity and familiarity that always seemed like a surprise. 'I suddenly thought that I don't know what you do, in your professional life. We never talked about that.'

'I'm a ghost-writer,' said Maude. 'I write other people's books for them.'

'How strange,' said Sadie. 'I've never met anyone who did that before. So what is all this?' she said. 'Is someone who can't string a sentence together planning a shattering exposé on Alexander Dent?'

Maude, used to secrecy and holding herself at bay, was suddenly seized with a violent desire to tell Sadie everything. She hesitated, knowing in the deep buried heart of her that if she did that she would start something she couldn't stop. She felt a surge of fear, a shaft of naked terror at the idea of being exposed; she also felt, in the same moment, a pulling tug of yearning. Everyone, after all, wants to be known; everyone wants to be understood.

'It's me,' said Maude, giving into the second impulse. There was something about Sadie, had been from the beginning, that brought the walls Maude had so carefully constructed tumbling down. She wondered what it was and why she felt so powerless to resist it.

'I'm writing about him,' she said, spacing the words out so that they were clear and distinct. 'Me. I am.'

She stopped, thinking how risible it sounded; she was nobody, what did she know? People had tried to write about Dent before, but since his wife's death he had become a recluse, harder to find than J.D. Salinger in the woods. He never talked to the press, he never gave interviews; he let people write articles and thin volumes based on his work, pulled from tenuous rumour and secondary sources. People didn't even know where he lived, although it was said that he had moved somewhere north of the border. But for years, since Maude had started to earn her living by writing, she had wanted to do something on him; she had a fantasy that she would somehow gain access that no one else had been permitted. She thought, in wild midnight dreams, that he might recognise a fellow sufferer, that if she told him what had happened to her on the same day he had killed his wife, he might be moved by the sinister coincidence of it. He might, at the very least, be curious, and Maude had once read that curiosity is the strongest human emotion. She thought if she told him about this bizarre confluence of fate that he might be moved to grant her an interview, something, a few words on the telephone, his benediction.

She knew that the real possibility of this happening was less than zero, and she felt ashamed, as she started telling some of this to Sadie: it sounded so childish and impossible and Sadie would surely laugh in her face.

'I've been obsessed with him for years,' she said, wondering if there was any way she could make it sound sensible and pointful. 'And I got good at writing, good enough, anyway; after all this time, I can carry a tune. There has been such vicious rubbish written about him, I thought that I could tell the real story. I thought if I could find a way of getting in touch with him he might want to set the record straight. After all these years. That's all.'

She trailed off, her voice sounding flat and miserable in the still basement room. Sadie must surely laugh; she must sneer and laugh until her sides ached.

Sadie did laugh, but not in derision.

'See?' she said. '*See?* I told them upstairs, I said this, I did. I knew that underneath all that silence and self-possession there beat the passionate heart of a true idealist. I told them so.'

Maude stared at her in astonishment. 'You think that I'm self-possessed?' she said.

If only Sadie knew, she thought. If only she knew the reason that Maude never spoke much was that she was afraid that her heart would split wide open all over the floor and make a mess and embarrass people and give herself away. If only Sadie knew that the silence and the monastic life were to do with her regimen of self-flagellation. All those times she had sat in that big room upstairs and not said much, as the rest of them talked and laughed and acted normal, there had been a furious battle raging in her, the second voice beckoning her towards small moments of pleasure and real life, and the first barking like a mastiff, furious that she should allow herself even a sliver of this.

'Self-contained like a still pool,' said Sadie, nodding. 'But there is something below the surface, and that's what it is, your passionate heart beating. And,' she said slyly, 'I know about your secret meetings with Dean, I know that he comes down here in the morning and tells you about his despair and you listen and you get it. I know that.'

It sounded as if she was talking about another woman altogether, someone Maude had read about in a book.

Then Sadie said something that surprised her even more.

'I know,' she said, 'that you have chosen to live some kind of hidden solitary life, and I don't ask you why, because that's not my business, and I also know that in some ways you resent me for coming and taking you out of it. I can see that you are torn, that there is something unwilling in you, and if I weren't so cussed and I couldn't see that beating heart so clearly, I expect I would leave you alone, like I should.'

Don't leave me alone, Maude found herself thinking, like a child; not now, don't leave me.

'I know what this is,' said Sadie, and for a falling moment Maude thought that her secret was out, that Sadie could read minds, could see right through into the dark spaces that lay underneath the façade she had so carefully constructed.

'I've seen it before,' said Sadie. She paused, as if she was about to say something and then changed her mind. 'In my work,' she said. 'When people get broken. I don't mean the things that happen to all of us, shitty childhoods and parents who don't understand and lovers leaving and jobs failing and dreams not coming true, I mean something worse than that, the things that aren't in the script. Sometimes something so unimaginably bad happens that people break, their hearts crack open as if they are beyond repair. In my experience,' said Sadie, and her eyes grew distant, as if she were talking to someone else, as if Maude was hardly there any more, 'when they get broken up like that, truly wrecked, they do two things: either they withdraw from the world, into their own internal twilight, or they go out and fuck themselves up with drink and drugs and sex and danger, stun themselves with substances and adrenalin, so they don't have to feel anything any more.'

She looked right at Maude with her good kind eyes, that had seen things, despite her not even being thirty yet.

'I think,' she said, 'that you are one of those people, and that's why you hide away in this room and write books with other people's names on the cover. And I also think that you should write your book, your real book, about Alexander Dent, because all that passion is sitting there in you however much you try to quell it, and you should go out and use it, because not everyone has it, and you could do something wonderful with it, if you would let yourself.'

Maude looked away. She was terrified because Sadie had guessed so accurately at the secret she thought she hid so well; at the same time she was swamped with gratitude because of the sympathy and utter lack of judgement that Sadie offered, something she had never dreamt she could receive. She was frightened because it felt like a door had opened, and she was glimpsing something beyond, something strange and unimagined, outside the drawn circle of her small closed world.

'I can't,' she said. 'It's foolish. He would never speak to me, why should he? I'm no one.'

'No,' said Sadie. There was some subterranean excitement humming in her, as if this was all her idea. 'No, you don't understand. You are someone. If you write him a good letter, he might say yes. You can't know he won't. It's ten years since he spoke to anyone at all; maybe now this is the time, maybe now he wants to say something. It could be one of those instances of perfect timing.'

'I can't,' said Maude. 'No. No. I can't do that.'

'Write to his publishers and they will send it on,' said Sadie. 'What have you got to lose?'

Nothing, thought Maude, but my chains.

The next day Sadie arrived very early, before Dean even. She seemed to know that Maude would be up.

Maude was sitting at her kitchen table, sitting staring into space, with her dark hair pushed behind her ears, her face whiter than ever, her ancient dressing-gown dragging on the floor. It was purple silk, with small brown holes in the fabric from burning cigarettes, the only thing she still had of her father's. She had barely known her father, he was a distant presence in her life and then he died, and she had sold every single thing in the house of her childhood, there were debts everywhere and the bank claimed most of it, but for some reason she kept the dressing-gown. She had worn it since she was eighteen, with its bagging elbows and fraying sleeves, and the small singed holes where her father had been careless with a smoke.

She felt paralysed – by hope, by confusion, by the calling voice of her old life and the siren song of the new one that Sadie had sketched for her so carelessly.

Sadie banged on the door and Maude went to let her in. They sat down and Sadie said, in her abrupt way (no small-talk for her, no genteel niceties, no throat-clearing): 'I'm on my way out of town,' she said, 'but I came to say I'm sorry. I'm not sure I should have said all those things that I said. I never did know what was my place or not.'

She looked at Maude with a searching, pleading look; asking to be forgiven, to be absolved for trespassing.

Maude shook her head. 'It's fine,' she said, although she knew that was not quite right. 'Of course it is,' she said, as if she was trying to convince herself. 'You can say what you want.'

There was a pause, and for once Sadie didn't seem to know what to say.

'You were right,' said Maude. 'Pretty much. You were right on the heart of the matter.'

Sadie gave a shadowed grimace with her mouth, twisting it into a smile.

'Doesn't make it any better,' she said. 'It's your life.'

There was another small, loaded silence. In it, Maude wondered if she would ever learn to become a real friend with this alluring woman. Sadie had guessed half of her secret, the broad brush outlines of it; she wondered if she would ever be able to tell the rest. She wanted all at once to confess, to let it out, to be shriven.

Instead, her mind veering away from the black spot, she said, 'How did you know all those things, the things you said?'

'Oh, well,' said Sadie. 'You know, I've seen it; I've seen it before. You get to looking below the surface, if you do my job long enough. And,' she said, 'you have no mirrors in your flat. You have books and pictures and things that other people have, but you don't have a single looking-glass.'

After Sadie had gone Maude sat and thought for a long time. She sat, in her kitchen, in her father's dressing-gown, looking out into the day. A tangle of twisted thoughts ran through her head, chasing themselves into knots. She didn't know what happened next. She had some confused memory, from a long time ago, before her life changed; some barely articulated memory of wanting to do something, to make her mark, to *be* someone. But that had all gone west the day her car had hit that child, as if fate or physics or whatever it was that ordered the universe had taken a hand, laughed in the face of her puny plan.

She had accepted for so long that she would never live any of those possible lives she had dreamt of when she was young; she knew that this dark hidden half-life had been decided for her, and she had become complicit, patrolling her punishment like a prison guard.

She had thought, a few years ago, of going to see the mother; had some bare notion of making amends. But she knew that there was no point in that, because she couldn't make the dead breathe again, and that was the only amend that would mean a damn. She felt that if she were a different person, stronger, *better*, she would have gone and worked in a children's home or trained to counsel abused infants or taken a job with the NSPCC. If she were one of those good strong women, she would have got in a van and driven to Romania and rescued a pack of the lost babies who lived in orphanages there. But she didn't have that strength; she shied away from the idea of having to face real children, each of them a small, ghostly reminder of the one she had killed.

Guilty, full of disgust at her weakness, she had taken the easy way out. She adopted foreign children instead, ones she would never have to see. There were advertisements every week, in the broadsheets, foreign aid charities showing grainy desperate pictures of poor children from struggling countries. For thirty-four pounds a month you could adopt one, thirty-four pounds a month was all it cost to feed and clothe a needy child, give it an education and the hope of something better.

She had twenty adoptees from all over the world, from

Pakistan and Uganda, Guatemala and Eritrea. Every three months, she got a report on their progress, and sometimes, heartbreakingly, bright crayon drawings: This is a cow, this is a tree, I send you greetings to London. You were allowed to write back, although not to a specific address: you were invited to send simple cards and letters via whatever agency it was, and some good concerned field-worker would vet them and pass them on. If she were a really honourable person, Maude thought, she would send postcards of red London buses and the domed cupola of St Paul's, but that was too close for comfort.

She could do this charity from one remove, that was what she could manage. She sent money, and she hoped that one day one of her twenty babies would grow up to be an engineer or a poet, and she might have made up in some small way for the hope that she had taken away. She did this, and she hated herself as she did it, and she knew that however many children she adopted, it would never eradicate the ugly stain of what she had done on that ordinary day in north London.

Maude knew that this was just another one of the twenty-seven things she could never tell Sadie, or the people upstairs; she knew that if they guessed the real dark heart of her secret they would recoil in revulsion. There had been moments, over the last month, when she had been given a glimpse of what it would be like to live a usual and known life, as if she had been taken backstage at a play somewhere, dazzled by the light, and seen what really went on behind the thick red curtains. She had, in forbidden, late-night moments, allowed herself to wonder what it would be like to have the ease and companionship that they held so lightly. But she also knew that would never be possible for her. She could never be more than a spectator, on the sidelines, always at a remove; she had no right to it; she would stay in her silent life, where she belonged.

For all that, she thought that she would write the letter to Alexander Dent. She would send it off and wait for the curt refusal, and she would subside again into her dark room, and she would ghost more books for people who could barely sign their own names and make some more money for her band of adoptees, and that would be an end to it.

She spent the rest of the day writing the letter. She took some care over it, and in the early evening she folded it up and put it into an envelope and walked along to the fat scarlet pillar-box on the corner and posted it off, and then she went home and waited for this man she had never met to tell her no.

Alexander Dent wrote back by return of post and said yes.

It was a qualified yes; but all the same Maude didn't believe it was true. She sat and stared at the letter in rank disbelief, wondering whether it was a hoax or a fraud.

He said that he was interested by her idea, that he would like to meet her, and discuss it further. He said that he didn't have a telephone and he never came to London. He said that if she would come to his house, they could talk about it. He gave her an address in Scotland. He asked, politely, that she should keep it to herself, since he took care to keep where he lived private.

No, Maude thought: this wasn't what was meant to happen. He was supposed to see straight through her and rebuke her for her presumption. He wasn't supposed to invite her to come and see him, this man who hadn't been seen in public for ten years. He guarded his privacy with a ferocity bordering on obsession; that was the official view, peddled in every article ever written about him. There were so many yards of print, so much speculation: the ostentatious death of his famous wife had seen to that. He wasn't just another writer, he was an enigma, and there was nothing the press liked more than that.

Maude didn't understand any of it; she didn't know what was happening. Everything was spinning out of control, and she wanted to turn and run away.

Sadie came round the day the letter arrived. She was beside herself with delight, as if this momentous thing had happened to her.

'You see?' she said. 'You see? This is what happens. You spend your life thinking I can't do this, I can't do that, this is not *allowed*. But if you take your courage and do the frightening thing, sometimes you are rewarded. You are. You see?'

She walked around the kitchen, lifted up on the balls of her feet with excitement.

'Imagine it,' she said. 'Imagine. All those literary lions and articulate critics and venerable academics who have been trying to get to him for years, and now you've done it. I think that strikes a blow for all of us little people.'

Maude stared at her in astonishment. Sadie was as far from the little people as anyone she could imagine; Sadie, with her brio and her determination and her unpredictable hair and her deep sympathy and her shining eyes. Sadie was one of the people who made a difference to things, who seemed to have some inviolable sense of the world and her place in it.

'He might still say no,' said Maude. 'He wants to meet me, that's all. That seems overwhelming, but once he sees me he's bound to think it's an insane idea and he will surely send me packing.'

'No, no,' said Sadie, laughing as if at some secret joke of her own. 'Accentuate the positive, come on, break the habit of a lifetime. Let's find a map and see the way. You should pack. Do you have any thermals?'

Maude looked out at the tropical sun which was still breaking all records for an Indian summer. 'No,' she said. 'I don't.'

Sadie packed Maude up, looked at the road map and plotted a route, right up into the high country, took a spare key and said she would come in and water the garden; and the next morning, very early, while the mist was still rising off the pavements and the heat of the day hadn't yet started to build, Maude found herself driving out to the west, towards Birmingham and the road to the north.

6

Britain is a small island, everything packed together right and tight and bounded on all sides by black sea; that is the official view. Maude was surprised by how long her drive was. It was a Sunday, and there was no traffic on the wide motorways. She pushed up quickly through the Midlands, through the bottleneck between Manchester and Liverpool, into the long stretch past Preston and Lancaster, and then suddenly, like a magic trick, the country opened up, the towns and buildings and industrial estates and rude power stations falling away, and the sky grew wide and endless over her head, and the flat lowlands gave way to the high mountains of the Lake District.

She had always thought of the lakes as a cliché, the province of earnest hill-walkers in vivid anoraks, loaded charabancs packed with American tourists burning with a desire to see old England, copies of Wordsworth tucked under their arms. Maude thought Wordsworth the most overrated of the great poets: she preferred the bleak melancholy of Eliot, the ironic romanticism of Auden, the knotted insanity of Robert Lowell. So when she thought of the lakes, she thought of guesthouses and chugging caravans and platitudes about daffodils and the green hills of home.

She wasn't expecting the country to be untamed and desolate. She wasn't expecting it to be so empty, bare indigo mountains stretching away either side of the road. It wasn't cosy and English and expected: it was disturbing, lonely country, the kind you might find in some distant blasted place, not in the cramped insularity of this little island state.

It stirred something in her and she shook her head and pressed hard on the accelerator, as if to get through it, put it behind her.

While she drove, she listened to music, the sad songs she liked best. The whole history of popular music, she sometimes thought, was composed of sad songs, right from the early scratched recordings of Bessie Smith singing about her lover man. There was a stage in the sixties when there was a rash of snappy sappy jangly songs, jokes about sunshine and laughter and things going the way they were supposed to. But most of it was about loss and yearning and the wrong man and the wrong woman and broken hearts and smashed promises and a world that didn't make any sense.

Maude wondered why that was. She wondered whether it was that the people who wrote the good stuff, the real three-in-the-morning tunes, were by nature the misfits: the freaks and the geeks, the lonely and the lost. They went into their silent rooms with a guitar for company and they wrote it all out and gave it music and maybe then they felt a little better about their bleeding hearts. Singers and songwriters, they weren't the shiny happy people, the ones who put their heads down and painted a smile on their faces and stared at the bright side. They were the ones who never fitted, who didn't talk right or look right or act right, who didn't know the rules (who didn't even know there *were* any rules). And then they went and put all their frustration and vexation and confusion into a song, and the other dislocated people, out there in the dark, heard it, one late night on the radio, and perhaps, for a moment, felt that they were less alone.

Maude sat up in the long nights when she didn't sleep and listened to the bleak songs written by the people who didn't fit in: Leonard Cohen, and Nick Drake, and Gram Parsons, and poor broken Lady Day. She listened to Edith Piaf, singing with desperate defiance about her lack of regrets; she listened to Bob Dylan and his simple twist of fate. They comforted her, these searching voices. But in the end, it didn't do many of them any good. Some of them broke through, the ragged bunch of survivors who cast off the drink and the drugs and the one-night stands, who settled down and never wrote much that was any good after that. But they lived at least, they didn't end up as fish food with a headstone where their life should have been. There were so many casualties: the suicides, the drug-overdosers, the gunshot victims; the drinkers, the jumpers, the drowners and the ones who just walked out into the traffic. And even those who did survive often lived in a half-light, lobotomised by coke and smack and bourbon and never finding the end of the rainbow. These are my people, Maude thought, when she listened to the ragged desperate voices, asking questions to which there were no answers; the ones who never really knew how life worked, however many limos and groupies and platinum credit cards they got.

She made tapes sometimes, in the evenings. She put together poignant compilations of her favourite songs, the ones that touched her heart and made it ache in her chest with recognition and fury. She had brought some with her now: she listened to the plaintive tunes as she drove through the bare grandeur of the north. She listened to 'Eleanor Rigby' (all those lonely people, where did they all come from?); she listened to 'I Got A Right To Sing The Blues', and 'Desolation Row', and 'Five Years' (David Bowie saying it was cold and it rained so he felt like an actor, which always hit a note in her that reverberated like a struck chord, however many times she heard it). Just before she reached Carlisle, she listened to some old Nashville boy singing, as if he knew, as if there was no other answer, that only love can break your heart.

She stopped then, exhausted suddenly, feverish and worn out, her bones aching with driving and thinking and remembering, because these songs were ghosts for her, the phantoms that peopled the years of her loneliness. She pulled into a service station, the gaudy neon of the filling station and the fast-food stop incongruous against the wild country beyond.

She bought a sandwich, and sat on the bonnet of her car, getting some air on her face, and she wondered what the hell she was doing and who did she think she was. The last song kept echoing in her head: *only love can break your heart*.

She wondered how it was that hearts were mended, in the end. Did they ever get mended, or did people just cover over the cracks, put on a brave face because that was the expected thing, and carry this fracture beneath suitable clothes and set expressions and fake lives, because that much hurt was not what people wanted to see; because it grew frightening in the end, seeing the raw edge of despair up close.

She thought she had heard somewhere that only love could *mend* your heart, but she wondered whether this was a myth, put about by playschool Pollyannas, trying to pretend that Santa Claus really existed and there was a tooth fairy, and in actual fact a pot of gold at the end of every rainbow. If Maude knew anything, she knew that rainbows were a big con: you followed them and followed them, and every time you got to where the end should be it had moved on another mile, taunting you with its implausibility.

But it didn't matter, in the end, if love broke your heart or mended it; her heart was finished, and that was where she had to leave it, in the dust, because of what she had done.

She was tired and confused, so far from home. Half of her wanted to turn back and forget the whole thing, go back to where she belonged. She had made a break for freedom, contaminated by Sadie's whirlwind certainty. The past weeks seemed like something from a dream. She wondered if she hadn't imagined the whole thing, that back in the real world Sadie and Ruby and Pearl and Dean would be sitting in the arched studio in the Talgarth Road, talking and eating and laughing and drinking rough red wine and listening to 'Wish You Were Here' and not knowing that anyone called Maude ever existed.

I can't drive like this, she thought. She got into her car and went to sleep.

When she woke it was late in the day. The country around her had taken on a still amber aspect. She started up the car and drove out to the slip road that led on to the motorway. She could turn north or south. She hesitated; maybe she should forget this improbable journey and go back, back to the smoke and the silence and the empty rooms of her life, her real life, her *deserved* life.

Then she thought, But no, this is the right thing,

because the more she thought about it the more she knew that Alexander Dent must surely be waiting to punish her for her importunity; and that was really what she had come for, that was her fate.

The first voice, coming through loud and clear on all frequencies, told her that she should go and take her medicine like a good girl, and then she could go back and it would put an end to this late summer madness. Maude thought: There is one road to take and it leads back to the beginning and nothing will mend my heart.

She drove north.

She had a good memory, precise and unforgiving (it was this recall that never let fade the picture of the small boy disintegrated on the tarmac in front of her murderous car) and she only had to stop and look at the map one more time. The road took her through the failing light past Lockerbie – another picture flashed into her mind, of a crumpled aeroplane nose lying on green grass, the pitiful poignant debris of people's belongings scattered around, a book, a briefcase, one shoe, curiously shiny and intact. She swerved round the outskirts of Glasgow and pushed up through Stirling, past Perth and the prosaic roundabouts of Dundee.

And then, beyond Forfar and Brechin, as she turned left off the main road and into the pass over Cairn O'Mount, it suddenly got wild, wilder than she could have expected. With two switchbacks she was on top of the world, the witching twilight turning the mountains into something mysterious and unimagined.

As she came over the far side and set north towards Inverness the country drew in again, dark forests and wide rivers, and the day died. Banks of clouds like cityscapes filled the horizon, and the weather broke. The last glimmer of light in the sky was extinguished as if someone had turned off a switch and a monsoon rain clapped down, hard as stones.

Maude kept on driving. There was nowhere to stop now; she was almost at journey's end. She felt ill and light-headed, the barbs of her self-reproach digging into her like needles. She was lost, miles from home. She knew the way, she could see it branded on her eyelids like a map, but she was lost all the same, her moorings torn, she was floating away on a high tide.

She drove on, doggedly, steering the car in the right direction. A set of headlights came streaming round the corner and Maude flinched and had to concentrate to keep the car on the road. The tarmac was slick and wet with rain, shining with danger, and the lights flashed past and were extinguished, swallowed up into the forest.

Alexander Dent had said that he lived in the shadow of Morven, not a great mountain, but a distinctive one. You can't miss it, he had written. But now there was only dark and slanting rain lit up like silver in her lights and Maude could barely see ten yards in front of her.

She found the turning, as he had described it; just as she thought she couldn't go on, there it was. She pulled off the road, her head burning. It's the driving, she thought, it's the distance; it's too much.

The drive was long and pitted, under an arcade of heavy trees, the rain coming down harder than ever. Maude put her foot down, speeding up, on the last lap. Her eyes were boiling and scratched with tiredness; she dreamt suddenly of warmth and light and a dry house and a bed with starched linen; and then there was the flash of something tan in her lights and she blinked and snapped her head upright and punched her foot down on the brake but it was too late.

No, no, not again; *not again.*

She had hit something.

Tears erupted out of her, the same tears she had cried the time before, in the street surrounded by polite English strangers. Time screeched to a halt and turned back on itself and she didn't know where she was, here or there; she couldn't understand why she was in a rain-filled dark when this happened on a bright Tuesday afternoon.

No, no, she heard her voice calling, out loud, into the night, and it brought back some sanity; her mind slotted back into real time, which was not London, not ten years ago. It was here and now and she was on her way to see Alexander Dent, she was on his drive, and she had hit something.

It was a deer. She didn't know enough about deer to tell which breed or even which sex it was, whether it was full-grown or just a yearling, but she knew enough about death to know that it was finished. From the dimmed light of the car headlights she could see the glistening tan of its hide, slick and wet with rain. She could see the individual hairs on its back, twenty different shades of dun and brown and chestnut, the white markings at its throat, the liquid eye turned towards her, in mild dead reproach. It had been a beautiful live creature and she had trashed and broken it; its neck was turned at a violent angle, cutting off life at the source.

The track was narrow and the animal was wedged under her wheels. She tried to drag it away, crying helpless childish sobs. She pulled on one of its spindle-thin legs, couldn't get a purchase, grazed her palm on the sharp hoof. Pain, she thought, that's right, that's what you deserve. She looked down dispassionately, as if her hand didn't belong to her, and saw blood washing away with the rain. The rain was so thick she could barely see through it, it fell like a wall, something actual and solid and impenetrable.

There was nothing to do. The creature was dead and gone and she couldn't move her car. She thought about sitting in the driving seat until light came, sitting vigil by the extinguished deer.

She knew she couldn't do that. She had to get to the house. It couldn't be far now. Just up the drive, Dent had written, keep going till you reach the end.

She walked, in the black and the rain, the reels of memory flashing through her head; the grief and desperation, the howling nothingness of what she had done all those years ago, unravelling within her, as if this second collision had unleashed something she had held tight and contained in her all this time.

She had cried, when it actually happened, in the street, crying into the arms of a phlegmatic policeman, saying, It's my fault, it's my fault, it's me, it's *me*. But immediately afterwards she put a guard round all that, reined it in, shut it down. She lived with her sense of culpability and the real knowledge that she could never let go again, never live as other people did, careless and messy and free; tears were an indulgence, something she wasn't allowed.

So she didn't cry again. The mother, she deserved tears, she had *earned* her tears: tears, after all, must invite sympathy, and that was another of the seventy things that Maude would not allow herself. So she had hidden it, buried it, deep inside, kept everything in check.

Now, with this second coming, this death revisited, it was as if all that control had been ripped away with one stroke. Maude felt as if the actual layer of skin covering her stomach had been torn away and that her guilt and despair were spilling out into the night.

She walked and walked, barely remembering how to put one foot in front of another. The woods were dark and deep, and the sliver of her mind that still held some thought in it wondered if it might be frightened, that this was where the demons and wood sprites and crazed axemen and creatures of the forest lived, but there wasn't room for that, because it was raining too hard and she was crying too hard and she had her hands held together over her belly as if physically to keep her guts from spilling out on to the ground and she knew that she had to put one foot in front of the other, one foot one foot, and keep walking or she would die.

She walked and walked; she couldn't tell how far or how long. Her watch, which was the old-fashioned kind you had to wind, was misted and clogged with water and even when she brought it right to her face she couldn't see the hands.

Loud gouting sobs tore out of her like waves until she thought she couldn't survive it, couldn't walk any more, should just give up and lie down there on the rutted path and let it all run away. It was cold, the temperature dropping so fast she could feel it: she would be like Captain Oates, walking out into the snow. She could lie down and it would be over, all the hurt and struggle and this wild, wracking grief.

But the first voice, still going against all the odds, told

her she had to go on, that dying was the easy option, the coward's way out. So she kept on walking, and just as she thought she might crumple and fall, with nothing animate left in her, not even the engine of her own shame, she saw a light.

She banged at the door, one arm still wrapped round her stomach; she had a fleeting vision of what Alexander Dent would see when he opened the door – an insane bedraggled figure, eyes slitted with crying, face red and swollen and drowned with rain – the woman who had come to write his life story.

Dent opened the door so abruptly that Maude stumbled forward, and before he could speak she looked up with beseeching eyes, barely able to see straight: his face was no more than a shadow against the hot yellow light coming from his hall. She said, 'I'm Maude, I'm Maude Strong,' and as the blackness poured in, grey first, then pitch ebony, she thought, This is it, this is what dying feels like, and then there was no more.

7

She woke up she didn't know how long later; she woke herself up with coughing. She had no moment of disorientation. She knew exactly where she was and what had happened. She felt drowned in shame and all she wanted to do was put her clothes on and run away.

It felt like someone had put a girder on her chest and she tried to sit up but she couldn't. She lay back and looked at the ceiling. The whole room seemed to be made of white wood; the ceilings were slanted in, as if she were on a ship. There were shutters at the window and limed floorboards and her bed was made of painted white metal, an old-fashioned bed, the kind they used to have in strict Victorian seminaries, and there were two pale plaid blankets over her, and a green tapestry rug on the floor and a small wooden table with a bottle of water and a glass on it, and a lamp, which was shedding a low light on the ceiling. She wondered where Alexander Dent was.

She was shaken with a long fit of coughing. She was hacking out thick pustules of slime from her lungs, and she reached over for a tissue and spat into it and thought with bitter satisfaction that it was entirely fitting that this was what she was bringing up because that was what she felt like, inside.

The coughing passed and she lay back and felt faint and ill and desperate, and she wondered if she would ever learn to grow into someone who wasn't such a falling-apart mess.

She went back to sleep; she woke twice in the night with coughing. She wondered if she was disturbing anyone, but no one came. She wondered, in a late-night moment of delirious half waking half dreaming, whether they had just put her in the attic and left her to die, like Mrs Rochester.

She woke early the next morning. The rough old linen, the kind that comes from France or Greece or some hot foreign place, was wrapped around her like a winding sheet and soaking from sweat. The girder across her chest was still there and although the room was dim from the shutters closed against the light, some early-morning sun was creeping round them, and even that was enough to make Maude wince. She hadn't been ill for years, not since she was a child and she developed a mystery illness that made her head feel like lead, and she had crawled on her hands and knees, because she couldn't lift her lead head to walk, down the stairs to her parents' room. Her mother looked distracted and annoyed, and called the doctor, who was young and modern and clearly excited by such violent symptoms; she prescribed huge doses of paracetamol and opening all the windows.

'But it's January,' said Maude's mother. She might not have known much about the world but everyone knew that you had to sweat out a fever; turn the heat up and dole out soup.

'Freezing air,' said the doctor, humming with pleasure. 'And pills every two hours,' she said. 'You'll see.'

'I'm dying,' said Maude, without melodrama. She was a literal child and that was what it felt like.

'Don't be absurd,' said her mother, who really wanted to get back to the British Museum.

'I'm dying,' said Maude, opening her red eyes a slit. 'And that doctor is killing me.'

She lay all day with her head heavy and filled with explosives; she had never felt anything like it in her life. Gales of frosty air came in, gusting across the room; she could see slate sky from the open windows. She sweated and cried and sweated and cried and rolled over and over, groaning, as if noise alone would alleviate the pain.

Then suddenly, at six that night, it was gone.

The doctor was smug as hell and said I told you so. Maude never got measles or mumps or even chicken pox; she never got sick again, but she always remembered that time.

Now, in her real life, she realised that in spite of the girder she had to get out of bed because she had to take a pee. Her legs were boneless and white and she wondered if she was going to have to crawl again, like when she was six. She thought that would be good: if she ran into Alexander Dent, he would surely hire her on the spot to write the truth about him.

By holding on to the solid metal frame of her bed and leaning over and catching the door knob, she managed to get across the room. She opened the door and leant on the jamb; there was a small landing outside, lit from a skylight which had sun pouring down from it like water. Maude screwed up her eyes and tried to hold herself together. There was a door opposite and that was her only choice. She managed to walk over to it and open it and it was the bathroom and she swung herself down on the wooden seat of the lavatory and felt like she had climbed Everest and should plant a flag.

I must be hysterical or delirious, she thought; I must be delusional and hallucinating and all fucked up. I wonder, she thought, if there is anyone else in this whole bloody house.

Days, hours, weeks later: the bedroom door opened and Alexander Dent walked in. The lintel of the door was low and he had to bend his head; it looked like a curious gesture of civility, some kind of outdated reverence, the contained movement that religious people make when they approach the altar.

Maude thought that her mind was wandering: it felt as if it had nothing to cling to, no centre; it was moving around her head as if it had never been there before.

'How are you?' Dent asked. There was a formality in his speech too: the stilted intonation of the recluse.

Maude felt a wash of shame spill over her. She wanted to get into her car and drive far away and forget that she had ever embarked on this misconceived journey. She shut her eyes for a moment to block out the light white room.

'I don't know,' she said. 'Terrible,' she said. 'I feel as if my chest is filled with stones.'

'You have had pneumonia,' he said. 'The doctor came. Do you remember?'

The shame roared up into a tidal wave and crashed over her. She had a horrible and vivid picture of herself sweating and raving: she could remember nothing about it. There had been too many people in her head; she couldn't remember which were dreamt and which were actual.

'No,' she said. 'I don't remember.'

'You had a high fever,' he said. 'You have been very ill.'

Maude thought it was too hackneyed to be true. It was bad enough that she was here at all; but a soaring temperature and raving fever; and no memory.

'Do you remember how you got here?' Alexander Dent said. His voice was steady and straight, with no pity in it. Maude was glad for that, at least.

'It was raining,' said Maude. 'There was a storm.'

Then it tumbled back into her mind and she saw the dark drive and the thin light of the headlamps and the black shape leaping out in front of her and the revolting jolt of impact.

'I hit a deer,' she said. 'Oh, God. I hit a deer.'

Her voice caught and stumbled and without meaning to she started to cry loud raw tears.

'I killed a deer,' she said.

Alexander Dent left her alone. Maude felt she was crying for everything she had ever known. She felt lost and unhinged, as if all the tight defences she had so carefully built up were crashing down around her and she didn't know if she would survive it.

Dent came back later with a tray. There was soup and bread and water and, surprisingly somehow, a bowl of strawberries. Maude was quiet and still now; she couldn't meet his eye.

'You should eat.' She heard his voice come into the still white room. 'You should eat something.'

He put the tray on a table by Maude's bed and left again. She was glad that he realised she wanted to be alone.

*   *   *

For two more days she lay in bed, watching the weather change outside her window. She could see sky and a green stretch of forested mountain rising into the distance. The clouds moved fast across the sky and she lay back, without energy or emotion, watching them go. She let her mind go slack and didn't think about anything; she felt as if there was a blank thing inside her.

Dent came and went. He brought her food and clean towels and tea in a squat china pot. The clothes she had arrived in had been laundered and sat in a neat pile on a chair against the wall. She looked at them and knew that soon she would have to put them on and get up, get back into the world and deal with the mess she had made of it. She didn't want to do that: she dreaded it in the lurking black way that you dread an exam you haven't studied for.

But on the next day, she got up. She knew she couldn't put it off any longer. She had stopped coughing; the weakness that invaded her was receding. She felt her body come back to life.

She knew that she had to go downstairs and face Dent. She knew she had to say goodbye and that it was all a horrible mistake. She hoped that he might be out, or locked in a room writing, so that she wouldn't have to face him. She could leave a note and get into her car and drive south, back the way she came, back to the silence of her dim basement room.

But when she got dressed and went downstairs he was sitting at a table in the window, reading, and he looked up, and said, 'So, are you ready to start?'

For a moment, she didn't know what he was talking about. The room receded and came back at her, as if she were watching it through a long lens. It was two storeys high with windows on all sides, so that half of it seemed like the sky, the mountains, the trees – as if there was no distinction between what was inside and what was out. The sun was shining, in a thicker, yellower way than it did in the south. It had some ancient viscous quality to it; it was old light, it had been here before.

The walls were painted bright white, and the sun lit them and made them gleam and glow against the blue shadows of the country outside. Alexander Dent sat in the middle of this, like a character in a play.

It was strange, Maude thought, her mind slightly detached, to know so well how someone looked from photographs and pictures, and then to see them in life. They look exactly the same, instantly recognisable, but also different in some indefinable way. The last photograph of Dent had been taken ten years ago, so of course he was literally different. He had aged: the dark fox red of his hair had faded to brown and there was grey in it, his eyes had dark lines round them, there was a hollowness in his face that there hadn't been before, when he was young and mighty and ruling the literary world. But it was more than that: he was in three dimensions now, not the flat still of a photograph. Maude found that intimidating, on top of everything else.

She knew, suddenly, what he meant, and she thought he was a fool; or perhaps he was playing with her, luring her with false promise before he brought the boom down and whacked her with the backlash of her own impertinence.

She didn't say anything because she didn't know what to say. She stood, mute, like a child waiting for its punishment.

'Do you want to?' said Alexander Dent.

A long time went by. Maude shook her head. 'I can't,' she said. 'Surely you must see that? I didn't think for a moment you were serious.'

Dent looked at her, raising his eyebrows. He had amber eyes that slanted a little, like a cat, she thought, her mind growing loose again. She thought she had never seen that colour before. Before, she had only seen him in black and white. He was too real, now; he had lived in her head for years, a pristine picture, untouched by reality, and now he was actual and present and she wanted to run away. She was nobody and he was somebody and there was no place for her here.

'You came all this way,' he said, 'because you thought I wasn't serious?'

Maude felt foolish and childish and at a loss. She ducked her head and wished she could just say goodbye and pick up her bag and go.

Dent smiled, a surprising broad smile, and got up and said, 'I'm hungry. Let's eat something. We'll eat, and you can tell me.'

I don't want to tell you, Maude shouted in her head; I don't want anything. I don't want pity and understanding. I want to be sent away with my tail between my legs.

She was too tired to say anything out loud. This bizarre journey, the crash, being ill, all this had drained everything out of her and it felt as if nothing had come to fill the gap. There was a space inside her; she felt light and impossible.

Dent led the way into the kitchen which was broad and low with fat windows looking out over a distant range of green hills. The floor was flagged with uneven stone and the walls were panelled and painted the same thick blue as the sky; there were old tallboys and sideboards arranged round the walls carrying china and glass and steel pots, and it was nothing like Maude had expected. There was something domestic about it, but exotic at the same time, no fitted cabinets and gleaming appliances, a kitchen from another era. There was a pewter range against the back wall, battered and marked from use, and Dent lifted the lid of one of the hobs and put a kettle on to boil.

'Sit down,' he said. He had a low contained voice with something cracked running through it. Maude realised that that also was what was different: she had seen his picture and read his words but she had never heard him speak.

She sat down at one end of a long wooden table covered in papers and books and herbs in pots and looked up at him mutely as if he could tell her what happened next.

He made a pot of pungent black coffee and a dish of eggs with olive oil and put them on the table with bread and butter and tomatoes and told her she should eat. She ate the food and she felt better. She realised that she liked this pale room with its wide view. She had pictured Dent living in a dark, closed house, something inhibited and cramped, hidden from the world. She hadn't expected all this light and space; all this generous open space.

'So,' he said, after a while. 'Do you want to tell me?'

'I don't know,' said Maude. She still couldn't meet his eye. 'I don't know what there is to tell.'

Dent smiled again; quizzical this time, and questioning. Maude noticed that his shirt had a darn in one sleeve and frayed cuffs. For some reason, she found this reassuring.

'There's a whole story there somewhere,' said Dent. 'It was just a deer, and you cried as if it was the end of the world. And now you seem to think that I got you here to tell you to leave. There's a whole bank of subtext that it doesn't take a genius to see.'

Maude flinched and looked away. She had never known she was so obvious. But Sadie had seen something too, so perhaps there was more written in her face than she had thought.

'I'm sorry,' said Dent. 'It's your private business. If you want to go, of course you must go. But I was interested in your idea and it seems wasteful to turn round and go back when you've come all this way.'

Maude suddenly realised she didn't know what day of the week it was.

'What day is it today?' she said.

'Friday,' said Dent, without a beat. 'It's Friday.'

There was a long silence and Dent did nothing to fill it. Maude had a shouting match hurling around in her head. All at once, she wanted to tell him everything, because she was worn out with carrying it with her, like a sack of cement over her shoulder; she was sick of fighting it and beating herself with it and not letting anyone see it. He was a complete stranger to her; he might not welcome sudden confession. But she felt she knew him in some way because she had read all the books over and over again, and if you really want to know a writer, don't read the biographies or the articles or the letters or the interviews, read the work, because that's where it all comes out. Not in the direct autobiographical way that people expect (Is that you? Is that your mother, your house, your childhood, *your smashed-up life?*); in a more subtle way. Everything the writer hopes and dreams and fears is there in the work; all the beliefs and the fragile hopes and the night terrors and the dogged faith in human nature.

Maude felt that she knew this man, but she only knew him on the page, in dense black print; it was something else sitting opposite him now, seeing him in flesh and bone and wanting to tell him the story of her life. She wondered fleetingly whether everyone wants to tell writers about their lives, because the temptation is too great; it might get written into a story, a paragraph, a cameo appearance, and all that strife and trouble is immortalised, at a tangent, in the authority of print.

Without meaning to, she started talking. Afterwards, she wondered what it was; whether it was because of Sadie, who had come along and started to chip at Maude's defences; or if it was the journey, the rash decision, the death of the deer, that took her back so immediately to the flat afternoon in north London; or all those things, building one on another, until there was nothing to do but give in. Or, she thought, perhaps it was something to do with Dent himself, something in his silent patience that invited confidence. She felt in some nebulous way that she owed him something: a raw confession in exchange for breaking into his contained life.

She opened her mouth before she could think about it more and began speaking; words jumbled out of her in no particular order.

'It was a punishment,' she said, and she saw something move in his face, surprise or recognition. 'Because that's how I live my life, that's what I deserve. I had an absurd idea, but I kept thinking about it, how I wanted to write something about you, about your work. I read your books over and over, and it started growing in me like an obsession. I knew I would never do anything about it, because why on earth would you want to talk to me, but there was a woman I met and she argued me into it. So I sent the letter and you replied and then I got it in my head that you would bring me up here to upbraid me for such presumption, and that seemed fitting, so that's how it happened.'

'But why the punishment?' said Dent, as if the rest of it made sense, as if he could understand something from this warped and rushed narrative. 'And why me?'

'Because,' said Maude, 'on the day you did . . . had . . . your accident, I mean, the day your wife died, the very same day, I was driving down a street in London and a child ran out into the road. I didn't see him, I didn't brake in time, and I killed him, and that's all.'

There was a really long silence this time. Maude sat in it, dazed with relief and revelation.

Alexander Dent was very still. His eyes clouded over as if they had gone back into the past, into some place Maude couldn't follow.

After a while, he looked over at her, across the long table, and he looked uncertain; or something else – vulnerable perhaps; as if someone had come along and stripped him naked and left him out in the rain. He's going to change his mind now, Maude thought, now he knows the truth. Now he can send me away and then it's done.

'My God,' he said, in a slow voice. 'All that. You've been carrying that for ten years, and you brought it here so you could be punished.'

But he didn't say it in a questioning way, he said it as if it made perfect sense, as if it was explicable and usual and the only expected thing.

'You know,' he said, shaking his head as if in apology, 'that I can't do that for you.'

'Yes,' said Maude. Everything rolled away from her and the world was suddenly filled with clarity. 'I know that.'

She started to laugh. 'You've given me a present instead,' she said, seeing it clearly now, as if someone had wiped a glass in front of her, so the view was distinct and true, instead of distorted by dirt and dust. 'It wasn't what I planned, but that's what's happened. Because you made me tell you, and now it's different, in the mere act of telling.'

Another pause; another silence. And then: 'You must have told someone,' Dent said. 'There must have been someone.'

'There was a therapist,' said Maude. Her voice was low and easy now, as if she knew she could say anything without fear of reprisal or misunderstanding. 'She said I could forgive myself. She didn't understand that wasn't the point. The point was that I should suffer, because of what I'd done. I couldn't bring back the dead, but I could suffer for it, as if that was some kind of reparation, as if in some way that would square the circle. I wasn't much good to her. She said it was an accident, she said it was one of those bad things that happen to good people. She said it could have happened to anyone. She wanted me to get better and get on with my life and I sat there telling her that wasn't the point, that it was an eye for an eye.'

'And then the whole world is blind,' Dent said.

Maude gave him a sharp questioning look and then she laughed again, the muscles in her throat tight and rusty from lack of use.

'That's what she said. That's the exact thing she said. She said: Then the whole world is blind.'

*   *   *

They sat for hours, at the kitchen table. When Maude looked up again it seemed the room had shifted, as if it was something familiar to her now. The light was fading and it was evening. She could barely remember what they talked about, that first day. They just talked. She hadn't done that for as long as she could remember. She thought perhaps she had never done that, even before the accident. She remembered the silent watchful child she had been, the introverted adolescent. It was the way she had been brought up: everyone was always talking in her house, but not to her; words were not her property. And now it felt as if the walls had come tumbling down and the voices in her head were out and running and Alexander Dent listened to her as if she were not mad or bad but someone who had a right to talk, a right to be heard.

It was six o'clock and she was exhausted with talking and revelation and the strangeness of this day. She fell silent, and she didn't know what happened next. Even after all this, she knew that she had no place here, that this day would stay as something still and out of time. She knew that it was something she would always remember and feel grateful for; she knew also that she should get up and thank him for it and drive away.

'Don't leave,' said Alexander Dent, into the tired pause. 'Not now.'

'I would like it,' he said, in his low serious voice, 'if you would stay.'

8

Maude woke early the next morning; the light was still a suggestion somewhere outside the open window. The raw air of the day came in and moved over her face, and she felt it like a kiss or a promise. Her mind lay flat, stilled in the cusp between dream and reality, rising from the unknown of sleep with nothing yet to fill it. In that quiet moment, she didn't think, she just felt the rough white sheets on her back, the wind on her face, the weight of the bedclothes on her legs.

She opened her eyes wider and raised herself up on her elbows and looked out at the mountains: an opaque light hit the trees in the distance and drew them in eight different shades of green.

She thought of what had happened yesterday, the long snaking afternoon of words running back through her head. For a moment she felt a shaft of terror, because she had revealed herself, but then she remembered Dent's voice when he asked her to stay. The fear drained away, and she felt something come to replace it so unknown to her that it took her a while to put a word to it. Safe; that's what it was. She felt safe.

She got up and reached into her overnight bag and put on her dressing-gown, her father's dressing-gown, its worn silk falling around her like a memory, and she went downstairs to the kitchen, feeling the cool wood of the stairs against her feet.

She made a cup of coffee and sat and drank it and watched the day outside the windows. It was before eight and there was a fine mist rising from the ground. The coffee tasted thin and bitter in her mouth and she took some sugar to sweeten it.

Dent walked in, dressed in dark trousers and a blue shirt, and smiled at her as if she had a right to be there. Maude looked up and suddenly felt conscious that she was not yet dressed – a stranger sitting in his kitchen, a stranger who had told him the most intimate thing in her life.

He sat down opposite her and smiled again. 'Did you sleep well?' he said, and it was so usual and mundane that Maude felt her shyness subside.

'Yes,' she said. 'Yes, I did.'

'Did you have any breakfast?' he said. She shook her head, and he got up and went into the larder and looked around. 'There's bacon,' he said. 'And peaches.'

They ate the peaches in their fingers and the juice ran down their hands. Dent cooked the bacon in an iron pan and made it into sandwiches with thick white bread and they ate those too and Maude thought that she had never seen a man who was so at home in a kitchen. But then she thought she hadn't seen that many men. She hadn't seen that many anyone.

'Is it strange,' she said, 'having someone here? When you are so used to being on your own?'

Dent shook his head. 'I'm not quite as reclusive as everyone thinks,' he said. 'I stepped out of the world when my wife died, at first because I needed time to get myself together and you can't do that in a crowd. But then the engine of the media started up and the whole thing turned into a freak show, and I couldn't face it. I

110

knew if I ever went back, into the limelight, the questions would be unbearable. So I moved here and no one much knows about it. But there are people I see. I have some friends near Inverness, and I have a daughter who visits, and there's Richard Hunter, who lives out the back.'

Maude looked questioning.

'There's an old stone house, it was a stable originally, and I converted it,' said Dent. 'I was going to use it as a studio, somewhere quiet, but then I met Richard and he came to live there instead. He is,' he said carefully, 'another one; a victim of fate, whatever you want to call it. His sister died. They were sailing together and she drowned. He tried to save her and he couldn't and he felt it was his fault. He drank, that was his escape, *his* punishment perhaps, and he had drunk away all his money and all his hope by the time I met him. I saw him in Glasgow once, on the street, and we started talking, and it turned out he had read everything I had ever written, and there was something there, so I gave him the house. It was barely habitable then, but he started working on it, and he gave up the bottle, and he got himself back. People think it's kindness,' he said, as if Maude had spoken, 'but it's not. You can't save people, but sometimes you can throw out a lifeline, and then you save yourself, a little.'

Maude nodded. She understood that. She had her band of orphans, and they were her lifeline, in a way; they made some of the unbearable bearable.

'Yes,' she said. 'Yes. It's whatever gets you through the night.'

'He's away at the moment,' Dent said. 'He went over to Orkney. Sometimes he gets tired of the mountains and it's flat as hell up there.'

'And anyway,' he said, getting up to clear away the empty plates, 'loneliness is in your soul; it's not to do with how many people you surround yourself with. Solitude never killed anyone, but living with someone and still being alone, that will kill you, in the end.'

Maude wondered afterwards if he was talking about his dead wife when he said that.

She went upstairs and dressed and when she came down Dent was sitting at the table in the main room, just as he had the day before. The sun had moved in through the windows and the mountains were blue in the distance and the white panelled walls were bright and clean in the light.

Maude looked around, taking it in as she had not been able to before. The floorboards were pale and worn and there was a long scarlet sofa against one wall and two armchairs with white carved frames and sagging cane seats; there was a low table and a ponyskin rug and a high marble fireplace with a Venetian mirror over it, flat and silver and figured with fine engraving.

The main part of the room was double height, two rows of windows at the front, set squarely one above the other, and the mountains out there were double height too, one range beyond another, blue and rolling as the sea. At the back, where Dent was sitting, the room reverted to normal height, and there was a round table, walnut or some exotic wood, and chairs in ageing bamboo.

There was nothing extraneous, no ornaments or mementoes, no curiosities or conversation pieces. Maude found it restful and cool; but there was something missing and for a moment she couldn't work out what it was.

'There are no books,' she said, suddenly getting it. She frowned. 'How curious,' she said. 'There are no bookshelves.'

'There's another room,' said Dent, 'across the hall, where . . . where I work. That's where the books are.'

Maude wanted to see this other room but felt it would be indelicate to ask and he didn't offer.

'So,' he said, 'do you want to start?'

She sat down opposite him and leant her elbows on the table. It was sturdy and solid and took her weight. 'I don't know,' she said.

Dent shook his head, as if he wasn't sure himself. 'I don't know either,' he said. 'It's something about your story, about the same day. It's like something from a Paul Auster novel, all that chance. People love chance, they call it fate and think it is trying to tell them something. I'm not immune to that.'

'Six hundred thousand people die every year in Britain,' said Maude. 'I looked it up once. I never could believe it was that many, but it's true. Think of that: six hundred thousand bereaved people, more than that, because it's never just one that's left behind, it's all the friends and families, the wives and daughters, the sons and lovers. All that grief. I sometimes walk the streets and wonder how the city goes on at all, with that weight of grief bearing down on it. I know that many of them will have been old or unloved, will have died quietly in their sleep. But a lot won't; and some will have been the victims of grotesque accidents like the one that I did. So there must be many other people who suffered the same thing on that day. It could be any of a thousand other people.'

'Yes,' said Dent. 'But they didn't come here, and you did.'

Maude gave a twisted smile. 'I did come,' she said. 'I still wonder how I did, but I did.'

'And perhaps,' said Dent, 'it was timing as well. Perhaps I find that I do want to talk, after all this time. What was it that you had in mind? Portrait of the artist as a broken man?'

Maude laughed. 'No,' she said. 'Not that. More that you might want to put your side of the story. All those years I was reading your books, I read every word of what was written about you, and about your marriage, and how they made your wife into some kind of martyr, and then it became a feeding frenzy. I thought it must drive you insane, all that speculation, all that speculative print; I thought it must be maddening for you, that the controversy of the life sometimes obscures the work.'

She stopped suddenly. She never talked. She never made speeches. She said yes and no and how terrible to Mr Seth, when he told her about the newest superbug that had got into New York on the backs of mosquitoes hidden in a shipment of tyres from Nigeria, and that Ebola would soon be stalking the streets of Queens; she said thank you and goodbye to the silent bookshop woman. And now she was making speeches.

Alexander Dent didn't seem to notice.

'There is that,' he said, and there was something unwilling in his voice that she couldn't identify. 'But then it is the work that survives, it is the work that speaks for you, and the acres of newsprint are in the end only tomorrow's fish-and-chip wrapping. Most writers don't bother with putting the record straight, they don't bother with the life because it's the work that counts.'

'Yes,' said Maude. 'Yes.'

He seemed to be making her argument for her, because now she was here, seeing him in life instead of on the page, she didn't want to do it, she wanted him to keep silent and let the work speak for him, because no one could ever take that away from him.

'There was Nabokov, I suppose,' said Dent. 'There was *Speak, Memory*. And Auster did *The Red Notebook*, and Amis wrote *Experience*, which told the truth about the teeth. Fitzgerald had *The Crack-up* and Updike did something, I can't remember what it was called. I would never do it myself,' he said. 'It's not in me. But you are a ghost-writer: I talk and you write. That's what you came here to do. And perhaps,' he said again, as if wondering himself, 'I do need to talk.'

There was a vulnerability running through him like a hairline fracture; Maude hadn't seen it before, and now she wondered that she hadn't. He had seemed so assured and certain when they talked the day before, and since she had been here she had been the one cracked and broken, opened wide by the death of the deer, bringing all the memories back to vivid, tearing life. She had been crying out in her sleep and full of fever, and he was the writer and he had the reputation and he was the strong one. She had assumed that he had somehow recovered from what had happened to him in a way that she had not been able to. But now, in the light, sunlit room, she saw the jagged gulf of his past open up, and she wanted suddenly, urgently, to comfort him. She looked away, so as not to betray herself, but perhaps he had seen something.

'It's all right,' he said. 'It's all right.'

'I don't know,' said Maude. 'I don't know that it's such a good idea.'

'Why don't we start?' said Alexander Dent. 'And then we'll see what happens.'

Maude turned on her tape-recorder, and Dent talked. He talked for five days. They paused sometimes to eat something, or get outside and walk in the clear northern air. But mostly he talked. As the words poured out of him and Maude recorded it all, she wondered whether, like her, he had essentially been silent for the last ten years, and now all those words that had been dammed up in him were coming out, in an unstoppable stream.

He talked at first about fiction, as if that were a safe place to start, something impersonal and known to him, something from his professional life.

'It's like a love affair,' he said. 'I heard someone interviewed on the radio, not long ago, a young male writer who is having a lot of commercial success; he said he didn't read. I was astounded by that, I didn't understand how you could write and not read. You forget about it sometimes, what it was that made you do it in the first place. It's something in you, some urgent desire to tell stories, to get all those imagined spectres in your head on to the page; it's a desire also to make sense of the world, because only fiction can do that. Life has no narrative, it's random and inexplicable and formless, and that's why people want to believe in something, because it makes the unbearable meaninglessness of it explicable. Fiction does that: it soothes a deep searching part of you, because you can take the chaos of the world and give it shape, give it sense.'

He paused and took out a pack of cigarettes and lit one

and smoked at it. 'I gave up for years,' he said. 'But then after Claudette it didn't seem to matter any more.'

Maude sat very still, wondering if he would talk about his wife then, but perhaps it was too early for that, and he went back to what he was most comfortable with, which was talking about words.

'Do you know Laura Riding?' he said, and Maude shook her head. She had read a lot, she had found a refuge in fiction, because however desperate and miserable the stories were, they always made sense, and her life made no sense at all. But she knew already that his breadth of knowledge made hers look like a shallow pool.

'No,' she said. 'Who was she?'

Alexander Dent smiled involuntarily as if he were talking about an old friend, someone he was so fond of that just the thought of them brought pleasure to him.

'She was a poet,' he said. 'She was an extraordinary woman. She was an American poet, and in 1938 she gave up poetry altogether and disappeared. Suddenly in 1962, she resurfaced, on the BBC of all places, I heard a recording of it years later. She said something that I always remembered and I think is the point of the whole thing. She said that we know we are explainable, and not explained. She said that until the missing story of ourselves is told, we shall go on quietly craving it.'

Dent put out his cigarette and smiled again and came back in a perfect circle to where he had started. 'That's what I mean about fiction being like love. It's for that exact reason that we write, and more than that, why we read. And as a writer you do forget sometimes that really you started because you fell in love with a book, that it moved something in you, like when you meet a person and look at them and feel your heart shift within you. You go on and you're working yourself, you have your head down; and then every so often you pick up a book and after a page or two that swoon in your heart comes again, because there is something so perfect there on the page. This is it, you think, this is what it is all about. We read to know who we are, someone else said, I can't remember who, and that's some of it. We read to know that we are not alone. But it's more complicated than that, and more so if it is what you *do*. Sometimes I think it's a tortured love, an unrequited love; there are times when you read something so beautiful that it wrenches you, because you know that you may never achieve that pitch of perfection yourself. There is a part of you, the arrogance that keeps you writing at all, that thinks, perhaps, perhaps, one day; and there is another part that is filled with envy; and then there is a practical part that reads something like the list of the party guests in Gatsby, one of the most perfect passages ever written, that says everything about yearning and wishing and the taunting impossibility of the American dream, and that practical part says, But look at Fitzgerald, he was a lush and an embarrassment and he sold himself out and died alone in a rented room in Hollywood. But it is love, for all that, however complicated it is, it is love, maybe the truest and most enduring love you will ever have.'

He stopped abruptly, and at the same time the tape in the machine came to an end and turned itself off with a sinuous click of minute machinery, and Alexander Dent looked up at Maude and laughed ruefully at himself and said, 'Is this what you wanted?' as if she might be bored or restive or regretting that she had ever asked him, and she looked back at him in amazement that he might have

118

any doubt, because she thought it was the most beautiful talk she had ever heard.

Afterwards, Maude looked back on that week as one of the most perfect times in her life; that week of talk. It was as if this bizarre chain of events had been the catalyst that allowed her to live again, like a normal person. Or, rather, that the crushing burden of guilt and shame and recrimination had been lifted for a moment, allowing her to see something else, something other than the grey expanse of her culpability. It was as if the wrenching tears she had cried for the deer had washed something from her. If she had been given to mysticism, she would have said that they had washed her clean, and although there was a secret part of her that felt that, she shied away from believing it; partly because she thought it too fantastical, too *simple*; partly because she was not sure how long this would last, whether it was just a gap, a caesura, a moment given to her when she could step out of her life and feel released. She wasn't so optimistic to think that it would always be like this. But when she had said to Alexander Dent that he had given her a present, she was telling the truth.

Because of this, this feeling of impermanence and unreality, she stopped thinking about herself and what she had done (all those silent years in her dim room, when there was nothing else to think about) and let herself be carried along on Dent's stream of talk.

There were moments when he stopped and gave her the same questioning look as he had on the first day, as if to say, is this all right, is this *allowed*?, and it never stopped surprising her, that he might have any doubt.

Perhaps, she thought, needing some justification herself, this was a release for him too; perhaps this was some kind of unburdening. He never used it as a confession, and until the very end, he barely talked about himself in intimate terms. He talked about his passion for writing and writers, and there were lines to be read between, but he didn't give her many personal details. He never talked about his childhood or his parents or his early love affairs; and most of all he barely mentioned his dead wife, who stood as a ghostly presence, silent, in the corner of the room.

On the fourth day, Dent talked for a long time about his third book, *Black Dawn*. This was the novel that made him famous; one moment he was not there, and the next he was known in eighteen different countries and no one could remember what they had done before he was there. It happens like that sometimes; not so often, because there aren't many people out there with that kind of talent, the kind that is so transparently real, so patently other, that it brings a kind of recognition with it, a vibrating chime of authenticity – this is the real thing, the real McCoy, and there is no doubt in anyone's mind, and the literary landscape is changed for ever.

In those days Dent was married and in the public eye because his wife took him there; she was famous long before he was. For a while, he had been the dark horse to her shooting star. He was a reluctant literary presence; his first two books had been sparsely but kindly reviewed, but had given barely any clue of the storming of the citadel that was to come. She was the diva, and he was the husband, the *writer*. In the dark gloomy days of the early seventies, the three-day week and the electricity black-outs had brought a kind of anarchy to England:

politics were a joke and the kids were angry and the novel (of course) was dead. The baton had been handed to the land of the free, where the Great American Novelists strode around Upper West Side salons like titans, a bourbon in one hand and someone else's wife in another. Writers in England were not courted and fêted as they are now, and no one knew that the tide was about to turn, that there was a new generation about to race out of the starting blocks (reports of my death were greatly exaggerated). So no one much had taken any notice of Alexander Dent, except a few dedicated literary periodicals, operating out of dank rooms in Soho, struggling through the harsh economic climate.

When *Black Dawn* was published it sent seismic ripples through the small pool that was then English literary life, and beyond. It was as if it was so good, so obviously the real article, that people remembered there was life in the novel after all, that it might just live to fight one more day.

So he became famous, his fame compounded by the notoriety of his dazzling wife, and in those dark days they shone like two brilliant burnished stars. But he was already reticent, and even though he went through the motions, spoke to interviewers, appeared in the newspapers, he never gave much away.

'I was superstitious about that book,' he said to Maude now. 'It meant so much to me. For a while it meant more than Claudette, and I don't think she ever forgave me for that. Mostly when you are writing you can't work out whether a book is any good or not. But maybe once in your whole writing life, you know that you are working on something that comes close to your ideal. It was like that for me then. All the time I was writing it I never had any doubt about it, and I remember developing a sudden tearing fear that I would die before it was finished. Every time I read about an air crash or a train disaster or a motorway pile-up I thought, That could have been me. Every time I went out to get a paper or a pack of cigarettes, I used to look at the trucks in the street and think, Is that mine? Each time they passed I felt a reprieve, that wasn't my truck, that wasn't the one coming for me.'

He looked up suddenly, realising what he had said. 'I'm sorry,' he said. 'I didn't mean . . .'

Maude shook her head. She was out of the world and it couldn't touch her now, not now. 'It's all right,' she said. 'Go on.'

Alexander Dent looked down at the tiny spools of the recorder turning slowly in their little metal box and smiled a twisted smile to himself, as if wondering what he was doing. 'And,' he said, 'there is always the fear that this will be your last book. There is the dread that you will wake up one morning and there will be no more words, that you will have used them all up, and then there will be nothing. So I wrote it fast and I didn't think about anything else for two years. I worked insane hours, I've never been able to do that since, eight or nine hours at a sitting, and sometimes through the night. So when it came out, I didn't want to talk about it. I felt superstitious, and also I felt curiously protective of it. I didn't want to deconstruct it and explain it and lay it out for everyone to see; I didn't want to disembowel it. I just wanted people to read it.'

Maude kept very still, afraid that the slightest distraction would divert him from the point. He let a pause go by, as if he was weighing something up in his mind.

'It was for Paul Celan, that book,' Dent said. 'Do you know him?'

'No,' said Maude; again, the wide spaces of her ignorance opening up under her.

'He was a poet,' he said. 'He was a poet and he died.'

The novel was about a writer, an exile, far from home, who walks the streets of Paris in a frenzied attempt to pull the threads of his fractured life together and still the voices in his head. When it came out, the critics made extraordinary comparisons: to Dostoevsky, to Conrad, to Joyce. 'Whenever,' said Dent at the time, with a stonewall modesty that sent interviewers into a spiral of adoration, 'anyone writes about someone who is walking a city, they bring those old names out of the hat. It's like a reflex action, they can't help it.'

Maude thought the critics were right, but it was more than that, because, in an entirely unfashionable way, it was a book with a great big beating heart at the centre of it. There was none of the ironic comic savagery that was modish just then. It was as romantic as it was bleak, it was haunted with hope for better things, that broken hearts and broken steps might somehow get mended, that aimless stumbling might transform itself into the fleetness of the athlete.

'I was in Paris,' said Dent, 'when I started writing it. Claudette had gone there to be photographed by some Left Bank character and she decided to stay. I was finished with my second book and I was in that time when you have to stop for a while, to think, to fill up again, because you're all emptied out. So I started walking in the day. I walked and walked, not knowing where I was going. One day I stopped in a café, not one of the famous ones where Sartre and de Beauvoir used to hold court, nowhere Hemingway or Gertrude Stein would have been seen dead in. I had the idea then that every café in Paris was a place of glamour and existential debate, filled with the ghosts of dead writers, but most of them aren't like that at all, they're just unremarkable places where people go to drink a beer at the end of a long day. It was one of those places, in a bleak street with no trees in it, and I sat and read a paper, and there was a man sitting on the next table, very thin and dark, with something bruised and wounded around the eyes. I saw that he only had one small *café noir* the whole time he was there, as if he couldn't afford anything more. They let you do that in Paris, they would never dream of moving you on. You could sit somewhere warm and dry all day for the price of a cup of black coffee no bigger than a child's hand.'

He stopped and took a breath. Maude could see that he had gone right back into that dingy café with the thin, starved stranger, as if it were yesterday instead of almost thirty years ago.

'I need a cup of coffee now,' he said. 'I haven't told stories like this for . . .' He shook his head. 'I was going to say ten years, but really I haven't told stories like this ever. I always wrote it down.'

He got up and stretched his legs and his arms and moved his head back and forth to release the tendons in his neck, and they went into the kitchen and he ground up the beans for coffee and made a big pot of it and they didn't speak at all. Maude was afraid of breaking the train of thought and Dent seemed to need a moment of silence in the middle of all that talk.

When they were sitting again with the coffee black and hot in thick white china cups, he took up again where he had left off, as if there had been no interruption.

'I suddenly realised,' he said, 'that I was hungry, so I ordered a ham sandwich, and then I took a chance and I asked the strange man in my rather stilted French if he would like to join me. He said was I English and I was surprised that he had a strong American accent. I had been wondering if he was Algerian; but that had as much to do with his stillness and poverty as his looks. He came and sat with me and I gave him half of my sandwich and as he ate it I knew that he hadn't eaten for maybe two days. It was the way he held himself back from wolfing it down with a kind of savage animal hunger; he was concentrating so hard on not betraying himself that he couldn't speak. I remember thinking, This is it, what separates us from the wild, that entirely human restraint, the thin line of civilisation.

'I was pleased to see him eat, as if he were an old friend who had fallen on hard times. I had never known poverty like that; I was struggling then, the first two novels were not bringing in much money, but there always was cash, there was always enough. There was never a fiver between me and the street; he knew something that I could only guess at.

'When he finished, something relaxed in him, and he looked up at me and smiled, and he had the sweetest smile I had ever seen in a man. Even though it was the afternoon I ordered brandy for both of us, and then we started to talk.

'He never told me why he had come to France. He said he was working on a novel, but that he did translations to keep him in money. I guessed the translation business was thin, that was obvious I suppose, but I didn't ask about that either, it seemed indelicate. He did though, tangentially, talk about hunger, but not his own. Peter, that was his name, he was obsessed with hunger. He talked for a long time of the Kafka short story about a hunger artist. He told me that Kafka died at forty-one of tuberculosis, but the disease became so bad in the end that he could not swallow, so before the sickness killed him he literally starved to death. Peter was struck with the grotesque irony of that; that the creator of the hunger artist should himself die of starvation.'

Dent paused again, for breath, for thought, for something. Maude looked down at the tape-recorder to make sure it was still moving, gathering all this talk into its small silver body.

'He was the one who told me about Celan,' he said. 'I didn't know much about him, although I should have done, he was the most important European poet since the war. But then in England we don't read that many foreign poets. We have too many poets of our own to revere. Or perhaps it's an insular thing, I'm not sure. But this American, from New York City, knew all about Paul Celan and he told me about him, that day. He was intoxicated with Celan; he had read all his poems three or four times over, and he still didn't understand half of it. He said that you felt you were absorbing the words through the skin, that you understood them with your heart and not your head. I ordered more brandy and we had become hilarious by this time and we were smoking ourselves into a frenzy. I felt the same heedless recklessness that you do when you first fall in love with someone, that's as close as I can come to describing it, it was such a strong vertiginous feeling. I didn't care what time it was or where I was supposed to be or whether I'd said I would be back; I just wanted this man to keep on talking.'

Dent looked up, pulled out of his memory, and gave

Maude a faltering smile; she saw again that strain of vulnerability running through him. She felt that in some way he was searching for her approval; or not quite that – permission, perhaps, that was closer.

She kept her face still and unsurprised so as to let him go on, unjudged; but also there was something in her that did not want to betray the thought that had run through her head when he talked about the intoxication of talk, of it feeling like falling, of it feeling like love. Like now, she had thought, like this. And she shut it down before it could get anywhere, because that was too far out of bounds even to contemplate.

'Go on,' she said.

'He told me,' said Dent, 'that Celan was born in Romania. He was a Jew. When the war came his parents were taken to a concentration camp. His father died, of typhus; his mother was shot in the neck. I remember that detail; it seemed especially shocking. I wondered how that fact survived, who knew it, who told it. There isn't that much known about Celan's private life: there were some letters that he wrote to Nelly Sachs, who was another Jewish poet who survived the war, she was haunted by it as he was, she was in and out of sanatoria, they gave her electric-shock treatment and still she won the Nobel Prize. They corresponded for years, but if you read the letters there is hardly any information in them, they are all abstractions. They are beautiful and full of hope and encouragement and love; in the last letter Celan wrote to her, he said, "All gladness, dear Nelly, all light!" That was the whole letter. A few months later he threw himself off a bridge into the Seine, and the day they buried him Nelly died herself, on the very same day they put him in the ground.

'So the parents were killed and he was taken to a labour camp. He managed to get out, and he ended up in Paris, and he married, and he started writing poetry. You would think that would be enough, for one man, enough to break your heart, but fate hadn't finished with him yet: his first child died, in infancy. There was another son, afterwards, whom Celan was very proud of, but the shadow of that first death must have hovered over him like a reminder of what went before. To escape death and then have it follow you like that, like a hound.

'He wrote and he won prizes, but he was haunted with feelings of persecution, and mostly they were real – you forget how much anti-Semitism survived the war: there was terrible hatred of the Jews through the fifties and sixties, and Nelly Sachs got it too, that was part of what drove her into an institution where they put electrodes to her head. Celan suffered mental collapse; he fought it and wrote and there is a haunting despair and fury in his poetry, but in the end words weren't enough, and he went to the bridge and he jumped.

'Peter told me this. It was the Pont Mirabeau. He said that he went there once a week and looked over the parapet and imagined the fall. I realised that I had walked over that bridge only that morning, that it had meant nothing to me, but I noticed the name. It was such a fine name for a bridge, and it stuck in my mind.

'He said something else about suicides, that in the old days they wouldn't bury them in consecrated ground, because they had gone against civil and religious law; they were cast out. He told me that James Joyce once said, "As if their hearts weren't broken enough already." Peter said he thought of that when he went and stood on the Pont Mirabeau. He said he thought of the last lines

Celan wrote to Nelly Sachs, and what it was that had finally caused his heart, which had stood so much, to break so irrevocably.'

Dent stopped again, as if wondering the same thing; as if knowing there was never any answer to that kind of question, that all suicide is as inexplicable as water.

'We sat there until midnight,' he said, 'and by that time we were very drunk and we had to support each other out into the street like two old men. We never kept in touch afterwards, as if that one day was so perfect and so out of time that anything else would sully it or erase it. He is rather famous now, he writes beautiful novels and I think he's not hungry any more. I went back to my hotel and I slept eight hours straight and I got up the next morning, and it was one of those strange things that sometimes happens, when you drink a furious amount and somehow you get away with it. I walked straight out of bed and put a clean sheet of paper in the typewriter and I started *Black Dawn*. It sounds youthful and improbable, but all the time I was writing it I felt as if I was writing it for Paul Celan, in some way I can't fully express, as if I wanted to try and heal his dead, broken heart, which his own words, in the end, had failed to do.

'You see,' he said, 'the curious thing was that Celan had only killed himself a few weeks before I met Peter in that café and he told me all those stories. I looked it up, in a newspaper archive; I looked for it in the library. The day he jumped was the exact same day that I had flown into Paris. I imagined circling over the city, coming into land, looking out of the window, unseeing and ignorant, at the very moment that he flew off the Pont Mirabeau. So I wrote it for him.'

There was a moment of still, the last words hanging in the air like smoke. Dent looked shy suddenly, as if this memory of his youthful idealistic self had gone against all the rules, the ones that say you have to be sceptical and wry and not make such rash statements.

Maude turned the recording machine off and said, 'That's enough.'

Dent looked up, startled, and to tell the truth, Maude had startled herself. But she knew he had to stop now, and more than that, she knew she had to stop. She felt the abyss of impossible dreams opening up in front of her and she needed to get out of the house.

The evening was still and lilac outside the window; the light was dying in the west. 'Let's go out,' she said. 'You need to walk. We've been sitting here too long.'

There was a small loch not far from the house. They walked over a thick-forested rise and down the other side, and the water spread out in front of them, silver and untouched and flat as a mirror. There were blue mountains in the distance and the air was thin and cool against Maude's face and there was the call of birds from the woods. She felt the tension that had built in her all day shift and flow away from her, into the limpid evening light.

They didn't say anything, as if words now would be pedestrian and irrelevant. Maude felt the near danger pass, on the other side of the road.

Later they went back to the house and Dent cooked a chicken, and they ate it in their fingers, with bread and red wine, and sat in the high white room, watching a programme on television about middle-aged women who went to Greece in the hope of enacting their own version of *Shirley Valentine*, and it was so shoddy and filled with cliché that it drove the ghosts away, and Maude went up to her bed, exhausted, and slept, for once, all night without waking.

9

It was on the last day that Dent talked into the recorder that he finally spoke about his wife.

He talked in the morning a little more about writing, about fiction, about other writers he admired. He didn't refer to anything he had said the previous day, as if there was nothing to add.

They ate an omelette for lunch and then they went back into the white room and Dent started again. 'Claudette,' he said, and then he paused. Maude kept very still. There was some fear in her, as if they were coming to it at last, and she wasn't sure that she wanted to hear. She felt that he had revealed enough, but it was his gig and she wasn't about to start telling him where the lines should be drawn in the sand.

'Claudette was the most beautiful thing I had ever seen,' Dent said, but there was no admiration in his voice. 'It sounds so obvious, now,' he said, looking up, looking at Maude. 'You must have seen the pictures. It was what she was famous for. There are so many pictures.'

There was a flinch in his voice as he said it, as if he could never escape from all those iconic images. Claudette Dent had lived on in pictures: photographs and paintings and vivid black and white sketches. So many of the great ones had used her at one time or another, so every time there was an exhibition or a retrospective there she was, up on the wall for everyone to see: life-size and luminous and caught in time. She was only thirty-nine when she died, there was none of the decline of fading beauty for her; it was enshrined always, in all its astonishing lushness. She survived in eternal glory, like all those who die young, who take on a life they never would have had if they had done the most mundane thing of all, grown old.

Maude wondered how many times Dent was confronted with those pictures. Even though he lived here surrounded by mountains, like a natural shield, he still read the papers. Even though he didn't inhabit the urban drag, he must see them, he must be reminded.

'But,' he said, and there was some unidentifiable irony in his voice now, 'the pictures don't do her justice. There are women who have that kind of bone structure that looks better flat, in two dimensions, so when you meet them in life there is a falling disappointment. But Claudette was the other way round. Those pictures show some of it but not all. There was a quality to her skin, a wildness that came burning out of her like a light, there was something about the way she moved that a camera couldn't catch. If she was in a room, you couldn't look at anyone else.'

He stopped, as if this wasn't the road he had meant to take, but now he had started he couldn't turn back. Maude wanted to say, Stop, enough, but she didn't have the words.

Dent took out a cigarette and lit it and drew hard on it, and his face was tight and closed with remembering. 'We were absurdly young when we met,' he said. 'Stupidly young. The most dangerous age, when you know nothing but you believe you know everything, when you think that you have the secret of the universe, the talisman of youth, the one that all the old people have forgotten. I had just had my first book published, and she was impressed by the fact I was a writer, because everyone else then was a rock star or a fashion designer or taking off to find themselves in the Hindu Kush. She was naturally cussed and I think she found something exotic in the fact that I sat in a room all day and invented things. There was an intellectual snobbism in her, she was reading Baudelaire in French and that was why she wanted to go to Paris. She had been in London since she was sixteen and she was famous even then; she acted as if she was twenty-five and she had already done everything, lovers of both sexes and dope and driving to Morocco on a whim in the back of someone's Rolls-Royce. She drew me along with her, I was powerless to resist. We got drunk one lunchtime and we walked into Chelsea register office and pulled two witnesses off the street, one was a stoned hippie, dressed from head to foot in purple velvet, and the other was a Chelsea pensioner, in his red uniform, medals strung along his chest like amulets. He was reluctant at first, he wasn't sure whether it was against the rules, but Claudette was so persuasive and so charming, and even though he was in his eighties and had seen two wars, he was no more immune to her than anyone else. So that was how we got married.'

He paused and took a breath and lit one cigarette from the glittering butt of the last and Maude wanted again to say stop.

'The disillusion came quickly,' Dent said, his voice falling into the silent room. 'She was in love with an idea, of what a writer would be. She had romantic notions of a Hemingway life, wild lunches and impetuous trips to Cuba to drink in bodegas with gambling men and death in the afternoon. But what it is, all it is, is sitting in a small room, facing a blank sheet of paper. You live in your head, with characters who become as real to you as the actual people in your life; you become ruthless and unforgiving, because you have to make the space for it, and most people don't think of it as a proper job, they think they can interrupt you at any moment, as if you are running on inspiration and you can turn it on and off like a tap. Claudette couldn't bear it that I wouldn't go out with her to every party and sit up all night, she hated it that I was thinking that I had to get up the next day and work. She thought that was how everyday people lived, the drones, the sad-sacks; not writers, writers could put on a mile through the night and still go out to lunch the next day and drink two bottles of Rioja.

'But you know,' Dent said, 'the funny thing is that for years, even after she had become disillusioned with the reality, she still clung to the idea. She read about us in the papers and the magazines and she believed that was the real thing, even though it so clearly wasn't. Life for her was performance and surface: she loved the way we seemed, even though she hated the way we were. So she went out and found solace elsewhere; she used to ask me why I didn't. It wasn't out of any intrinsic goodness. I think I had a horrible desire to hold the moral high ground, which is a revolting thing to want. So the gulf between us grew wider and I withdrew into my work, and after a while I found I didn't mind any more. It was that which really drove her crazy, because part of it was to get a rise from me, some reaction, and when I didn't give her that I don't think she could ever forgive me. I wonder, now, whether the desert that my emotional life became made me hate her, in some buried part of myself;

I wonder if it was that that I was hiding from, because I couldn't bear to admit it, even to myself.

'And ever since, ever since the . . . the accident, there has been a part of me that wonders whether I did really see her, a part that wonders whether there was a sliver of my unconscious that knew she was there, that stopped me for a crucial second before I put my foot on the brake—'

'Don't,' said Maude, and her voice broke harsh and loud into the room. 'Don't say it.'

Dent looked up and she looked away, to left and right, and tried to sound reasonable again.

'I mean,' she said, pulling her voice down into a low rational register, 'and you know this, that language has a power, and once it's out there, once you've said it aloud, then it becomes a fact, and there's no going back.'

'But I say it,' he said, 'in my head. Every day I say it. The words are there, they're just not spoken. And you of all people – you are the one person who would understand.'

'No,' said Maude, and there was the frightened urgency back in her voice. 'That's not right. It's not real, all this: it's come about by a mess of chance and you are giving it a significance it doesn't have.'

She was pleading with him now, asking him to help her out. She could see the danger again, like silver ice on the surface of deep water: one more step and it would crack and they would both drown.

She felt panic grow in her like a mushroom cloud. She snapped the recorder off and took the tape out and held it up in front of him. 'It's all here,' she said. 'That's all it is. Seventeen of these plastic casings,' she said. She had counted them the night before: seventeen hours of talk

136

that no one would ever hear. 'I'm going to destroy them,' she said. 'I'm going to burn them up and then they never existed and I'm going back to London and it will be like all this never happened.'

'It is too late,' said Alexander Dent. 'It's too late for that.'

'No,' said Maude, 'no, it's not. You don't mean that. The genie can go back in its bottle and you will go back to your life and after a while this will seem like a dream, like a distant memory, like something that never happened.'

'Why are you so afraid?' said Dent.

'I'm afraid,' said Maude, 'because this wasn't in the script and because there are things I know and because this was never meant to be revealed and *because*.'

She would have gone then. She stood up; she put the tape in her pocket and turned to go. She was going to walk out and not care what he thought about it and drive back the way she came. She would forget about all this; she would go back to her dark basement room, where she was meant to be.

But as she stood up he stood too, and he walked round the table between them and he caught her hand and the moment she felt the strength and heat of it holding hers she knew she would never get to the door. He was too close to her, she was aware of his physical presence as if there was some fierce current coming out of him, running from his body to hers. She wanted, as she had before, to say, Stop, stop, but there was nothing she could do. He pulled on her hand, and her mind was still saying, No, stop, not this, and then she suddenly gave in, something collapsing in her like a sigh.

She closed her eyes and leant forward and felt for the

first time his straight shoulder against hers. He kissed her and his lips were cool and dry and it was a hesitant kiss as if to say, Is this right, is this what you want? The voices in her head stopped for once, silenced, and there was only her body which was saying, This, *this*.

Dent drew back and touched her face and then he bent and kissed her again and she didn't know what she was doing or what her name was and she felt like she was falling and her last thought was that this was what he had talked about, and then there was nothing.

She woke in the sun the next morning; sun again, she thought, northern sun. Before thought, there was just feeling, some hilarity rising in her like smoke, some spreading delight. She felt irresponsible and foolish; sun, she thought, this far north, but it must be autumn, it must be the time of decay and woodsmoke, of mists and damp. And there was sun still coming in her bedroom window, but then she realised it was not her bedroom (how had she come to think of it as *hers*?) it was a strange room, bigger and more solid than her small fastness.

She saw that there was the same white space, the same wooden floor, the same squat window frames, bringing the light in with them. But there were four windows instead of two, and a sturdy carved wardrobe painted in some reminiscent dusty blue, and a long table against one wall, covered in books and stray coins and random pieces of paper and a small ivory box, and other things she couldn't identify. There was a four-foot gilded mirror tilted against another wall, reflecting a slice of the bed and the window behind her and the distant view of the mountains, those azure mountains that seemed to be everywhere she looked. The air smelt cool and new and clean.

She remembered who she was and where she was and what had happened the night before and she looked to her right and saw the long body of Alexander Dent sleeping beside her.

He was translucent and still in the early light. He was lying on his back with one arm folded over his torso, and the sheet was pulled half-way down his body and she could see his wide spare chest, the shoulders set far apart, the line of his collarbones sliding up through his fine skin. There were dark flat moles and a splay of fainter freckles against the pale of his skin and a sweep of hair running up from his belly button; his ribcage rose and fell with his breathing and she couldn't believe that he wouldn't wake, with the weight of her eyes on him.

She thought that she might feel shame or regret, but looking at him now, she only felt desire. She caught a sudden echo of the fear she had felt the day before, when she knew that this was going to happen and she would have done anything to prevent it. It seemed to her now that it was inevitable and she didn't fully understand why she had felt that she had to stop it.

She wanted him to wake up but she didn't want to wake him.

She wanted him to wake up and reach for her and touch her and fuck her.

She moved on to her side and lay with her face near his, watching him. From this angle she could see him up close, she could see the straight slope of his nose and the pale curve of his eyelid and the tender tilt of his mouth. He had skin she had never seen on a man before, dense, dun skin, fine and flat, with some kind of sheen on it.

She thought it was the most lovely thing she had ever seen.

She moved forward, and laid her nose against his shoulder, and smelt the clean salt smell that came off him. He smelt of air and sea and sand. She wondered how that happened; she didn't know enough about other men to compare, but she remembered Ruby saying one night, in that high green room in the Talgarth Road, that you can always tell when someone has something angry and hidden inside, because they smell bitter, like almonds.

Maude wondered whether she should let him sleep or be bold and run her hand over him and wake him. She breathed slowly through her nose and then she sighed through her mouth and she blew gently on him. She stretched her legs and felt her feet touch his; she turned on the thick white sheets and she heard him make a noise in the back of his throat and she lay very still, suddenly frightened of disturbing him. For a moment it seemed that he was sighing in his sleep, and she lay back and started to relax. She felt his left hand move up her thigh and even then she thought it was still in sleep, but the hand settled into a steady rhythm and she moved closer and eased her leg over his. As she turned she could see his face, lying still and eyes closed against the pillow, but then she saw him start to smile, and the hand moved all the way up, and she knew he was awake.

The bed creaked as he turned towards her, and his eyes were still closed but his mouth opened against hers, and she whispered into it, Yes now, yes there. She slid her thigh up against his hip so that he could move into her, and there was no sound and it was as if they were sleepwalking. She was rocking against him, and it was quiet and minute and instinctive and slow. She closed her eyes and her head fell back and she could feel him smiling against her, and then it was the same as before and she didn't know who she was or what day of the week it was or where they were, and his hand was holding her steady in the small of her back and there was a sound in the room and after a while she realised that it was her voice, saying, Yes now, yes there, yes.

When it was over she lay on her side and curved her body against his and put her face in his neck and let him hold on to her. She breathed slowly and kept her eyes closed and she wanted to hide in him. She felt that soon she would have to open her eyes, that they would separate, get up, get dressed; that she would have to face the world. Everything had changed and she felt unsure about that and she wanted to lie for ever in this still suspended unreality. She wanted to stay with his arms locked about her and his leg heavy over hers and feel safe. She had never felt safe like this in her life and she couldn't bear the idea that that would change.

He lay very still for a long time and then he moved one arm and put his hand up and stroked her black hair and she felt it and she smiled.

She must have gone back to sleep and when she woke again the light was farther into the room and Dent was lying on his side watching her, one arm still over her.

She felt shy suddenly, because this was so strange. Not just because of him, but because she didn't do this: she always woke up on her own, and now there was someone there and everything was different and she didn't know how any of it worked.

He smiled at her and his face was very close and she felt the shyness grow in her.

'Are you all right?' he said. There was something hesitant in his voice, as if he was feeling the strangeness of it too.

'Yes,' she said. 'Are you?'

'Yes,' said Dent. 'Yes. I am.'

Maude thought that if she were another kind of woman she would have made a joke or teased him, said something sharp and witty and contained. She felt her absolute lack of experience and this time it didn't armour her, but left her exposed and afraid.

'I don't know,' she said, quietly, 'what happens next.'

Dent laughed, as if she had said something funny. He pulled her to him and he kissed her and he said, 'I don't know either.'

He laughed some more, and Maude felt herself starting to smile, from sheer contagion, and he said, 'I don't know anything,' and for some reason this made her feel brave, and she looked at him and raised her eyebrows, and said, 'But you are supposed to know, you're the man of the world, you're supposed to know how it works.'

He laughed again, and he kept on holding her and she was glad.

'You mean because I am the *older* man,' he said. 'That's what man of the world means. I'm fifty,' he said.

Maude said, 'I'm thirty-five.'

Dent frowned.

'Does that matter?' he said. 'Does it matter? Fifteen years.'

'Matter for what?' said Maude.

'For this,' he said. 'For you and me. For us.'

She lay very still and the fear hit her round the back of

the head as if to remind her that it hadn't gone away. The safety and the certainty fell away and she was left with the space of her own terror.

She didn't know what this was; now, in the open light of day, she thought it was a moment of insanity, an unscripted explosion, after all that talking, all that revelation. For a while, last night, and when she first woke, in the still dawn, she had thought that everything was different, that she was different, but now she knew that some things stayed the same. Something had shifted in her over the last week, but there are no magic wands, not in this lifetime, and the frightened part of her said, clear and definite, that this was not what she deserved, that this could only be one night, that there would be no more.

So when he said *us*, she didn't know what he meant, because there could be no future for this. She wondered if he was trying to work out how to ask her to go, without being brutal about it.

The old defences came running back as if they had never been away, and she moved away from him and got out of the bed and reached for her shirt; she put it on quickly to cover her nakedness and it was as if the last few hours had been an aberration. She didn't feel safe and warm and certain any more, she felt cold and exposed.

'I don't know,' she said, and she could hear her voice coming out harsh and abrupt. 'I should go.'

'Go where?' he said.

'Just go,' she said.

She felt that she had been given a glimpse of something perfect, something that other people knew; as if he had opened the low door in the wall for her and she had looked through it and seen a garden full of sunshine. But now the door closed again and she was left outside and that fleeting glimpse would only ever be a memory.

'Just go,' she said again.

She looked around, trying to see where she had left the rest of her clothes. The bed creaked and Dent came round and stood in front of her and put his hands on her shoulders. She turned her face away, not wanting to betray herself.

'Maude,' he said. It was, she thought irrelevantly, the first time he had said her name. 'What are you doing? What is this?'

She shook her head.

'I don't . . .' she said. 'I just . . . I have to . . .'

'What did you think this was?' said Dent, and his voice was straight and urgent. 'Did you think this was some fit of lunacy, that I was, I don't know, *using* you, for some comfort, after I told you all those things? That it's finished now and you have to go?'

Maude brought her eyes up to look at him. His face was so pale and beautiful that it pulled at her heart.

'Yes,' she said, her voice rising. She heard it and she didn't care any more; she couldn't make more of a fool of herself than she had already.

'Yes,' she said. 'That's what it is, of course that's what it is, and I'm going now, like I should have done before, and you won't have to think about it any more, because that's all it was.'

'That's not what it was,' said Dent. 'You can't think that.'

'I can,' said Maude. 'Yes, I can.'

'No,' said Dent. 'It wasn't that. It was something. It is something.'

144

Maude sat down abruptly on the side of the bed, the fight gone out of her.

'I don't understand anything,' she said. 'I don't know what you want.'

Dent sat next to her and looked away from her into the white room. Although he wasn't touching her she could feel his body; she could feel the heat of it, across the small space that separated them.

'I want you to stay,' he said. 'If you want to.'

There was a silence and Maude didn't know what to say in it. Twenty different emotions tore around inside her; a hundred random thoughts.

Dent took a deep breath. 'I don't know how to ask for this,' he said. 'I was shut in, in this silent life, for ten years, ever since the accident. You know that, because you did it too. And I had given up any thought of anything . . . anything, like this, happening. I walled myself off because that was safe and that was right and then you arrived and there was all that talk and I told you things I had never told anyone, and all the time I was thinking, wondering. I was hoping you would stay.'

He can't be asking for this, Maude thought. This doesn't happen. This doesn't happen to me. She kept her eyes cast down, away from him, and she couldn't speak because she didn't know what to say.

'You want to know what I want,' Dent said, into her silence. 'It frightens me in about ten different ways to tell you. But there isn't anything to lose. I want you to stay here, with me. I know that perhaps I shouldn't say this, it's only been such a brief time, but life is short as hell and you have to live it and you have to take chances and I feel as if I've wasted enough of it as it is. I want,' he said, 'you to live with me and be my love. That's all.'

Maude sat like a rock, petrified with disbelief. He didn't say that, she thought, no, no, he didn't, he couldn't say that. She would turn round and find that it was a joke, a mirage, and she would be back in her lonely room, and she would laugh at herself for being such a fool and dreaming such a dream.

But she didn't wake up, she was still there and she could feel him beside her, waiting for her answer, and it was real and it was true.

'Yes,' she said.

'Yes, what?' he said.

'Yes, *please*,' said Maude, and it hit her as if she were on a rollercoaster, roaring down a white rail slope with the wind blasting in her face. She knew it was true, and she started laughing, like it was the best joke in the world.

'Yes please, yes please,' she said, and Dent started laughing too, and they turned and held on to each other, rocking with laughter and fear and relief, and she thought, I don't care, I don't care any more, and to hell with it, and this is true and everything *is* different, and there is no going back, and I don't care.

10

It was October now and the country was lit up with wild soaring colours. The hills were purple and red and dark green and the trees were dying with flaming defiance.

The weather, like a dream, held. The sun still shone, although the heat had gone out of it. The days were cool and still and limpid with sunshine; the light was yellow and cinematic, thicker and older than the light in London.

In the first weeks, they did the things that lovers do. They told each other stories about their lives, they revealed secrets and invented jokes that no one else would understand, they slept together in Dent's high white bed, tucked like spoons against each other, breathing in time.

Dent drove Maude out into the wild country towards Inverness, where the mountains opened up like a book and the thin black ribbon of road unravelled over a vast high wilderness, with nothing between it and the wide sky, and there was not a house or a human for miles and miles. It was as if they were driving over the roof of the world.

Maude had never seen country like it. She felt as if she were thousands of miles from anything she knew, in some foreign place; she could hardly understand that London was only five hundred miles away, in the same island, the same landmass. This seemed to have nothing to do with anything she had ever known before.

One day Dent took her west, to a hidden valley with a shining silver loch at the end of it, ringed by sheer blue mountains, falling down in vertical cliffs to the water. They drove along a single-track road, flanked by mossy grass and silver birch woods; the tree trunks were white and narrow and elegant, leaning into each other like society women at a 1920s cocktail party, but the leaves were bright gleaming scarlet against the sky. They passed through a narrow gorge, where a waterfall pounded down into a black river, and it seemed very secret and contained, and when Maude was least expecting it they turned a corner and the glen opened up in front of them: an ancient glacial valley, half a mile wide, where a river wandered lazily through the flat land. They followed the river to its end, and there was the loch, long and glittering and perfect, with a thin sliver of white beach at its head, and a far ring of high blue mountains.

There were deer on the valley floor, a vast herd of them, maybe a hundred or more, moving slowly along the river, and the feeling of foreignness hit Maude again. It made her think of pictures she had seen of South America, something about the fat winding river and the vivid foreign colours; and again, watching the deer moving after their leader, it reminded her of untamed animals wandering across the veldt on some African plain.

She hadn't known that Scotland was going to be like this. She knew that it was another country, but she didn't know that it would *feel* like another country.

They got out of the car and walked down to the water.

Dent held her hand. (Like teenagers, like young lovers everywhere, like *new* lovers, they had to touch each other all the time; there was the urgent desire for some small contact, the warm thrill of skin on skin, some reminder of sex, of lying naked with each other.)

The air was cool and clear against Maude's face; ahead of her, the water was still and unbroken. Birds flew in pairs like Spitfires, wheeling over the loch in perfect formation.

There was something powerful and mysterious and old here, something more than the raging beauty of it, which hit you in the stomach like a shock. Maude started to see why people grew mystical about natural beauty. They were so ancient and unchanging, these mountains; they had been formed millions of years ago, and they stood here still, oblivious to the rushing changes of human society. They had been here for aeons before she was ever dreamt of: they would stand here for another million years after she had gone. She felt perspective fall on her like a coat.

They walked for a while and there wasn't another person there and it was as if all this gleaming display was just for them. Maude didn't say anything because she felt that there weren't any words to do justice to it, anything that wouldn't sound like an inadequate platitude. She looked at it and felt it in her and didn't try to put a name on it.

They stopped by the water and Dent stood behind her and put his arms around her. She leant against him and he was strong and solid at her back, as if he was planted in the earth. She found it strange that something could be so new and strange (this man, this writer, whom she had admired and wondered about for years, now standing, with his arms around her waist) and so familiar and comfortable at the same time. It was as if she had never known him and she had always known him and she didn't know whether it was like that for everyone, or whether it was something between them; whether it was some kind of sign or barometer – this is not infatuation or lust or insanity, this is the real thing. She couldn't bring herself to use the word love, not yet, not now; it was too frightening and imponderable. It had some power of its own and she knew that once it was out there you could never take it back and it could wreck everything in a stroke. She had no idea how she knew this, but she did.

After a while, she said, 'Thank you for bringing me here,' and he leant his chin on her shoulder and said, so quietly that she could barely hear it, 'This is what saved me, in the end, I think this is what did it.'

She turned round and looked at him and she wanted to cry, because he had been so alone for so long, and when you come along and love someone as strongly and as unexpectedly as this the idea of anything causing them pain is unbearable to you.

'I don't believe in God,' Dent said, smiling at her with his quizzical self-mocking smile. 'But I do believe in this.'

He started to say something else and then he changed his mind and stopped; Maude wanted to ask him what it was, but she didn't. Weeks later, she did ask him, and he remembered exactly and he said, 'I was going to say that you also were what saved me, but it was too early then and I couldn't say it because that is too much of a burden to give anyone, when you've only known them for so short a time,' and Maude looked at him and said, 'That is what I hoped you were thinking, even so.'

*   *   *

There were days, right at the beginning, when Maude felt the strangeness of it very much. It was not just the foreignness of him, but of having a love affair at all. She had never done it, ever. There had been the boy at university to whom she threw her virginity; there had been a couple of men, before the accident, but somehow they never got going, her heart was never in it. And then since the accident, barely anything.

There had been one night when she had been late at a meeting with her publisher, and she was tired and she stopped for a drink at a bar in Soho on the way home, and someone picked her up and she said yes before she meant to, loneliness roaring in her like a torrent. He took her to his flat, which was one room and a bath, although he was older than she. He said he was a poet, which explained the room. He played her Dinah Washington records and spoke to her softly and took her to bed and was tentative and gentle and without passion or technique and Maude lay there and felt nothing; not pity, not intimacy, not yearning; just nothing. He called her several times after that. She let him leave long messages on her answering-machine while she sat in her kitchen and listened and never picked up the receiver. (Now, opened up as she was by exhilaration and delight, she thought of him and wished that she knew where he was so she could ring and apologise; then, it had just been another small notch on the bedpost of her miserable existence.)

So she had no knowledge, as other women of her age would, of the small details of living with someone. She didn't know about things like the bathroom – was she supposed to shut the door, or was that considered rude and unfriendly, when you were getting naked with someone? She didn't know how much she was allowed to ask for, how much she was allowed to take. She didn't know how many questions she could ask, how much of his personal business was still private. He told her a lot, but there were still things that he skirted round, and she had a burning need to know now, to know everything about him.

There were other times when her absolute ignorance freed her from form or expectation and she let this new unknown feeling take her and she did exactly what she wanted and didn't care about rules or expectations.

Dent thought it was funny.

'You're so wild,' he said. 'All those years in the dark and now you are so wild.'

He was surprised by her ability to let everything go and not think about the consequences.

'How do you do that?' he said.

'I don't know,' said Maude. 'I don't know anything. You're the writer. You're the old man, you should know.'

There was a heedless thing in her and she felt it take her and it was like being drunk or lawless and she didn't care.

'I know it in theory, in my head,' said Dent. 'I don't know that I can do it in life.'

'Get in touch with your female side and live a little,' said Maude, remembering Ruby, in her high studio room.

'Do you mind that I'm old?' Dent said, and for some reason this made her laugh out loud.

'Fifty,' she said, stuttering with laughter. 'Well, you know. It's what you make it. You're pretty sexy for an old bloke.'

He minded about this and he never seemed sure whether she was joking or not.

'Why aren't you afraid of growing old?' said Dent.

'Are you?' said Maude.

'Maybe,' said Dent.

'Women have a different thing about death,' said Maude, and she thought it was curious how she could say that word now and it was just a word. 'We know it's going to happen to us so we don't get such a shock when we hit the middle years and know that it's more than speculation. I think it's something to do with being able to give birth. You're so much in at the dirty end that you don't have time to get precious about immortality.'

'But women do care,' said Dent.

'Not in the same way,' said Maude, remembering her afternoons with Rita Lane. 'It's more cosmetic, because every single agency ever invented has been telling us for the last five hundred years that the moment we get over thirty-five no one will want to go to bed with us any more and that makes us sad.

'Age,' she said, kissing his hard shoulder and smelling his salt smell, 'is nothing, it's just a random scratch on the page. You have a good strong body and a beautiful clever face and all I want to do is go to bed with you and does that mean fifty is no good?'

Dent smiled and kissed her back.

Maude laughed some more, in a way she would never have dreamt of three weeks ago; she laughed with the devil in her and she was entirely abandoned. 'It is lucky though,' she said, 'I must admit, that you haven't developed a roly little paunch and a nice line in bunions and a scraggy bit of male pattern baldness, otherwise fifty might not look quite so sexy after all.'

Dent sat back and looked shocked. 'But women always say that none of that matters to them,' he said. 'All those beautiful women who go out with ugly dwarfish men, you love us for our sense of humour, you know that's true.'

'Yeah, yeah,' said Maude. 'But women also say, every time they are asked, that size doesn't matter either, and we all know that's a big fat lie.'

Dent shook his head.

'You can take my clothes off now, if you want,' Maude said.

Dent said, 'It's four o'clock in the afternoon,' and Maude looked at him and laughed at him and leant against him and kissed him and then they went upstairs.

Dent was right: Maude did have a wildness in her. Because there was no experience for her to fall back on, she gave up on trying to work out how she should behave and followed her instincts, because it seemed to her that they were all she had. She felt like a wanderer having to navigate her way across a strange country with only the sun to guide her. There were no rules: she knew nothing and she had nothing to lose.

She was intoxicated with him physically; she wanted to touch him all the time and she wanted to be naked with him and she could never get enough. 'One more time,' she said, 'just one more.'

She had no inhibitions when she was in bed with him. It was as if she was making up for all that sex she had never had. She laughed and talked and gasped out loud; she pushed him and pulled at him and rolled him over. She had a fierceness in her, a crazy determination – she would sit on top of him, pushing him with her hips, wanting him to come, wanting to make him. 'Go on, go on,' she would say intently, and when she herself came she would cry out in triumph and fall back on the mattress and smile and laugh some more; she would kiss him on his shoulder or on his thigh or on his face, whatever she was nearest, wherever she had fallen. She would stretch like a cat and sometimes fall into an instant sleep so he was left watching her in the middle of a sentence, and other times she would turn the light off and talk to him, quietly, in the dark.

Other times still she was gentle and yielding and tired and defenceless and she would ask him to hold her so she could feel his skin against hers and the warmth of his body on her and the smell of him, that clean smell she loved. 'You smell of the sea,' she said, 'you smell of water and salt and sand.' In other moods she would run her hand over the features of his face as if she were reading Braille and she would list them in a sing-song voice – 'Look at your lovely eyes, look at your high brow, look at your aquiline nose' – until he would laugh and tell her to stop.

Once, she cried afterwards.

'What?' Dent said, pulling her against him. 'What is it?'

She looked up at him as if they had never met and tears slid out of her eyes and on to the pillow. Then something shifted in her face and the crying stopped as quickly as it had started. She wiped the tears off her cheeks with the back of her hand and her eyes came into focus and she recognised him and she said, 'It's just feeling, that's all. It's not good or bad, it's not happy or sad, it's just feeling.'

She could have four orgasms in a row and sometimes

when he touched her she would come at once in quick shallow movements and then she would smile half in pride and half in shame and say, 'My body is such a cheap date.'

For a month they lived in an enchanted circle, cut off from the world.

They talked and drove over the mountains and walked outside and they ate long lunches and played music and had sex, over and over again. All the time, Maude felt this new unstoppable feeling building in her. Sometimes, if she paused to think about it long enough, it frightened her because it was so unfamiliar and she didn't know what it meant or what she should do with it. She wasn't sure whether Dent felt it too, even though he had said what he had said at the beginning, and she wanted to ask but she didn't know how. She was afraid if it was put into words it might disappear as fast as it came.

At the end of that first month, one Friday night, very late, in the still cool of the dark, she rolled off him and lay on her side, looking at his face in the silver light that came in from the moon outside, which was full and sailing past the window like a ship on a high sea. He never closed the shutters, and she liked that.

Dent lay on his back, looking up at the ceiling, his eyes open and unblinking. Maude touched his cheek and it was warm and familiar against her hand and she wanted to tell him everything.

'What did I do before you?' she said.

Dent turned and looked at her and his eyes were dark and desolate.

'What did you do?' he said.

'I sat in my lonely room and that was all,' said Maude.

The memory of it came back at her like a wave and she shuddered with it. 'I sat and blamed myself and knew that I could only ever be half a person.'

'It wasn't your fault,' said Dent. He frowned. 'There must have been a part of you that knew that,' he said, 'and yet you went on taking all the responsibility for what happened.'

'There were children there,' said Maude, 'on the pavement. I saw them, out of the corner of my eye. There was a group of children walking, and I should have slowed down and I didn't. They took me to court because you can be prosecuted for that, it's something about due care. They said I should have taken due care and I didn't, and I agreed with them, but my lawyers were so bloody good they won. I felt like a fraud, because some fat man in a wig got me off on a technicality. And everyone said, Oh, you know, it could have happened to anyone, but it didn't, it happened to me. I dream, you see, that's one of the things I always did, I used to do, ever since I was a child. I would go off into a little daze, into some imaginary world. I think it was because there wasn't anyone ever much to talk to. My mother used to sneer at me for that, she didn't have a dreaming bone in her body. And I think maybe I was dreaming, in the car, I wasn't concentrating, and I should have been, because I knew there were children on the pavement and school was out, and I should have been taking due care. So after it happened, I thought if it had been anyone else it wouldn't have happened, and that child would be alive. It's because it was *me* in the car that he died. It was as if all those inchoate feelings I'd always had of not fitting, being out of step, of not being good enough, were confirmed.'

157

Dent didn't say anything. Sometimes he seemed to know that there wasn't anything to say.

'It was just across from his front door,' said Maude. 'He was crossing the road to go home. Three more yards, ten seconds either way, and everything would have been different. He would still be alive. I think of that. That was one of the things I did for all those years, while I sat in my room, I thought of that.'

She paused. Dent looked at her and she knew that she didn't need to say anything else, that he understood absolutely.

'I took myself out of the world,' she said, 'and then there was nothing. There was space, that was all. There was an empty space, and now it is filled up and I don't know what to do with it.'

There was a silence for a while and Maude wondered what he was thinking. She wanted to be able to run a line into his head and see everything that was in there. She found it strange that she could be so close to him, so naked with him, and still there was a gap, a distance, because she couldn't ever quite know what he was thinking.

She wanted to ask but she had seen enough films and read enough books to know that that was the question men most dread from women.

'I'm not used to this,' Dent said, after a while. 'I don't think I know what to do with it either.'

Maude was curious. 'You must know more than I do,' she said. 'You have had this before, you were married. There was that.'

Dent shook his head. 'It wasn't the same,' he said. 'I don't know why, but it wasn't. We were too young, maybe that was it. Then it went sour, it went bad, and there was recrimination and resentment and misunderstanding where love used to be, if it was love. Whatever it was. It was different, that's all.'

Maude wanted to ask how and why and what this was now, this new thing, what this felt like to him, but she kept quiet.

'It was the past,' said Dent, 'which is a foreign country. This is different,' he said. 'This is like something I heard other people talk about and never knew, almost never believed in, as if they were making it up, to see how credulous I could be. It feels like a homecoming, like a boat coming into harbour.'

Oh, thought Maude, don't say anything like that unless you really mean it. Don't say it because it is late and the moon is shining and we just had sex and there is nothing to stop you.

She wanted him to go on talking and she wanted him to stop and she took his hand and held it hard because she was scared.

'I love you,' he said. 'That's what it is.'

As he said it Maude felt something in her falling and she held her breath and couldn't let it go.

'I want you to stay,' he said, and the words came out low and fast. 'Not just for a week, not just for a month. I want you to stay for good. Would you do that?'

Maude couldn't speak. Everything stopped and the room was black and silent and she had a hundred words in her head, but none that seemed to make any sense.

'I'm sorry,' said Dent, into the long space of her silence. 'Is that too much? Is it too much to ask?'

Suddenly Maude realised that he was serious and that this was real and not a dream and she started to laugh, with relief and exhilaration and abandon.

'What?' said Dent. 'Is it funny?'

'I can't . . .' said Maude. 'I don't . . .' she said. The laughter rolled away from her and she felt a wide calm fall on her like snow on a still day.

'It's not funny,' she said. 'It's not. I just never thought this would happen.'

'So what do you think?' he said. His voice was stilted and he was very still and she thought perhaps she had hurt him and she wanted to explain.

'It's terror,' she said. 'All this time I've been carrying this feeling around for you and I didn't know if you felt the same, whether it was something that would pass, it was just passion or madness or I don't know what. I wouldn't let myself think about it because it was all so sudden and strange. I thought one day it might blow out or burn up and I didn't know that you would say that. So that's why I laughed. It was release of tension, that's all.'

He turned his head and looked at her, and she looked straight into his serious eyes, and she said, 'I love you more than I ever thought it would be possible to love anyone, and all I want is to stay with you and I don't care about anything else, and that's all.'

Then he started to laugh too and he pulled her hard against him and they lay tight together in the high white bed, as if they were shipwrecked on some churning sea, as if they let go of each other they would drown.

Maude thought, as she felt all the fear and the years of loneliness fall away from her: I must remember this, I must never forget this, because it's the kind of thing that you only ever get once in your life. I must, she thought, never forget.

The next day they woke early and had breakfast in the low blue kitchen. Dent made eggs and ham and there was bread and jam and Maude ate it all because she had never been so hungry in her life. She felt safe and free now and she could say anything.

'I need to work again,' she said, although that was not necessarily what she had meant to say. But once she said it she knew it was true: she suddenly knew that her work was important to her, even if it was someone else's name on the spine.

'I'm not going to write about you,' she said, and she smiled up at him with some teasing slide in it, 'because it wouldn't be appropriate, not now.'

Dent smiled back and leant his elbows on the table and she loved the way that the light hit his pale clever face. His eyes were still clouded from sleep and there was a faint red line against one cheek where the pillow had marked it.

He said, 'I think you are right.'

'Anyway,' said Maude. 'I want all that to be our secret. It's between us and that's where it should stay. But there was another job I was offered before and it might still be open and I think I should do it.'

'There's a room,' said Dent. 'There's an empty room I use to store things. There's a desk in there and a window looking out over the hills and you could have it.'

'That will do for me,' said Maude. 'I'm going to telephone my editor and see if it's still on.' She ate some more bread with scarlet jam on it and she thought she had never tasted anything so good before. 'And you will need to get back to work yourself,' she said. 'I've kept you from it long enough.'

A shadow passed over Dent's face that she couldn't identify and later she was to think of it again.

'Yes,' he said. 'Yes.'

Maude thought the shadow was a fear that real life would intrude and spoil this fantasy island that they had built themselves. After what he had said last night she felt like the strong one, and she got up abruptly and walked round the table and folded her arms round his shoulders and put her hand in his hair and held his head close to hers.

'It won't change anything,' she said quietly, feeling the rough of his cheek where he hadn't shaved yet. 'We can go into real life, into normal life, and it will seem as if it has always been this way.' She sat back down and smiled at him as if she could fix everything because he had given her the key to the universe.

'This is what grown-ups do,' she said. 'I've been feeling as if I'm eighteen years old, as if there was nothing in all those lost years and I'm starting again like an adolescent. Now I want to do what grown-ups do. We'll work and we'll be in love and it will be fine.'

Sitting there then, in the beginning of the day, with the certainty of his love keeping her armoured against any possibility, she really believed it was as simple as that.

She drove down the rutted track to the red telephone box that Dent used to make calls, and she rang up Joan Bellow and asked if the explorer was still looking for a writer.

'I've moved away from London,' she said. 'So if he wants to do it face to face it might be a problem.'

Joan didn't sound surprised. She didn't ask why Maude had suddenly upped and left the Talgarth Road. She said that they hadn't got anyone else and that the intrepid hero wanted to do tapes and get them transcribed and written up.

'He's not used to much human contact,' she said. 'He wants to talk the whole thing into a machine and send it off in the post and get a book back like magic.'

'I'll do it then,' said Maude.

They talked about the sharp end: money and time. Maude didn't use an agent, but she had been working with Joan so long that she knew she would get a fair deal. They haggled, mildly, out of habit, agreed a date and a price and a percentage, and Maude put the telephone down and knew she was in the world and found that she was glad.

Then she rang Sadie. 'It's all very unexpected,' she said. 'But I'm going to stay.'

'Well,' said Sadie, her voice carrying clear and familiar down the line, 'do you want to run that by me again?'

'It's a long story,' Maude said. 'I'll tell you some other time. But it's crazy and it's real and I never was so happy in my life, ever; I never dreamt of this.'

She knew Sadie would understand this and she did.

'That is,' said Sadie, 'the best thing I ever heard. So are you really going to stay?'

'Yes,' said Maude. 'He asked me to stay and I'm going to stay, and I need to do something about the flat.'

They talked about logistics for a while and it turned out that Sadie's lease was coming up and in the end they agreed that she would rent Maude's flat. 'I'd like to be near the others,' Sadie said. 'And I have a strange fondness for your place. It's dark and strange and I like that. I'll keep it nice for you, until you decide what you want to do.'

'I'm pleased to think of you in it,' said Maude. She thought that with Sadie there, that dank dim basement would be lit up with something else, some of the life and certainty and fearlessness that Sadie carried with her, and that would be enough to drive the ghosts away. Maude smiled, liking the idea of that.

They talked some more, to get everything straight and sorted, and then Sadie said, as if she shouldn't, 'So is it?' and Maude said, 'Yes, yes, it is,' and they didn't need to say any more.

11

Maude got the tapes from the rugged old wanderer and Dent cleared out the small room for her and they made it into a study. Maude drove into the nearest village and bought pens and paper and other small essentials and blinded the shopkeeper with the smile that she couldn't keep off her face. She arranged her computer and set up an e-mail account.

'You do realise,' she said to Dent, 'that you have a telephone socket here?'

'Yes,' he said, very seriously.

'But you don't have a telephone?' she said.

'No,' he said. 'I don't.'

'We could get one,' said Maude.

'Or not,' said Dent, and she laughed and let it go.

They started to keep a small daily routine. They woke early and had breakfast and Dent read the paper and then Maude went up and had a bath, which was her thinking time, getting into the day. There was a window at the end of the bathroom and she could lie there and watch the weather moving across the sky. By the time she came down, Dent had gone into his study, and she went into hers, and she began to know the gravelled voice of the explorer as if he were her friend; she wrote notes and started to think about the shape of the book. She felt her writing muscles come back, hard and clean, and because she was in love and all her senses were heightened, she liked this feeling; she realised it was the first time she had had it unencumbered by the old weight of loss and guilt that she carried with her like a cross on her back.

They ate lunch together and took a walk if the weather was fine. Dent pointed out the various mountains to her, and she started to know their names. She began to look for the gulls when they came in from the storms on the coast, crowding together like fat white gossips, squabbling and calling into the day. She watched for buzzards floating through the sky like gliders, and craned her neck to see the lone heron that came soaring in like an extra-terrestrial being, hardly like a bird at all. In the woods there were tiny agile red squirrels, fleeting and nervous, nothing like their fat grey cousins that sat like terrorists in Hyde Park, daring pedestrians to mess with them. When it rained, she watched the burn rise and burst its banks, so the water lay on the flat ground gleaming like a mirror.

In the afternoon they returned to their separate rooms, and finished at around five and came out and had a pot of coffee and sometimes cake and Maude would put her arms round Dent and kiss him all over his face and suddenly be eaten with not seeing him for so many hours. Sometimes she would take him up to bed before dinner because she couldn't wait for the night. He pretended to be shocked, but she knew that he wasn't shocked at all; she knew, without him having to tell her, that he liked it and needed it, just the same as she did.

'Love,' she said, in one of those forbidden afternoons, 'doesn't last for long like this. This is the wild part when there is no rhyme or reason. Romantic love is a kind of madness,' she said. 'Did you know that shrinks sometimes refuse to treat clients in the early throes of love because they are too insane to do a thing with?'

'Surely that would be the time they need the couch most,' said Dent.

'So you see,' said Maude, running her hand over his chest, with its flat smooth skin and its short pelt of hair, 'we should take advantage of this time, because it will burn low in a while and then it will be tea and slippers and once a month, if we're lucky.'

Dent looked at her. The lines around his eyes were etched deep, but the dark shadows that had been there when Maude first arrived had faded.

'Slippers maybe,' he said. 'But never once a month.'

Maude sometimes took a walk by herself, when Dent was working. The light was drawing in, it was dark by four o'clock. In the witching dusk hour, when the clouds built like islands in the sky and made shapes that she had never seen before, she walked round the house and caught the last of the day and let her thoughts settle. Sometimes there was a wild sunset, vulgar and technicolour, lit with pink and orange and purple; other times there was something more subtle and gleaming, eight different shades of blue, which was the kind she liked best. She had never seen so many different kinds of cloud in one sky. On some afternoons there were thick cumulonimbus monsters rising up behind the mountains like dust clouds, and then, higher up, faint horse-tail cirrus trails, translucent and ephemeral, and, beyond those, long opaque streaks of mauve, as if some ghostly painter had trailed a thick brush over the sky.

They filled her with some nameless emotion, these solitary evenings. It felt as if all this beauty, all this gratuitous display, was for her, sent by some outside agency, to tell her that she was in the right place. She forgot all the mad and bad things, she felt that the world would go on spinning in inexplicable beauty until the end of time. She had never known this feeling, even before the accident, and she wondered if it was something that other people knew. She wondered whether she could see it now because she was in love and all her senses were heightened. She wondered if she had come here and there was no Dent, no love, it would have touched her in the same way. She wondered whether the people who had lived here for ever felt it in the same way she did, or whether they were so used to it that they scarcely noticed.

In these solitary walks, she tried to slot the raging thoughts that lived in her into neat holes, but she never succeeded. There was some searching desire in her for order and certainty; but in the end she knew that each day would be different and there were no guarantees. She had moments of feeling weak and grateful for the snaking chain of chance that had brought her to Dent's door, and she wished that she knew a god to pray to or thank. And then she felt the springing reassurance of turf under her feet, and the cold metal smell of the outdoors in her face, and she thought that there were no answers, to any of it, and she should just take it as it came, and not ask too many questions. She would laugh at herself, and go in for her tea, where she knew she would find Dent waiting for her.

One morning, Dent said, at breakfast, 'Richard is coming back tomorrow.'

Maude had forgotten about Richard Hunter, who

lived out the back. She felt a sudden childish resentment, as if someone was going to come and break into her idyll.

'Oh,' she said 'That's nice.'

Dent looked at her, and said, 'It won't change anything.'

'I don't want anything to change,' she said. 'But things will anyway. It just seems soon, that's all.'

'Nothing will change,' said Dent. 'He lives a quiet and solitary life. Sometimes I don't see him for days on end.'

Maude knew it would change things, she felt it shift in her like a stomach ache. Because this Richard was part of Dent's guilt, of his penance, of his old life. She didn't know what was between them but knowing Dent now as she did, she knew it would run deep, and she couldn't guess at it, and it frightened her.

Richard Hunter came up the drive in a twenty-year-old green Land Rover the next day at lunchtime. Maude and Dent were out walking and the car came roughly round the bend, breaking the quiet. Dent waved and Richard Hunter stopped and leant out and said, 'Hello, Al,' and Dent said, 'Hello, Richard, how was the north?' He held Maude's hand tight, and he drew her close to him and said, 'This is Maude, she's staying here now.' Maude said, 'How do you do,' in a shy voice and Richard Hunter looked right at her and said, 'Hello, Maude, pleased to meet you,' and Maude knew right then that he hated her.

Later, she tried to rationalise it. If she were close as brothers with someone and went away for a few weeks and came back to find them shacked up with a stranger, how would she feel? Perhaps she was being dramatic and it wasn't hatred at all, perhaps Richard Hunter was just the quiet type. But she knew what she knew and she couldn't tell Dent about it, because he loved this man, and she must try to love him too. It was the first secret between them and she feared it.

They didn't see Richard for a few days after that. As Dent said, he kept himself to himself. Maude had an irrational feeling that he was watching them from somewhere, but she knew this was foolish and unlikely. He was just a wounded man who had been down on his luck and now he lived out the back. His cottage was set round a corner, behind a small copse of trees. Maude couldn't see it from the main house, but now he was back she felt it there like a shadow.

'Tell me more about Richard,' she said to Dent. They were sitting in the big white room. The shutters were closed and the fire was cracking and the lights were low and there was a faint smell of woodsmoke. Maude was lying along the red sofa with her feet in Dent's lap.

'I told you,' he said.

'Don't be mysterious,' said Maude. 'This is me you're talking to.'

Dent smiled. 'I know that,' he said. 'I feel as if we have been sitting here talking all my life.'

Maude stretched her neck and turned round and laid her back against him so he could hold on to her. She felt his chin on her hair and she forgot about Richard and she let the wave of love that lived in her come up and crash over her. Sometimes she wondered how long this feeling would go on. She wondered what it would be like when they were old.

'Sometimes I get frightened,' she said. 'As if this isn't allowed. How can I be allowed to be this happy?'

'You are,' said Dent. 'Everyone is.'

'But hardly anyone ever is,' said Maude. 'Some people never get it like this. Some people go their whole lives without knowing what this feels like. Or they get it, and it's the wrong one, or the wrong time, and it all gets twisted and broken, and they're left with the pieces and no idea how to pick them up.'

'We got lucky,' said Dent. 'That's all.'

'But it seems unfair,' said Maude. 'Sometimes I think I'm going to have to pay for it.'

'You paid for it,' said Dent, and Maude could hear in his voice that he was very serious. She turned round so that she could see his face and he looked back at her and his eyes were full of the dark.

'You paid,' he said. 'For ten years you paid. And that's enough. That's enough for anyone. You can let it go now, and be free.'

Later, lying against him in bed, feeling his long strong body against hers, like a sea wall against the world, she wanted to thank him, but she couldn't find the words.

She had read enough to know that you can't save someone, hard as you try. Dent had said that, in the first week, when he was talking about something else, and she knew it was true. She knew that you had to do that for yourself. But she felt, in some barely defined way, that they had rescued each other; that if it wasn't for him she would have been sentenced to a lifetime in that lonely room, and it left her breathless at her luck. The old voices came back from time to time, distant and broken up like radio static, shadows from the past, before everything changed. The old voices that said she didn't deserve this, that this was cheating, that this wasn't the *point*. But now she only had to look at Dent to still those voices, because he was here and present and real, and he had given her his heart.

Don't let that change, she thought, lying in the dark. Don't let anything come to change that; because loving this man is the best thing I ever did in my life; the only thing I ever did that counts.

Richard Hunter came into the kitchen the next day at lunchtime.

Maude was sitting at the long table, dreamily eating a peach. It wasn't the season for peaches, Dent went and got them from some shop, where they were imported from a far sunny place, because he knew she liked them, even though they came out a little downy and thick at this time of year. She was thinking of the Antarctic wastes and her intrepid explorer. Filled with love as she was, it seemed she had love enough for the world, and she was growing a passion for this reticent English man, with his old-fashioned stoicism and his burning desire to conquer the wild white spaces of the frozen continent. She had started to think of him as a combina-tion of Captain Oates and Jack London, but there was something else as well, some sense of poetry, of Thoreau in the woods, despite his public-school reserve and honest self-deprecation.

So she got a shock when Richard walked in without knocking and said 'Where's Al?'

Maude started and looked up and brought her eyes into focus, back from the snowdrifts and sun blindness. She felt a shock of resentment at the way Richard said *Al* like that. She never called Dent Al or Alexander, even; she didn't use obvious endearments, love or sweetheart or darling. She called him Dent, because that was the way she had always thought of him. Sometimes she thought it strange that she should love him and sleep with him and live with him and call him by his surname, but the way she said it, it came out soft and secret. It was her name for him and she hated it that Richard called him Al and she knew it made no sense but it was what she felt.

'Hello,' she said, hoping none of this showed in her face. Dent said she showed everything in her face. He said it was one of the things he loved in her. He said he loved to watch the shadows of her changing face.

Now she kept it straight and still because she didn't want to give herself away to Richard Hunter.

'He's gone to get food,' she said. 'He's gone shopping.'

'Oh,' said Richard, but he made no move to go.

'I'm going to make coffee,' said Maude, although she wasn't at all. She thought that she should be friendly, because Richard lived out the back and there was some subterranean bond between him and Dent that she couldn't quite guess at, and she knew that she would have to live with that and make the best of it. 'Would you like some?' she said.

Richard looked at her for a moment, as if considering something; then he nodded curtly and sat down. 'That would be fine,' he said.

He had a flat white face and a square chin with a cleft in it; his hair was thin and brown and his eyes were small and set close together under a low forehead.

Maude made herself busy with the coffee, grinding the beans and cooking them up on the stove, and then it was done and she brought it to the table and sat down, and all the while Richard Hunter said nothing.

Maude wondered what he did with his time, in his small stone house, behind its screen of tall evergreen trees. 'There,' she said, pouring the coffee into white cups. 'There's sugar and milk.'

Richard took his coffee black. Maude thought she should have known that he would do that.

'So,' he said, looking at her. 'You came from London.'

'Yes,' she said. 'That's where I came from.'

She thought of London. She thought if Ruby or Pearl or Sadie were here, they would crack a joke or ask a leading question; with their urban certainties and worldly sense, they would know what to do with this silent strange man. But they weren't here and she was; she was conscious of her long years of solitude, which left her without resources when it came to this kind of thing. Dent said she was more of the world than she thought she was, but it wasn't any use to her now.

She wondered if she should tell Richard Hunter that she had come here to interview Dent and then stayed, but it seemed too personal. Perhaps Dent would tell him, but it didn't seem to be her decision to take.

'It's beautiful here,' she said, and she heard it come out lame and thin into the room. 'With the mountains and all. I lived in the Talgarth Road before,' she said, 'between the road and the railway.'

'And now you're with Al,' said Richard.

'Yes,' said Maude, ducking her head. 'Yes, I am.'

'Did he tell you about me?' said Richard.

Maude nodded. 'He told me a little,' she said. 'That he met you when you were . . . you were in a difficult situation, and you came to live here, and that's all really.'

Would it make you feel better, she thought – the old voices firing up in her head again, the furious and bitter voices, sensing an ally – if I told you I killed a child, and that's why I'm here?

Richard shifted in his chair; of all the chairs around the long wood table, he had chosen the one right next to Maude. He was too close to her: Maude wanted the reassuring heft of the table between them, but there was only a bare space, and his stocky body filled it, and there was something menacing in that, and she wanted to move away.

'Did he tell you my sister died?' he said.

Maude nodded, and looked away from him. She drank at her coffee. It was too hot and left a singed red taste in her mouth. 'Yes,' she said. 'I'm sorry. I'm sorry about that. It's a terrible thing to happen.'

She heard the words come out, small and inadequate, and she didn't know what else to say to him.

'It was my fault,' said Richard. 'Did he tell you that?'

'No,' said Maude, shaking her head. 'No. He said it was an accident.'

'It wasn't an accident,' said Richard Hunter, and then the door slammed and Dent walked in and Maude was never so glad to see anyone in her life.

Richard stood up and said 'Al, I need to talk to you,' and the two men went out of the back door and Maude could see them through the window, talking quietly together, and she kept hearing Richard's voice in her head, saying: It wasn't an accident.

Afterwards, she thought he must have meant that he felt about it the way she felt about what she had done: culpable, guilty, to blame; the old saw – bad things happening to good people. But in the moment he said it, she had a blinding flash in her head, clear as a film clip, of the boat and the sea and the tearing wind, and instead of Richard putting his hand out to try to save his flailing sister, him pushing her head under, deliberate and meant and with purpose. Afterwards, she told herself that this was wrong and foolish; but the picture stayed in her head, and she never lost it.

12

Dent had a passion for jazz. In the still nights when he and Maude sat in the high white room with the fire cracking in the grate and the black sky outside the windows, he played her the music he loved. He played her Charlie Mingus and Charlie Parker and Stan Getz and Ornette Coleman and Albert Ayler and other lost names that she had never heard before. He played her *Sketches of Spain* and *Kind of Blue* and the early Thelonius Monk recording of ''Round Midnight' with John Coltrane on tenor sax. He loved the music, but he loved the stories as well, the tainted lives of love and despair and drugs and drink and a sliding twilight of broken dreams. He said that he thought it strange that all anyone ever wanted was to be happy, but that the stories that fascinated people most, that moved them and drew them in, were the sad stories.

'We remember the fuck-ups and the suicides,' he said, 'the ones who never made it, who were always searching for something that wasn't there. Why is that?'

It was two months in now; Maude felt she had been here with him for ever. The love that lived in her grew like an animate thing. Every day was new to her, a surprise; she had no points of reference for this, only things she had picked up second-hand, from the late-night movies she watched and the books she read. People wrote about love all the time, but it seemed to her now that it came from a distance. Or, rather, that it was always the kind of love that is impossible, that finishes in tears and heartbreak and disaster, forbidden love, that ends with a body on the train tracks, *Anna Karenina* love, doomed love. Perhaps it was the same thing that Dent spoke about, that we all want to be happy and we all want to live with someone and love them well, but the stories we read are about the other side of it, the dark side.

'Happiness writes white,' said Dent. 'It doesn't show up on the page. I know that, everyone says that, it's an old trope. But I'm not sure I know why it is so.'

'It should be the greatest challenge of all then,' said Maude. 'For a writer. It's what they all should be trying to do, if it's the hardest thing.'

'Maybe,' said Dent. 'Maybe you are right.'

November was cold; the weather drew in from the east with bitter winds and hard diamond skies. The frost glittered thick and white in the mornings and the last defiantly flaming leaves fell from the trees, leaving the branches bare and black against the mountains. It grew dark early and Dent turned on the lights and lit the fire and he and Maude drew together against the cold. London seemed a long way away, in another time and another life.

One Friday night, Dent said they were going out. They never went out and Maude didn't care about that. She had never been used to having any other life apart from herself; now she had Dent she didn't need anyone else. She had him, and her Antarctic explorer, who was growing more real and vivid to her day by day; she sent long e-mails to Sadie, who told her the news. That was enough for one person, she thought; that was enough for her.

'Where are we going?' she said.

'It's a secret,' said Dent, smiling with it. 'You'll see.'

They drove out into the night and Maude couldn't see where they were going. There was no other traffic on the road and she sat back and let the blackness go by. She felt hidden and safe in the car, with Dent, going to wherever they were going. He put some music on the stereo and the yearning sound of a muted trumpet came into the small space and Maude smiled in the dark.

'Will there be people?' she said.

'Yes,' he said. 'There will be people.'

'And what will they think?' she said.

'I don't know,' he said. 'But it doesn't matter. I don't care what anyone thinks, they can think what they like.'

'I think that Richard thinks something,' said Maude. 'But I'm not sure what it is. I think he wonders how it was that I arrived just like that, and I stayed.'

'Maybe,' said Dent.

'Did you tell him anything?' said Maude.

'No,' he said. 'He didn't ask.'

They pulled up a while later outside a stone building, a squat grey tower; cars were drawn up in a line and lights poured out into the indigo night. There was a fat amber hunter's moon out, hanging low in the sky, running through the clouds, turning them gold and silver and white.

'What is this?' said Maude.

'You'll see,' Dent said.

The door was open and they went in and there was a small ochre hall and Dent led her downstairs. She didn't know what she expected, but when they got there it was a surprise all the same. It was like a night-club; there was a low room with dark red walls and tables and candles everywhere and chairs and bottles of wine and thick unbreakable glasses and people all around, talking and laughing like they came here all the time.

'It's a party,' said Maude. 'Is that what it is?'

'Sort of,' said Dent.

A stocky man with dark brown hair and shoulders like a quarterback and a wide open face came over when he saw them and put his arm around Dent and said, 'You made it,' and Dent smiled and said, 'Yes, we did, the roads were open.'

'The forecast is for snow,' said the man to Maude, as if they had met before. 'It comes down fast over the mountains and then the road is blocked and there's nothing you can do about that, even with four-wheel-drive.'

'This is Mickey,' said Dent. 'Mickey, this is Maude.'

'Hello, Maude,' said Mickey. His even face fell into a smile and Maude, who had begun to feel shy, stopped and smiled back, because anyone could see that this man wasn't thinking anything, he was just pleased to see her, whoever she was.

'Hello,' she said.

Dent went to get a drink. As he crossed the room, people turned and said hello and shook his hand, and Maude thought it was strange because she had always pictured him apart and alone, like she had been, and now it was clear that that was not the whole story at all.

Mickey smiled at her again, and said, 'Alexander said you were coming,' and Maude looked up in sudden alarm, and he put a hand on her arm, as if he saw it, and said, 'It's a good thing, it's a wonderful thing, because he's a fine man and he's been alone for a long time.'

He reminded her a little of Dean, in his directness, and she felt reassured.

'I wasn't,' she said. 'I didn't.' She stopped and shook her head.

'Is this your house?' she said.

'Yes,' said Mickey. 'And my brother William's as well.' He pointed over to the corner where another dark-haired man was talking to two younger women. William was taller and older, but all the rest was pretty much the same. They both wore jeans and black jumpers and they reminded Maude somehow of the Beats, or something later perhaps, some sixties thing. She could imagine them smoking reefer and playing the guitar and reading Richard Brautigan and listening to Bob Dylan before he went electric.

'I think it's a lovely house,' said Maude.

'Thank you,' said Mickey. 'We think so too. Now you're settled in, you can come and visit. In the summer we have writers up here, there's a barn that we converted, and they sleep there in dormitories and write masterpieces about death and desire.'

'Is that true?' said Maude, laughing in surprise.

'Well,' said Mickey, smiling back at her and raising one eyebrow, as if he had seen enough of the world not to be surprised much by anything, 'they think they are masterpieces, and who am I to tell them different?'

'Is that how you know Alexander?' she said, wondering whether they went all the way back or whether it was a writing thing or what it was.

'No,' said Mickey. 'He got stuck one time, driving over the hill, when the snow came in without warning, and we gave him a bed for the night, and that's how we know him. I didn't know who he was for a long time; I don't read much. I farm sheep and write music and I don't have so much time for fiction. But one day there was an article about him in the Sunday papers and I recognised the photograph and then I knew. I never asked him about it. He told me later. It was late one night, and he told me the story, and I didn't say that I knew it already, because it seemed as if it was his to tell.'

Dent came back with glasses of red wine and gave one to Maude, and Mickey said, 'I like your girl, Alexander,' and she didn't mind that he said girl, even though she hadn't been a girl for years, because it sounded all right, here in this dark smoky room.

'I like her too,' said Dent, and Maude smiled because she was here with him, in a crowd, and everyone knew that she was his girl.

She couldn't work out who all these people were; they were not necessarily what she would have expected, in the middle of nowhere, in farming country, in this harsh mountainous landscape. Urban people, she suddenly realised, had no idea what went on outside the city limits. She perhaps had a vague thought of doughty hill farmers, or dropped-out hippies, eating tofu and milking their own goats. She had held a shadowy notion that the country was full of hard-bitten people with Land Rovers and sleek working dogs and battered green coats and ruddy complexions from going out in all weathers; and then the lord in his castle, the embattled Scottish aristocracy, railing against Westminster and its apparatchiks and the liberal menace.

She realised now that she didn't know a thing about it.

The people here were mostly young, in their thirties perhaps, and curiously stylish, no thornproof tweed or knitted lisle in sight. She drank her red wine and let Dent move away from her, and she forgot to be shy, and she talked to people; she said, Hello, I'm Maude, without feeling that she had to explain herself. They didn't ask her awkward questions or give her suspicious what-the-hell-are-you-doing-here looks; one or two said, Oh, yes, you're with Alexander, as if that said plenty.

There were artists and musicians and one man who ran an Internet business from something that used to be a cowshed. There was a computer technician ('I'm writing a software manual,' he said, laughing at himself as if to do it before she could) and a woman with mournful eyes who built water features. 'I'd like to call them fountains,' she said, 'but everyone would fall on the floor if I said that.' There was a man with a suggestive look who made a whisky liqueur. 'I go to Glasgow,' he said, 'where the distillery is, and pour in the secret ingredient and then we sell caseloads to malls in Tennessee.' There was a woman with short peroxide hair who worked for a wildlife organisation and was saving the wolf in Eastern Europe. 'Is that wolf in trouble?' said Maude, feeling laughter rise in her, and the woman looked out from under low black eyebrows and said, 'That wolf is in deep shit.'

Who are these people? Maude thought, as the evening pulled and flowed around her. What am I doing here?

It was nothing she would have expected. And Dent was right in the centre of it and they knew him and they loved him and some of them had read his books and some of them didn't care less and they accepted her without question, because she was with him, so she must be all right.

Perhaps I am all right, she thought, perhaps after all I am all right.

Then the music started, and she realised why Dent came here. Three men and two women walked into the back of the room and started to play: a saxophone, two trumpets, a drum and a double bass. They played old-fashioned improvised jazz, and she realised why she had thought that Mickey and William had that nostalgic boho look to them, because that was what the music was. The room fell quiet to listen, and the crowd moved into tight groups; couples drew together, shoulder to shoulder – against one wall Maude saw a slender woman with red hair twisted up on her head like a question mark lean against William; he put his arm round her and drew her in, and Maude thought that was what this kind of music did, it made you want to hold on to someone and let everything go into the night because nothing else mattered very much. Dent came through the crush towards her and she realised that he had been looking for her and it made her feel glad and still.

He looked at her to see what she made of it and she smiled and he seemed to relax, as if he was not sure what she would have thought. He pulled her into him, so that she was standing against his chest, with his arm across her front. She dropped her chin on to his forearm and felt the heat and strength of it; she could feel his chest against her back, and his face was in her hair, and there was no telling where one of them started and the other one ended. The music was playing into the room with some kind of urgent melancholy and it was like every film you ever saw about those lost smoky days when everyone wore black and demonstrated in the streets and knew that they could save the world, when they weren't walking around third-floor apartments barefoot and having sex in the afternoons.

The music grew and shifted, went faster, spiralling into some kind of crazy celebration. A man with a bodhrán drum joined the musicians, and later a woman in purple velvet got up and started to sing. She sang 'Night and Day', and 'I've Got You Under My Skin', and the old Bessie Smith number about my daddy taking me for a buggy ride. She had a voice like sand and glue and she was older than the rest, and she wore her age on her face like a badge, as if it wasn't something to fear.

Maude turned her face up to Dent and touched his cheek and kissed him on the mouth and he kissed her back, even though there was a room full of people there, and she felt his lips cool and dry against hers, and she thought, This is what it is like, to be with someone, to be in a pair, to be loved and wanted, and she had the feeling again of wanting to remember it, because it was something she had never imagined.

The party moved into the night. People shifted and laughed and drank red wine and smoked too many cigarettes.

Maude turned round and found that Mickey was back beside her.

'So,' he said, 'what do you think?'

'I think,' said Maude, and she felt herself smiling with pleasure, the sort of smile that was new to her, that she was learning as she went along, 'I think that it's fine here.'

'Yes,' said Mickey, looking around the room. 'I do too.'

Later, the woman with red hair came over. 'My name is Violet,' she said. 'I know that you are Maude.'

'Yes,' said Maude. 'That's who I am.'

'You came with Alexander,' said Violet. She had a square face and eyes that weren't quite blue and weren't quite grey and a fast smile that came and went in her like quicksilver. There was something loose and unstructured about her, as if she wasn't used to playing by the rules. She had freckles over the bridge of her nose and a wide mouth and she seemed lit with some inner laughter, as if she got the joke.

'Yes,' said Maude. 'I did. That's who I came with.'

'I live here,' said Violet, as if she thought it was important to get the information out, before they could move on to the main action. 'I live with William. I was in London for years, I was an urban girl, and then I met Will and I came for the weekend and I never went back.'

'Me too,' said Maude, and she started to laugh for no reason. 'That's what I did.'

'It's a hell of a way to live your life,' said Violet, and she smiled at Maude with swift complicity, as if they already had a secret. Maude wondered if they would see each other again, if this woman would be part of her life, if they would be friends, spend winters together and talk about the snowdrifts and how it was all sunshine in the south, while they dealt with the weather.

'I like Alexander,' said Violet. Her heavy eyebrows drew together and she looked serious and certain. 'It was terrible what happened to him. I'm glad he has someone now.' She stopped, and some of her certainty fell away and she suddenly looked young and doubtful. 'I don't know if I should say that,' she said. 'But it's what I think. I hope you don't mind.'

Maude said, 'I don't mind at all.'

Then the music started again and they smiled at each

other, as if to say the ice is broken now and there will be more later, when there is time, and Violet moved away, with a little sway in her walk, and Maude saw her go over to William and lean against him again, as they had stood before, letting the music take them.

13

Around midnight, the party started to thin out. People picked up their coats and went out into the dark night. 'See you next time,' they said, as if there was no doubt that there would be a next time. Maude thought that perhaps she should learn some of those assumptions that other people knew.

The candles were burning low and empty wine bottles stood like sentinels and the ones who weren't ready to go yet gathered together around a table in the middle of the room. William and Violet sat close together, and Mickey came and sat too, and the man who had played the double bass, whose name was Edgar. He told Maude he had a French mother and had lived in Paris when he was young.

'I was very Rive Gauche,' he said. 'Mostly gauche, actually. I smoked too many Gitanes in a self-conscious way and played in a dive in the Marais and dated silent model boys who had no hips and I thought I was the thing. And then I got bored and came to Scotland and stopped trying to make a point.'

'Why Scotland?' said Maude. It seemed such a long way from Paris, from the classical architecture and the wide boulevards and the pavement cafés, where even the taxi drivers talked about Sartre.

'Why not?' said Edgar. 'Space and freedom and no traffic jams. And there still is a dive to play in. Actually,' he said, looking slightly sheepish, 'I saw *Local Hero* when I was younger and I always thought about that red telephone box and the aurora borealis and everyone knowing each other. Some people dream of a house in Provence or a shack in Hawaii. I dreamt of Scotland.'

'I can see that,' said Maude seriously, who had never thought of it in her life, until she came here and fell in love. 'It's not strange.'

Edgar smiled. He had a straight smile and even teeth, and suddenly Maude wanted to tell him everything. She couldn't tell whether it was him, or because it was late and she had drunk many glasses of red wine, or whether it was just because she was happy.

'A little,' he said. 'Perhaps it is a little. But I don't really care any more.'

'What do you do,' said Maude, 'when you're not playing in this dive?'

'I make tables,' said Edgar. 'I make furniture, all kinds. But I like tables best. There are people who will pay any kind of money for a really good table.'

The man who had played the trumpet came and sat down next to Edgar. He had very blue eyes, even in this dim light, and he wore a dark blue shirt to go with them, and he had a pointed face that would have been girlish except for his nose, which had been broken. He laughed and put his arm around Edgar's shoulders.

'They pay through their teeth,' he said. 'And they keep us in gin and cigarettes.'

'This is Christy,' said Edgar. 'Did you meet Maude? She's with Alexander.'

Christy smiled gravely and shook Maude's hand over the table. 'I heard that,' he said. 'I'm glad for you,' he said.

How did they all know that it was a good thing? Maude wondered. She wasn't used to being approved of; she wasn't used to this. She found she liked it.

Dent sat down by her and she leant her shoulder against his. The woman who had sung the blues came and sat beyond him; she reached over and stole a cigarette from a packet on the table, and told Maude that her name was Nora, and then there were no more people, it was just the eight of them, in the empty room, with the candles guttering in their holders and throwing improbable shadows on the walls.

They talked late-night inconsequential talk, and Maude was happy to sit and listen, to let it roll over her. Dent's arm was warm against hers and she was having a good time.

Later, as she was growing tired and wondering if they should go, the door opened, and a man she had seen earlier came into the room.

'Paolo,' said Mickey. 'I thought you went home.'

Paolo held up his hands. 'The snow's come in,' he said. 'The road is blocked. No home for me tonight.'

Mickey smiled round at the table. 'No home for anyone else, then. You're here for the duration.'

Violet showed Maude and Dent to a bedroom near the top of the house. The plaster was flaking on the walls and the floorboards were bare and there was a high bed made out of dark wood covered in a scarlet satin eiderdown. Maude thought it looked like something from an opera.

Violet opened the window. 'It's hot,' she said. 'All Mickey's money goes on heating, he hates the cold. Which some people might think strange in a sheep farmer.'

Outside the window, the snow fell in ghostly silence. Maude felt insulated, cut off from the world. She wanted to stay in this room with its scarlet bed for ever.

'Does this happen often?' she said to Violet.

Violet smiled her quick smile. 'Once or twice every winter,' she said. 'You meet old men up here who will tell you how they used to be snowed in for five months each year, in the old days. We get it easy, they say, with all this global warming.'

'Well, thank you,' said Maude. 'This is lovely.'

'I like this room,' said Violet. 'I slept here when I first arrived,' she said, giving Maude another of those complicit looks, as if they were on the same side, and perhaps they were. 'There's a bathroom next door; there are new toothbrushes and things.'

She gave Maude a kiss on the cheek and Maude was reminded suddenly of Ruby, and the first time she had gone upstairs to that wide green studio and how thin and doubtful she had felt. Violet waved at Dent and went out, shutting the door quietly behind her, and they were left alone.

'This,' said Maude, 'is the most romantic thing that ever happened to me. Did you plan it all?'

Dent kissed her, and she could feel his mouth smiling against hers. 'All of it,' he said. 'Even the snow.'

The next day rose white with sun. The snow had settled in a high shining mass, leaving the country unrecognisable. Maude couldn't remember the last time she had seen snow. It made her feel excited, like a child.

She and Dent walked down a winding stone staircase to the kitchen, a low square room that took up the whole of the ground floor. It was filled with light from the windows on all sides. It was part kitchen, part living room, part office, filled with furniture and business and flowers in pots. At one end, a huge stone urn stood, incongruous under the low ceiling; opposite it, there was a tree in a galvanised-iron tub.

'The tree was Violet's idea,' said William, seeing Maude look at it.

He was wearing a dressing-gown and pyjama bottoms and there was dark stubble on his face and Maude was certain there must be a copy of *Howl* in his back pocket. He acted as if they met at breakfast every day.

Mickey and Violet were sitting at a scrubbed white table in the middle of the room, reading the papers. 'The road to the village is fine,' Mickey was saying. 'It's blocked at Cockbridge, like always. Same old, same old. Paolo got home, dug his way out with a shovel.'

He looked up as Maude and Dent sat down. 'Good morning,' he said. 'Look at you two, so clean and innocent. Why are you up so early?'

Maude blinked in shy surprise, but Dent didn't seem to mind. Perhaps he was used to Mickey.

'Shame to waste such a day,' he said blandly.

'Edgar and Christy are wasting it even as we speak,' said Mickey.

'That's very naughty,' said Violet, 'and you don't know that's true.'

She was wearing an Aran jersey over her nightdress and a pair of muddy black gumboots. Maude looked at the fashion magazines sometimes, and every so often they got bored of shoots in Miami or Bali, and went off to Connemara and photographed some etiolated model wearing just this kind of look – an old man's cardigan over a couture ballgown, some printed chiffon slip with hiking boots. In the pictures it always looked phoney and pointless, but on Violet it looked natural and fitting, as if she had just got up and reached for something warm so she could go and feed the chickens.

She smiled at Maude and poured her a cup of coffee. Maude smiled back. She was struck with Violet's absolute ease and sense of place, the assurance that allowed her to sit in her nightdress and her bare face with a stranger and make morning conversation and be entirely herself, without need for embellishment or explanation. Maude wondered if she would ever feel like that. The old years were sloughing off her like a snake's skin; but like a snake, she felt she still had many more skins to shed.

William made plates of sausages and eggs, and they ate them with ketchup and bread.

Nora arrived later, as they were finishing. She was fully made up, her lips red as berries in winter, her eyelids an unlikely shade of emerald green and her dyed black hair skewered up on her head with a lacquered chopstick. She was wearing her dress from last night, which was episcopal purple velvet to the floor.

'Don't shake those sausages at me,' she said to William, as if he were an errant schoolboy. 'I'd like a cup of coffee and that's all.'

She smiled a faded smile at Maude and sat down and lit up a cigarette and looked around the long windows into the white of the day. 'Well,' she said. 'We're not getting out of here in a hurry. I hope you girls don't have any work to do,' she said, looking at William and Mickey.

'It's the weekend,' said Mickey. 'The animals are fed. We'll entertain you all day long.'

'That's what I like,' said Nora. 'I want long and winding stories and revelation in the afternoon.'

In the late morning, they went for a walk. The sun was shining still, out of a flawless sky. It glittered on the snow, gleaming points of light shooting off the white.

The ground sloped away from the house towards a river valley, through a winding skein of firs. The snow lay heavy on the dark green arms of the trees – sometimes a branch bent gently under the weight, letting its load fall on to the ground with a shivering slide. The world was muffled with it; their steps sounded in small contained thuds.

Violet and William wandered behind the rest; Violet made a curving path, too busy watching the sky to see where she was going. Mickey and Dent walked strongly ahead, as if they had some deadline to meet.

In the middle, Nora and Maude walked together. Nora was still wearing her long velvet dress, although in deference to the weather she had borrowed a bagging tweed coat from Mickey, which looked as though it had last been used some time around 1933. She had also borrowed a pair of Wellingtons, in sturdy black rubber, normally used by William, so they were three sizes too big, and Nora had had to stuff them with several pairs of socks. She walked staunchly in them, with heavy steps.

They walked in silence for a while, getting the measure of the sloping ground, leaning their weight back, watching for the treacherous places where the snow masked dips and gullies.

They came out of the woods into flatter terrain, and they could see the black sinuous slide of the river reflecting the sun, which was low in the sky, flooding the land with slanting ochre light.

'So,' said Nora, looking ahead to the two black figures in front of them, Mickey and Dent, walking fast, turning right along the riverbank and walking up to the higher ground, their heads bent in talk. 'You are with Alexander.'

Maude thought back to last night, when people had said that. You're with Alexander. Sometimes as a statement, sometimes a question: You're with Alexander now.

'Yes,' she said. 'That's who I am with.'

She didn't have the feeling with Nora, as she had with Edgar, of wanting to tell everything. She couldn't tell whether it was because they were out in the day, in the bright light, instead of in the dim shadow of the basement room, or whether it was something to do with Nora herself.

Nora said, 'It's all right,' as if she read Maude's mind.

Maude turned her head sharply and looked at her. Nora kept walking right along, her profile etched ebony against the brightness beyond.

'It's not a test,' she said. 'You might perhaps feel a little strange here, because we all know each other, and we know Alexander. But we're not thinking anything much except that we are pleased, because we love him.'

Maude was confused. That was half of what she was thinking, but there was another half that was thinking something more, something that she couldn't put into words.

'I don't know,' she said. 'I don't know what I think.'

There was a pause and Nora kept on walking, and there was a smile around her mouth, as if she had secrets to tell.

'Go on,' said Maude. 'Say what you are thinking.'

'This thing,' said Nora, gesturing with her hand, 'this little group, whatever, this is new for him. I mean, they have only known him for a few years, and then by chance. They meet every so often to listen to jazz, because that's the thing that keeps them together, and he has told some of them the real story. But you see, I knew him from before.'

Maude felt a piercing shaft of jealousy. Nora was around the same age as Dent, maybe a few years older; perhaps, she thought, that was the reason she didn't want to tell Nora everything. Perhaps she and Dent had been lovers, perhaps there was a whole story there that Maude couldn't guess at. The spaces of the unknown past opened up in front of her like black ice.

'Oh,' she said, because she couldn't open her mouth very wide, suddenly.

'No,' said Nora, stopping and laughing and looking at her. 'No, no, nothing like that. My, but you're touchy.'

Maude laughed despite herself. She looked back at Nora, and they gave each other a measured glance, just for a beat, and it was as if some understanding ran between them, and then they started walking again, in step, through the fat white snow.

'That's better,' said Nora. 'That's more the thing.'

They had come to the river and the ground was dropping away beneath them again. There was a cutting wind coming from the east, and they turned their faces from it and veered right along the riverbank. The range of mountains in the distance was gleaming translucent with the low rays of the sun, and Maude brought her head up and saw the view and felt better.

'I'm sorry,' she said. 'It's just that all this is so new to me, and there are so many things I don't know. He told me a lot of it, of his story, but I am conscious that there are gaps.'

'I know,' said Nora, and all of a sudden she seemed like an ally to Maude, on her side. 'I did know him before,' she said. 'I knew him when he was married, you see, we met in Paris.'

Paris, thought Maude, everything came back to Paris. It was where Edgar had come from, where Dent had met that hungry writer. Which film was it where the heroine said, 'We'll always have Paris'? But Maude had never had Paris, she had never been there in her life.

'Tell me about Paris,' she said.

She remembered another film, another one of the hundreds of flickering pictures she had watched in her old life, when she sat in her dark room with only fictional characters for company. In this film, the heroine was a writer, talented and passionate, but no good at life. 'Why do they always end up alone?' she said. 'All those women in those stories, why do they always end up alone?' But the line Maude remembered now, walking through the snow, was about Paris: 'I was very young, Paris was very old.'

'Tell me,' Maude said. 'I need to know.'

Nora turned and looked at her and Maude felt that it had come out wrong, too abrupt and urgent, that she needed to explain.

'When we first met,' she said, 'he talked all the time. I had come up to talk to him about his life, I was going to write about it. He talked for five days without stopping. And then we fell in love and now I'm with him, and he doesn't talk so much any more. It's as if he told me everything I needed to know. But I keep seeing the spaces and I know him so little and I want to know more. I want to know everything, but I'm not sure whether that's too much to ask.'

They stopped then, and watched the river run past them. The water was black and oily, with some glimmering sheen on it from the sun and the reflected white of the snow.

'In the summer,' Nora said, 'this river is translucent and green and you can see the stones on the bottom. You can see right through it.'

They walked back up the hill, towards the trees.

'It's always like that in the beginning,' said Nora. 'All love affairs are different, but they are also all the same.'

'I never had one before,' said Maude. 'I'm thirty-five years old and I never had a proper affair before.'

She said this fast, before she quite meant to; hearing it, the words hovering in the still air, she realised how peculiar it sounded. 'Something happened to me, when I was young,' she said, trying to explain. 'I cut myself off from the world, because that seemed like the only thing to do, and then I came here and there was Dent. I am having a love affair, and I should be at the age when I know how it works, and I don't, and it makes me feel afraid. Sometimes it makes me feel free like a bird, because there are no rules, but sometimes I get frightened.'

Nora laughed, which was not what Maude expected. 'You know, the strange thing,' said Nora, 'is that no matter how many times you fall in love, no matter how many times you go round the block, it always feels like that. You get there and you think I should know how this works, I did it before, but the curious thing is that you never do know.'

'Is that the truth?' said Maude. 'Or are you kindly saying it to make me feel better?'

'Oh, no,' said Nora, laughing a knowing salty laugh. 'No, no. It's the absolute God's own truth. There aren't many things that I know are true for sure, but that's one of them. Every damn time is like the first time.'

They breasted the top of the rise, and the house came back into sight. It was square and brown, in weathered stone; it was solid and reassuring against the snow and the mountains and the trees.

There was a bench to the left, set out to get the best of the view. Nora swept the snow off it with her tweed arm and sat down.

Maude sat beside her, and they looked out over the long sloping hill. The sky was bright staring blue against the white mountains, but clouds were starting to build in the west.

'That's why I was in Paris,' Nora said, 'because I was in love. And I didn't know what was going on or what it all meant. I was young and I believed in love, that it should come before everything else, that nothing else mattered that much. I think I read *By Grand Central Station I Sat Down and Wept* one too many times, I used to carry it round with me like some dog-eared handbook. I was sitting for artists, what they called a life model, because what the hell else were you going to do if you were in Paris and in love, and that was how I met Claudette. She was sitting for everyone just then, like it had never been done before, dazzling everyone with her beauty.'

Nora smiled with the memory and raised her eyebrows so Maude could see her green painted eyelids. 'I always thought she was rather dull,' she said. 'There was the beauty, which made you stare, and then there wasn't much else. I sometimes think, with the true beauties, men and women both, that they never need to develop much character or sense of humour, they don't need jokes, they only have to stalk into a room and everyone wants to be close to them. I liked Alexander, because he had plenty to say. Oh, yes, he was the interesting one. He was the deep one. I took one look at him and thought, Now there's a dark horse. Claudette just ran around fucking all those artists and photographers, but he had the right stuff.'

'So she just slept with everyone and didn't care?' said Maude.

'Oh, yes,' said Nora. 'She drank, that was her thing. And when she drank, she didn't care about anything, so she took her clothes off. Remember that line – There were so many people you just had to meet, without your clothes? I love that song, although it's too low for me, I can't sing a word of it.'

'Did she break his heart?' said Maude.

Nora looked at her. 'Why should you ask that?' she said.

'I think about broken hearts,' said Maude. 'It's one of the things I think about.'

Nora nodded, as if that was allowed. 'I don't know,' she said slowly. 'I think it was her revenge, more than anything, because he was so wrapped up in his work, she could never quite get to him. I don't think he ever loved her the way she wanted to be loved. It's hard to tell; you can never truly guess the secrets of a relationship between a man and a woman, not the whole truth. I saw them a lot in those days, but I couldn't do more than assume what was going on.

'I'll tell you what, though,' she said, thoughtfully. 'I

think his heart did break when she died, not because he loved her so much, but because he never could. She wasn't very lovable, for all that blatant beauty. You didn't warm to her. She was dramatic and demanding and spoilt; she was all surface. I think he felt in some way that if he had loved her more she wouldn't have died, he would have seen her. By the end, he couldn't see her at all.'

'Yes,' said Maude. 'I understand that.'

There was a pause and they sat, looking ahead, the stone bench cold and hard under them.

'The allure of the wounded man,' said Nora, with a rueful shrug of her shoulders. 'It's always such a strong pull.'

'It's not just that,' said Maude, not taking offence. 'I am wounded too. It's more like he understands.'

'I think it is love he feels now,' said Nora, 'and I probably shouldn't say that, but I do say it anyway, and to hell with it. I never saw him look like this before.'

'Do you think that love can mend a broken heart?' said Maude.

Nora laughed again, and there was something nostalgic and yearning in it, as if she had wondered the same thing, somewhere along the line.

'I don't know,' she said. 'I don't know how that happens. But I'll tell you something – I think even the most broken hearts get mended somehow. The human heart is more resilient than you might think. People piece their hearts back together in the most curious and dogged ways.

'But,' she said, in quite another voice, 'I don't know why I'm keeping you here, talking about love. We should go in and have our lunch.'

So they got up and walked towards the house, and behind them the clouds moved in, across the sun, casting a dull shadow over the mountains.

It was almost one o'clock when they got back. Edgar and Christy were cooking.

'It's the least we could do,' said Edgar, who was wearing a blue and white striped apron over his clothes. He looked clean and efficient.

'You naughty girls,' said Nora. 'Have you been having sex all morning while we were walking the hills?'

'Not *all* morning,' said Christy.

They sat round the big wooden table and ate risotto with mushrooms. Mickey opened a bottle of red wine, and they drank it with their food.

In the afternoon, William lit a fire, and they sat on long sofas and read the papers and Violet and Christy played backgammon for high stakes.

Maude felt heavy from the wine. She went upstairs and slept on the high wooden bed, and when she woke up it was dark, and for a moment she didn't know where she was. For a moment she thought that she was back in her old life, with the familiar drop in her stomach that she always felt when she woke to face another empty day. Then the door opened, and Dent came in, and she remembered, and she was so glad that she started to cry without meaning to.

Dent came over and put his arms around her shoulders and held her tight to him.

'What?' he said. 'What is it?'

'Nothing,' said Maude, the tears passing. She felt the warmth of his body and it brought calm back to her, and she looked up at him and smiled. 'I forgot for a moment, where I was. I thought I was back in my old life. I forgot there was you.'

'It's all right,' said Dent. 'Sometimes I feel like that too.'

'You do?' she said.

'Yes,' he said. 'I do.'

'We need to talk more,' said Maude. 'It's as if there was all that talk and everything got said and now we are taking things for granted. I don't want to do that. I want to know everything about you. I want to know that you still feel the same.'

Dent looked at her very closely. 'I feel the same,' he said. 'I feel more the same every day.'

'You have to tell me that,' said Maude. 'Otherwise I forget and I get frightened.'

'Don't be frightened,' said Dent. 'I love you. I do.'

'Yes,' said Maude. 'That's what you have to say. That's the correct response.'

Dent laughed. 'Thank you,' he said.

'Do you want a bath?' he said. 'There's supper soon.'

'Yes,' said Maude. 'I'll have a bath.'

For a moment she wondered if he was changing the subject. She felt that there was something more she wanted to say, or wanted him to say, but it was a fleeting and incoherent thought, and she felt that it was to do with waking up in a strange room with the disoriented feeling that afternoon sleeping brings. That's all it is, she thought. That's all.

They ate dinner together, and William made lamb with rosemary and potatoes, and there was talk and laughter, and later Christy played the guitar and Nora sang sad songs, and the next day Maude woke early and the sky was dull with rain. She looked out of the window and saw that a thaw had come, and she knew the road would be open and there was no reason to stay here any more, and she felt a piercing regret.

14

The days fell back into a routine. The weather stayed hard and cold, and the skies were low and threatening.

Maude went back to work, as if that weekend over the mountains was something from a fantasy. The life of the doughty explorer opened up in front of her as she transcribed his tapes. He was clear and linear, starting with his mother dying in childbirth, and his silent childhood with a father who never forgave him for it. He glossed over bullied schooldays in a flat monotone; lonely adolescence; early manhood in a chilly London flat. And then he met a man (in a pie shop, of all places) who told him about Ernest Shackleton and an obsession was born.

The explorer spoke about the Antarctic as if it were a lover, he recited its history as if it were an epic poem. He talked of the Polynesian legend: of the chief Ui-te-Rangiora setting out in the war canoe *Te-lui-O-Atea*, heading south until the ocean was covered in white powder and great white rocks rose high into the sky. The ancient Greeks called the constellation of stars above the North Pole Arctos; later they gave the South Pole constellation a name too, anti-Arctos. Aristotle claimed that the earth was a sphere, and that the northern landmass of Eurasia must be balanced by some then-unknown southern continent, which he called Antarktikos. For a thousand years afterwards his ideas were branded as heresy, but then the time of the great sea voyages came, the age of Marco Polo, Columbus, Magellan, and people understood for the first time that the earth was not flat, that sailors would not fall off the edge into the unimagined spaces beyond.

When America was first charted in the sixteenth century, map-makers assumed a great and rich country to the south of Africa; ships sailed out in search of it. In 1578, Francis Drake set out to enter the South Seas and claim suzerainty over all lands not already in the hands of a Christian prince; in the *Golden Hind*, he discovered Cape Horn. Almost a hundred years later, a London merchant, Antonio de la Roché, sighted an Antarctic island to the south of 54 degrees latitude.

Other names followed; the explorer lovingly outlined every one. Yves Joseph de Kerguelen-Tremarec, who was imprisoned in the eighteenth century for telling stories about a southern paradise, Jacob Roggeveen, Captain Cook, the first man to sail south of the Antarctic circle, William Smith and Edward Bransfield, with their disputed claim to be first to land on the mainland; the Russian Thaddeus Bellingshausen in the *Vostok*, Robert Fildes in the *Cora*, Captain John Davis in the *Cecilia*; the great Scottish sealer James Weddell in the *Jane*, Henry Foster in the *Chanticleer*, Dumont d'Urville in the *Zelée*, Lieutenant Charles Wilkes in the *Vincennes*.

The long-dead names rolled out fluent and vivid. Maude loved the sound of them, those wonderful lost names. She played that part of the tape over and over, wondering at how this litany of dead men and forgotten ships could conjure up something so immediate and evocative. This history of adventure came out in stark contrast to the stilted recital of the explorer's personal life. Reticent and English, he seemed constrained when talking about himself. He liked the abstract; he talked freely of the ice and snow and the wide white uncharted spaces that had haunted his imagination since he was a lonely young man, in a cramped bedsit with only a stuttering gas fire for company. He worked in insurance, writing policies for ships that set off all over the world, and every time one went south, his dreams went with it.

Then came the journeys themselves, each described in meticulous detail. First the preparation, the hope and excitement, the dreams of conquest. And then the reality, the wild white spaces, the icefields, the treacherous crevasses, the snowblindness, the searing sun, the sudden storms blocking out the division between land and sky. He glossed over the physical pain, the terror, the gnawing frostbite and peeling fingers, the blistered lips.

As Maude went on, through each expedition, she realised that the thing he barely spoke of was that every trip he took ended in failure. He wasn't part of the triumphant Steger and Étienne trek; he watched in admiration as Stroud and Fiennes returned in glory from the first unsupported crossing of the Antarctic continent. She realised, as she read her notes, why she had never heard of him. His were the expeditions that ended in crashing disappointment, dogged by bad weather, ill luck, faulty machinery. He never managed to do what he might have wished, but there was no bitterness in him.

'I saw the South Pole,' he said, his voice carrying strongly on to the tape. 'I saw a place that is still wild, untameable, almost beyond imagination.'

Right at the end of the last tape, there was a fractional pause, and then, on a different note, more personal, more muted, he said: 'I don't know who you are, because I didn't ask, and I don't think we shall meet, but you are transcribing my notes, and you will write my book, and you must be wondering what is the point of it all. I know a fellow who works at a publishing house, and he suggested it. He said it would be the kind of thing that the British would like, since they appreciate honourable failure more than heroic conquest. If I were a proud man, I expect I should have said no. But exploration doesn't pay, and I am over sixty now, and I need the money. So that's what you have, a story of failure, for cash.'

There was a dry note in his voice as he spoke the last sentence, as if he could laugh at himself enough to see the bitter joke in this.

Maude sat and thought about it for a long time after she typed the last lines into her computer. It was growing dark now and the light in her room was dim; a hesitant new moon was starting to gleam over the distant shadow of the mountains. She could smell the faint scent of woodsmoke and pine needles in the air coming in from the half-open window.

She had always thought of her life as a failure, ever since that afternoon in north London she had known that was the verdict. And now there was Dent, and she started to see that perhaps she wasn't such a failure after all. It was as if the fact that she could love this man, that she could hold him and soothe him and make him happy, was a sort of achievement, something that would balance the life she had taken away. But she wondered now what achievement was, what success was, what was the opposite of failure. The old explorer said he had failed, but she thought differently. She thought there was something noble and true about him; he had fought his own frailty and lived his dream, even if it would never get into the record books. He had done it with a rare integrity: half-way through one of the tapes he said that he had never married because he felt that such a perilous way of living wasn't fair on anyone else. 'I couldn't leave a family at home while I went out to test my own hubris,' he said. 'I'm sorry,' he said, quickly, in his gruff voice, 'that sounds unbearably pompous. But I never saw why I should drag someone else into a life that they hadn't chosen, when I never knew if I should come back alive.' Maude wondered how many other men would be so rigorous.

She wanted to write to him and tell him that he wasn't a failure at all, that he was a shining success, that his dreams had come true, whatever he thought about it. She knew she couldn't do that, so she determined that she would write his story as well as she had ever written anything. She would put everything she knew into it, all this new passion and life she had, and she would make the world see that he was a hero after all.

It's all perspective, she thought, looking out into the dark night. Nothing is good or bad but thinking makes it so. If she never wrote a book again, this one would make it worth it.

She was fired with it when she came out of her study that evening. Dent was in the kitchen. He looked up when she came in.

'Do you,' she said, 'ever feel, when you are writing, that sometimes you can make a difference to things? That we are all unimaginably puny and unimportant when it comes down to it, in the great sweep of history, in the vast space of the universe, but that sometimes we can put some small scratch on the surface, something that counts?'

She barely knew what she was saying, and she knew as it came out that it sounded high-flown and improbable, not her place. He was the real writer, it was his job and his territory, and she was someone who wrote invisible prose and never got her name on the spine of a book. But it was what she felt, and she knew that she could say anything to him and he would understand.

He frowned and she thought that perhaps she had spoken out of turn, that some of her certainty was misplaced. 'I don't think of it like that,' he said. His voice had an edge to it that she had never heard before, and because she was all strung up from finishing her tapes she took it hard, in the gut, and she wished she had never spoken.

It was the first time he had said anything to her in that way, and it was as if something splintered in her. 'No,' she said, her voice low and fast. 'No, of course not, it was stupid of me.'

She walked back out of the kitchen and she didn't know where to go, because this was his house; she was living here, but there was nothing here that belonged to her. It was his, everything chosen and arranged long before she was thought of. All she had was her computer and a suitcase of clothes and she suddenly realised that she was no more than a lodger. She wasn't at home here, this wasn't her place; she was just staying, until her time ran out.

She went outside. The night was dark and still and cold, and she looked up at the stars, scattered over the arched indigo above her, and for the first time since she had been with Dent she felt utterly, irredeemably alone. Nothing had prepared her for it. She didn't know that you could be with someone and feel so alone.

She heard him come out behind her. She heard the door open, and his measured steps sound on the gravel. She stood, immobile, petrified, looking out into the dark. She wanted to cry and she wanted to shout and she didn't know what for. I am crying for the moon, she thought.

'I'm sorry,' Dent said. He was standing close behind her, she could feel the heat and presence of him, but he didn't touch her. 'I am,' he said. 'I spoke too fast.'

'It's all right,' she said, although she knew that was not quite true.

'It's not all right,' he said. 'There's something, and I don't know what it is, and you should tell me. I mean,' he said, as if correcting himself, 'you should be able to tell me.'

She turned and looked at him, and his face was serious and shadowed in the dim light. 'It's your place,' she said, and her voice broke a little as she said it. 'All this, it's yours. I have no things here, no books or records or meaningless objects. It's happened so quickly and we're acting as if it's settled and taken for granted, but the fact is I am a guest in your house, and I don't know you very well, and even though I was lonely as hell in my dark basement room, it was mine, it was *my* place, it was where I belonged.'

'No,' said Dent. 'That's not right.'

'It's how I feel,' said Maude. 'I can't help it. There was that house we visited, and it was the house of more than one person, they were dug in. This, now, this – it feels like we are on holiday, one of those wild passionate things that happens under a hot foreign sun, when all the rules are suspended. It's not real.'

'It is real,' said Dent. 'It is. We can make it feel more real. I want you to stay, I meant what I said.'

'I know,' said Maude.

She shook her head and walked a couple of paces down the hill and stopped and turned and looked at him again.

'I *don't* know,' she said.

'I can sell it,' said Dent. 'We could get somewhere together. You could make it yours.'

'No,' said Maude. 'That's not it. I don't want a solution. I want . . . something. I don't know what I want. I want us to talk more; I want my books to sit alongside yours. I want it to feel more permanent, as if it will not dissolve if I look at it too hard.'

Dent walked towards her and pulled her into his arms and held on to her, and she smelt the faint scent of salt and air that always hung about him, and she clung on to his hard wide chest and her stomach was tight as a drum with unnameable fears.

'I'm sorry,' she said. 'I am. It was all so perfect and now I feel lost and I don't know why.'

'It couldn't be easy,' said Dent. 'It's easy when people are young and unscarred and untouched by life and trouble; then it seems like a straight road leading to the horizon. Perhaps that's what it is. It happened so fast that we thought it would be easy, when in fact it's complicated as hell and we have to face that.'

Maude knew that wasn't quite it. It sounded so explicable and right, the way he said it; it was almost right, veering round what was really there, but it wasn't it. She couldn't explain it to him any more, because she couldn't explain it to herself, and she was cold and chilled and she wanted to be close to him. She said, 'Yes, perhaps that's what it is,' and he led her back inside, and they went to bed, and she took her clothes off and fucked him hard, as if to try and lose herself in that vertiginous physical sensation, but that still wasn't it. After it was finished she rolled off him, and she turned her back on him and lay straight as a board, all the unspoken fear held tight and rolled inside her like a lead ball, and she wanted to cry, but she couldn't because he might hear her.

Dent lay beside her, breathing steadily, controlled, in and out, until she thought he was asleep. She felt there was a gap between them, a chasm, uncharted, and although it was only a few inches, it felt like the Grand Canyon to her. It was something she hadn't expected, and she felt entirely alone. She wondered if it was the end of everything, if all this had just been a mirage; she had dreamt that she was free, and it was nothing but make-believe, to get her through the worst of the night.

She wasn't sure if she slept or not. It seemed a moment later that she looked at the clock on the bedside table (his clock, of course, nothing here was hers, his strange clock) and the two dim green points said 3 a.m. Three o'clock in the morning, she thought: in the real dark night of the soul, it is always three o'clock in the morning.

'We could get married,' Dent said, behind her.

She wondered for a moment if she were dreaming; but his voice was strong and low and real. 'We could get married and have children,' he said. 'Would you marry me?'

'Are you doing this to make me feel better?' she said. The ball of lead was still low in her belly, as if she were pregnant with it.

'No,' he said, and she knew then that she was not dreaming, that he had been awake all this time. 'It's what I want. I love you and I need you and I want it for good, in sickness and in health. I want to marry you and grow old with you and make a home with you and make children with you and be together always. That's what I want.'

For a fleeting second Maude felt delight that he should say that. At the same time, the exact same time, as if she were in one of those slick post-modern movies, where they run two stories on the same split screen, she knew that was not it; it was not the answer.

More than that, she knew it wasn't what she wanted. Something from her past, from long ago, came up and swamped her, and she knew that she was about to be irrational and destructive and she would have done anything to stop it.

'That's not it,' she said.

'Why not?' he said.

She heard his voice behind her shoulder, she could see his clear long face in her mind; she couldn't look at it.

'Because,' she said. 'It's not the answer.'

'I don't know the question,' he said. He turned in the bed, she heard the sheets move against his body and felt the weight of the mattress shift. There was a part of her that wanted to turn and fling herself against him and hold him and hold him and say, Please understand, please forgive me, please get it; please know that there is something so frightened and complicated in me that I can't give it words but I want you to name it because you are the writer, you are the man who can conjure nothing into words, you can make sense of it all. She wanted to say – even though she knew it wasn't allowed, and it never worked, not in the hard light of day – she wanted to say: Please save me.

'Marry me,' he said. 'Say yes. Say you will.'

The voice in her head rose higher: *That's not the answer*. Everyone thinks that is the answer, but it's not. The question is more complicated than that; that's not the panacea to all ills, to the late-night terrors, to all the spectres and fears.

'You don't understand,' she said, and her voice was tight and coiled with it, all the things she didn't understand, all the things he didn't understand.

'Yes,' he said. 'Yes, I do. Marry me.'

And then she really was up and running, not just in her mind but in her body, out of the bed, across the room, pulling on her clothes in the dark, stubbing her toe against the wardrobe, knocking her calf against the hard wood of the bed.

'No, no,' she said. 'Fuck it,' she said, as she bashed her elbow against the arm of a chair.

She was dressing now, she hardly knew what in. She had to get clothes on her naked body and get out of this house.

'What?' he said. In the thin light that came from the window she could see him raise himself up on one elbow, trying to make her out in the dark.

He was confused with sleep and the lateness of every-thing. 'What is it?' he said. 'Where are you going?'

She stopped, in the middle of the room, mid-flight.

'Marriage isn't it,' she said. 'Don't you *see*? That's not the answer. How many happy marriages do you see? There are about four perfect ones in the whole world. Everyone says, Oh look at those ones, the flawless ones, that last and last, where they are still in love, and they are still best friends, and they rely on each other and make each other laugh and they never get bored or cat around and it's the alpha and omega. But mostly it doesn't happen like that. For so many people marriage is the end of everything, the end of the tenderness. It's a year of novelty and then it's swords drawn and sheathed silences and barbed remarks and careless betrayals and horrible insidious subterranean resentment and hostility. People say it's the answer to everything and it's the answer to nothing.'

Dent was sitting up now, trying to see her. Maude stood in the centre of the room, dressed, tensed to run.

'No,' he said. 'That's not it. It can be right. It can be better. It's not the answer, but it's something. It's a leap of faith, a gauntlet to the unknown.'

'No,' said Maude, and her voice was rising and she couldn't stop it. She knew she was making no sense, but she also knew that she was speaking the truth. She wanted desperately for him to get it, all the things that she could hardly understand herself; she wanted, more than she had ever wanted anything, for him to be on her side.

'I don't want a *gauntlet*,' she said. 'It's not so simple, you say let's get married and suddenly it's wine and roses. But it's not like that. This is real life and it's not like that.'

'It could be like that,' said Dent. 'It could. Marry me. Be brave and say yes. I want to love you and have children with you and we can do that.'

'I can't,' said Maude, and her voice cracked with it. 'Don't you see? How can I have a child? How can I have a child after what I have done? Don't you *get* it?'

It was strange how neither of them moved.

'You have to forgive yourself,' he said, and his voice was low and rational. 'You know that. You can do that. We could have a child together, and you would love it, and it would be new life, it would be like a symbol. And you could forgive yourself.'

'What if I couldn't?' Maude said. 'Sometimes women don't love their children. They pretend they do because everyone says they must, that they are programmed with love. But sometimes they hate and resent their children and it's all a fake and a phoney, and then I would be doing double death, double betrayal, and it would be the same old thing all over again.'

'You would love it,' said Dent.

Through all this he stayed sane and still and reasonable, as if he had all the answers. 'You would,' he said. 'You have a good generous beating heart, and we would have a baby and you would love it.'

'Women do terrible things to their children,' said Maude, as if he hadn't spoken. 'They carry them around for forty long weeks, in their bellies, and they bear them and feed them and then they do terrible things to them. What if I was like my mother? What if I was cold and distant and then I died?'

'You're being irrational,' he said, and his voice was still low and calm and she heard it and she wanted to hit him, she wanted to shout and spit and hurt him. 'This is irrational,' he said again, in that same voice. 'This is late-night terrors, this is morbid.'

'Yes,' said Maude. 'It may be that, but it's what I feel and don't tell me how I should feel and don't tell me what's right or wrong, because you don't have to do that part, you don't have to spit it out between your legs, you don't have to yell and swear with the pain, so don't tell me that you know about it, because you don't. Don't tell me that it will be fine and it's the answer.'

And then she really was running, as if her body all at once could move after all this static talk. She tore out of the room and down the stairs, hitting her side against the wall because she wouldn't stop to turn on the lights. She got to the front door and she ran through it and left it open behind her; she fumbled her way into her car and stabbed the key into the ignition and turned the engine over. It caught first time, and she pulled the lights on, so they illuminated the arcade of dark green trees, and there was a scree of gravel under her tyres as she drove out into the night, as if the devil were at her back.

She drove fast for a while, not knowing where she was going, the smooth oiled black of the road under her tyres, her mind wiped blank from thinking.

And then she stopped and she pulled the car over and she sat, looking out of the narrow rectangle of wind-screen, the night growing lucid through the glass, the moon riding unheeding over the shadowed lisp of the mountains. She remembered something she had read once: damaged people, it said, are dangerous because they know they can survive. She thought that was all wrong. Damaged people are terrified, she knew then, sitting in the fag-end of the empty night, that they won't survive, paralysed by the fear that however much they paper over the cracks all it takes is one chip, one tear, and everything opens up wide, the gaping wounds uncovered, deeper and more unfathomable than before. Damaged people are terrified that whatever they do, however hard they try, they will never get mended, and it's no good ever dreaming that love can mend your heart, because for some hearts there isn't enough love in the whole world to make a damn's worth of difference.

I don't know what I am doing, she thought. What am I doing here?

It was after five when she got back. It was dark as night but she knew that it was morning. She didn't know what she would say or why she had acted as she had. She pushed open the door, feeling it hard and cold against her hand, and she wasn't sure what she would find.

Dent was sitting downstairs, on the red sofa, in a green paisley dressing-gown; sitting upright and awake, waiting for her. The fire was dead in the grate but the smell of peat smoke was still strong in the room.

'I'm sorry,' she said, looking right at him. 'Did I spoil everything?'

He looked back at her and his face was very white. He shook his head and smiled a half-smile and he didn't say anything. He went over to the record player and he chose a record and put it on, wiping the flat vinyl surface of it with his sleeve and blowing gently on it to take away the dust and laying the needle in the groove. It crackled a little and then it settled in and it was Ella Fitzgerald singing 'It's Only A Paper Moon'.

All the time Maude stayed standing in the doorway, and when it was a minute or so in, and she heard the chorus, she smiled. She walked over to Dent and stood straight in front of him and looked up into his clear eyes and said, 'So it's that simple, I just have to believe in you?' and he looked back at her and said, 'Yes, you should have more faith.'

She dropped her head and felt an ache in her neck from terror and exhaustion and she shut her eyes and let her body lean forward. He was there to catch her and he left the record to play as he guided her up the stairs, so she heard the voice growing fainter and fainter behind her. When they got to the bedroom, she said, 'I'm too tired for anything, I'm too tired even to get undressed.' He said 'That's all right,' and he sat down on the bed and pulled her gently down beside him. He drew the bedclothes up over her, and she smiled a little, and she said again, 'Did I spoil everything?' and he said, 'Nothing is spoilt.' She said, 'Will you hold on to me?' and she felt him lay himself down beside her, fitting his body in behind hers, and without knowing why she knew that this danger was past.

15

They didn't talk about that night again. It was as if something was settled between them. Maude wouldn't marry him, but he wanted her to. He wanted her to stay, and she wanted to stay, and they would work from that.

Maude thought this was what happened; there was the early passionate part when nothing mattered and the world receded and everything was perfect and there were no horizons to look over. And then something came and shattered the dream world, broke the illusions. After that, it either disintegrated altogether, or it survived and grew stronger.

It couldn't be perfect, Maude thought, not after everything. Nothing is perfect and everything has cracks in it and it's all a question of degrees.

How do I know all this, she thought, how did I get all this worked out?

But she did know it, from whatever – all those books she read, and films she watched, and dreams she dreamed. She knew also that they had weathered their first big storm, and she took comfort from that.

She felt in a way that she could barely explain, even in the privacy of her own head, that because all that senseless terror had come out, the jagged scarring edges of her broken self, because he had seen it and not turned away, that there was something more real for her here now, something that she could rely on. He could have said it was spoilt, it was too much, but he hadn't. She thought that was worth more than diamonds.

Dent took her shopping at the weekends, to strange lost roadside arcades and antique shops and boot sales and told her to buy things, so that she could put them in the house and make it hers. She bought a fat armchair in worn green leather, with tight bronze wheels on its legs, so she could move it across the floor. She bought two engraved bottles in thin red glass, and a tiny blue picture of a seascape somewhere out west. The man who sold it to her was American: he had come to live on the east coast from Philadelphia twenty years before and grown obsessed with nineteenth-century Scottish artists. He told her the painter was called Thomas Bunting and had worked in Aberdeen at the turn of the century. Aberdeen, thought Maude, the silver city, the granite city; on a grey day it could look bleaker than any place on earth, but when the sun came out it shone like polished pewter. Maude thought that must be a fine thing for a painter to look at, the shining silver walls and the ephemeral light and the wide space of the harbour where the seagulls wheeled and quarrelled like white darts in the sky. She carried her picture away like a trophy, and hung it in the bedroom she shared with Dent, so it was the first thing she saw when she woke up in the morning.

With each object, Maude felt a sense of belonging and reassurance: this is mine, that is mine, she thought, here in this house. Dent wanted to pay for everything but she wouldn't let him. 'I have all this cash,' she said. 'I still get cash from Rita, after all these years. I never spent any money, except for the orphans. I want these things to be mine.'

Dent encouraged her to move the furniture and rearrange the kitchen and get more linen for the bed. They bought plants for the garden, even though it was the wrong time of year, and they planted them together, dug them into the hard cold earth, and Dent said they could watch them grow in the spring. It's a long time until the spring, Maude thought, but she didn't say so.

She still felt there were too many parts of him that she didn't know, but she thought now that she could wait it out, let things unravel in their own time. It takes years to know someone, she thought; you never know the heart of anyone else.

'It's as if he has some secret,' she wrote to Sadie, via e-mail. 'It's as if there is some dark secret at the heart of him, and one day I shall find out what it is.'

'Perhaps everyone has a secret,' wrote Sadie, by return of post.

Maude saw Richard sometimes, driving off in his Land Rover, or walking down by the burn at the bottom of the hill. She wondered sometimes whether this secret she guessed in Dent had anything to do with Richard Hunter.

It was coming up to Christmas. Dent dragged in a fat conical fir tree and put it by the fire, and because he had no decorations Maude went into Aberdeen, where the Christmas lights were shimmering against the gleaming granite walls of the city, and the pavements were as crowded as if it were a street party, and coloured banners fluttered in the chill evening air. She bought fairy lights and baubles and they hung them on the tree until it looked like a carnival. Maude arranged more lights in the windows and put candles everywhere and Dent brought in logs and pine cones for the fire, so that everything was festive as a bell.

'There are people coming,' he said, the night before Christmas Eve. 'Tomorrow. My daughter, and her friends.'

Maude looked up at him with shock. She was pushing cloves into an orange to make a pomander. She had read an article about it in a magazine, and it seemed such an outlandish thing to do she hadn't been able to resist. Her fingers were tender and red from the points of the cloves and stained yellow from the orange peel, and the stinging citrus scent was in her nostrils, mingled with the spicy smell of the cloves, which reminded her of something, she wasn't sure what.

'*People*,' she said. 'Your *daughter*. Subtitles for the hard of hearing. You can't do that to me, just like that.'

'I forgot,' said Dent, looking mildly shifty. 'She comes every year.'

Maude knew that Dent had a daughter, from the things that she had read about him, before they met. But he had never once said anything about a child, the whole time Maude had been there, and she hadn't asked. She thought there were some things that he should volunteer, in his own time.

'You never talk about her,' Maude said. 'That's so curious. Why do you never talk about her?'

'I got used to never talking about anything,' said Dent.

Maude gave him a sceptical look through her eyelashes.

'Oh all right,' he said. 'I don't know. I just don't. She's very private. She didn't like being known as my daughter, with everything that happened and all the publicity. She changed her name. So I suppose we keep each other in separate parts of our lives and we see each other at Christmas, and that's all.'

'You could have told me she was coming,' said Maude, letting it go. She was learning to let things go, that was one of the things she was learning. 'Is there enough food?'

'I got a goose,' said Dent.

'Your goose is *cooked*,' said Maude.

'William and Violet and Mickey are coming as well,' said Dent, looking out of the window.

'You know what's strange?' said Maude, sitting back in her chair and starting to laugh. 'Just as I think that you are some kind of anomaly, the kind of thing they don't make any more, you do something that makes me think men are all the same.'

'I can't help it,' said Dent, turning back to her and smiling a sheepish smile. 'I'm biologically programmed.'

'That's *your* excuse,' said Maude.

The next day, after lunch, Sadie walked through the door into the kitchen, kissed Dent on the cheek, and said, 'Hello, Alexander.'

Dent kissed her back, and said, 'Hello, Cal.'

Maude said: 'I don't understand.'

Sadie, who was wearing a scarlet coat and stacked boots, as if she were going to a film premiere or a fashion shoot, pulled off her gloves and sat down and started to laugh.

'Oh, Maude,' she said. 'Don't be confused. This is my dad. For real.'

Maude looked from one of them to the other and suddenly she got it. All at once she remembered the strange expression on Sadie's face the first time she came to Maude's flat and saw the long shelf of books by Alexander Dent. She remembered Sadie telling her she must write to him, that he might want to talk to her.

'Oh,' she said, the pieces falling into place so quickly that she wondered she had never got it before. 'I see,' she said. Suspicion chased in hard on the heels of her comprehension. 'This whole thing was a set-up, wasn't it?' she said.

'No, no,' said Sadie, shaking her head, so her long dark hair flew about her face like flags. 'Not at all. Chance, that's all. A simple twist of fate.'

'You set it up,' said Maude. She didn't know whether to laugh or spit.

'I did one thing,' said Sadie. 'When you said you were thinking of writing something on him, I wrote to him and said he should see you. That's all. All the rest of it was your own work. I have to say, I wasn't expecting you to drive away and never come back. That wasn't in the grand plan at all.'

'Oh,' said Maude, in exasperation. 'I don't know what I think.'

'Don't think,' said Sadie. 'Laugh and have a drink and wonder at how curious life is. Come on, Alexander,' she said to Dent, 'break open the bubbly.'

'It's three in the afternoon,' said Dent.

'It's *Christmas*,' said Sadie. 'We three kings of Orient are. 'Tis the season. Holly and the ivy. You know the thing.'

She looked around and stretched her neck. 'Dean is bringing in the bags,' she said.

'Dean is here,' said Maude.

'Dean is here?' said Sadie, as if that were only to be expected. 'And Ruby somewhere. They have no family, so they come here, for the festive season.'

'Do they all know?' said Maude.

'Of course we know,' said Ruby, walking in. 'Don't put on that face, the wind will change and then where will we be?'

'What wind?' said Dean.

'You brought the bags,' said Sadie, looking at him with love. He kissed her flat on the mouth and said, 'Of course I brought the bags,' and Maude started to laugh despite herself, because she didn't understand one word of it.

So here was a whole new thing for her to deal with. Dent springing the absent daughter on her had haunted her sleep the night before: she had imagined some silent resentful teenager staring at her with mute suspicion over the goose. (This was irrational, she thought: if she had done her maths she would have realised a daughter would be Sadie's age.) Now, she had to be in a couple with Dent in front of Sadie and Ruby and Dean, who had known her before, in her previous incarnation, and all of a sudden she found she didn't know where to look or how to act or what to do with her hands.

Everyone went off in different directions to unpack and settle themselves in, and Maude was left in the empty kitchen, not knowing anything. Later, Ruby came down and found her standing there, at a loss.

'Here you are,' said Ruby.

'Let's have tea,' Maude said, because she didn't know what else to say. She felt that she had been found out in something. It was so obvious that she and Dent were sleeping together, and he was Sadie's father, and Sadie wasn't that much younger than she was, and it made her feel twisted inside.

'Just let's have a nice cup of tea,' said Ruby, joining in the spirit of the thing. 'Come on,' she said, looking around, 'put the kettle on.'

Maude looked at her and started laughing. 'Oh,' she said. 'Oh, this wasn't what I was expecting.'

'I said we should have called first,' said Ruby, as Sadie walked in. 'Did I say that?'

'I wanted to it to be a surprise,' said Sadie, who was hugely enjoying the joke. 'And, anyway, there isn't a telephone here.'

'Where's Dean?' said Ruby.

'He's doing some male-bonding thing with Alexander,' said Sadie. 'They've gone to the woodshed or whatever it is that men do.'

Maude sat down.

'We're making tea,' said Ruby, getting some cups off the shelf and putting them down on the table, as if making a point.

'Maude needs a black whisky,' said Sadie.

They drank whisky in the end, even though it was the middle of the afternoon. Sadie said they should get a little drunk because sometimes it made things more explicable.

'Let's get tight,' she said. 'And then I can tell you all my secrets and you won't be cross any more.'

'I'm not cross,' said Maude, although she wondered if she was.

'I would be,' said Ruby. 'That's breaking the code.'

'You're supposed to be on my side,' said Sadie, giving her a stern look. 'Anyway, all it was was some harmless encouragement.' She laughed, a little guilty, and looked at Maude. 'I told him he should see you, that's all it was. I didn't tell him to fall in love or any of that stuff. You did that part, all by yourself.'

There was a pause when Sadie said that because it was still too new and there was something strange about it, although none of them could exactly have said what it was.

'It's too much coincidence,' said Maude, although she knew it was more than that. 'How does this happen? This doesn't happen in real life.'

She had been growing used to real life, to some knowledge of living in the world, rather than the refracted fictional version she had gleaned from books and films and old sad songs. Now this was something too improbable and she didn't like it. She remembered what Dent had said about chance and fate, and how alluring that is, and she wondered. She wasn't sure she liked it at all.

'Oh no,' said Sadie. 'I know all about this. Coincidence happens in life, that's the whole point. They don't put it in books because everyone stretches their eyes and says that's too much suspension of disbelief. If you get to thinking about probability too closely it will make your head spin.'

'You can get to the point now,' said Ruby. 'If you want.'

'Maude is fretting,' said Sadie, patiently, 'because she was obsessed with Alexander's books for years and then I appeared on her doorstep, and now it turns out we are related, and she doesn't like that.'

'Also you could have told her,' said Ruby.

It was back to that high green room, Maude thought, watching them, that room where they both bickered and teased and knew exactly what to say, while she was left, silent and other.

'See, Maude,' said Sadie, putting her chin on her hands, just like Maude remembered from those times in the Talgarth Road. 'It is extraordinary, but probability makes no sense. Every week someone wins the lottery, which is fourteen million to one. Fourteen million to one, how does that make any sense at all? But every week it happens to a perfectly ordinary person. And you hear all those stories about people going to India and standing on a deserted railway station somewhere outside Calcutta and running into the person who taught them English at primary school.'

'I don't know,' said Maude.

'I'll tell you a story,' said Sadie, who was on a roll now, not to be stopped. 'There was a girl who Ruby and I were at school with.'

'Not this old chestnut,' said Ruby, shaking her head.

'You know it makes sense,' said Sadie, unrepentant.

'It is a good story,' said Ruby to Maude, 'and funnily enough, it's all true.'

'This girl,' said Sadie, 'had an uncle who died in a car crash when he was twenty-one. He was beautiful and gilded and it was 1966 and everyone loved him and he drove his Lotus into a truck somewhere in Chelsea on a dark winter night. Years later, this girl's stepfather ran off with a fat rich woman he met on an aeroplane, so she and her mother were left with no home and not much cash, and they went to live in a rented basement near the Earl's Court Road. One day, the landlady said to my friend, Is your uncle who I think he is? And it turned out that the landlady lived in Chelsea in the sixties, just off Redcliffe Square, and at two o'clock one morning she heard a great crash and she went down to see what it was, and she found the smashed Lotus. The driver had swerved to save his passenger, some leggy model in a fur coat, and the radio had come out in the shock of the collision, on its entrails, and was still playing at full blast, and the model was so stoned that she was dancing in the street. The landlady said, I saw your uncle bleeding to death over the steering-wheel, while this girl danced in the street. And the strange thing was that my friend had always heard a story like that, but she never believed it, she thought it too far-fetched. And now, almost exactly twenty years after the event, she was lodging in the basement of the one person who was an actual eye-witness to the way her uncle died, and she knew that those rumours were true after all. So you see, this kind of thing happens all the time.'

'Is that true?' said Maude.

Sadie twisted her face into a smile. 'It's the truest story I know,' she said. 'That's all.'

'Oh, have some more whisky and let's not think about it so much,' said Ruby. 'I want to have a happy Christmas and anyway, we're all a long time gone.'

Maude shook her head and shrugged her shoulders. She thought suddenly, that despite everything, she was glad to have them there, even if there was a part of her that was still disconcerted and suspicious. There was something comforting about having the two women in the kitchen with her. She realised that there were things she might say to them that Dent wouldn't necessarily understand. This thought shocked her, but also excited her, in a subterranean way.

'What's the deal with Dean?' she said, in a new voice, and Sadie heard it and gave Maude a sharp look from under her eyebrows and took a moment, as if in acknowledgement, and said, 'Well, we seem to be consoling each other.'

'Not before time,' said Ruby, drinking her drink.

'It's not *that* obvious,' said Sadie. 'I hate to be obvious.'

'It is to me,' said Ruby.

'So the most commitment-phobic man in the world?' said Maude.

'Went back to his wife,' said Sadie.

'You knew that would happen,' said Ruby.

'He said he was separated. He said he was never going back, whatever happened,' said Sadie.

'Yeah yeah,' said Ruby, looking right at her.

'Oh, all right,' said Sadie. 'I was heartbroken but not surprised. And then,' she added thoughtfully, 'there was the small matter of the other couple of dillies he was running on the side.'

'And it still didn't stop you smoking,' said Ruby.

'When your lover leaves you, you have to have something to do with your hands,' said Sadie, with dignity.

Ruby gave her a hard look. Sadie gave a sigh and said to Maude, as if she had a right to know: 'I was a falling-apart mess, if you really want to know. I suppose I knew in my dark heart that it was never going anywhere, but I did love him, and he lied and cheated and I felt like a fool. I believed every plausible thing he told me, and I took care not to see the parts I didn't want to look at too closely. I knew that I was better off without him, but when the full extent of his duplicity came out into the light I don't think I've ever felt so brutally betrayed in my life. I kept saying, over and over, I have my health, I have my job, I have the world at my feet, but I felt as if someone had paraded me around town with a big fat dunce's cap stuck on my head so everyone could point and laugh.'

'Now you know,' said Ruby. 'Most people get cheated on, sooner or later. With me, of course, it was sooner.'

Maude looked at Ruby in surprise. She had assumed that Ruby could do anything, was invulnerable. She didn't know why she had thought that, but she had.

'Twenty-six years old,' said Ruby, seeing the look. 'Packed full of illusion. And one day I walked in, and there was another woman in my bed, and she wasn't doing the crossword, that's for sure.'

'All this happens?' said Maude. 'In real life?' She realised suddenly that she had taken herself so thoroughly out of the world that she had started to believe that life mostly happened in the movies.

'All this happens,' said Sadie, 'and yet we go on thinking it only happens to other people.'

'Is that why you are still on your own?' said Maude to Ruby.

Ruby shrugged up her shoulders and gave a small tight smile. 'Three years on,' she said. 'And still the memory of it is burnt on my retinas. So every time someone comes along and gives me sweet talk, I remember all those lies, and I can't trust it. There are many pleasures to life alone,' she said, and Maude knew that she believed it, 'but it would be nice to have the choice.'

'They don't understand that part,' said Sadie, 'when they lie to you. They don't understand that it's not just the hurt and the humiliation. I don't think they realise that it stays with you like a scar, like some ugly livid thing that throbs with shame in the still watches of the night.'

'But now you have Dean,' said Maude.

Sadie nodded. 'I know there isn't ever anything such as safety,' she said. 'But I know him well enough to see that he will only tell me the truth. Doesn't mean we'll always stay together with roses running over the door. But it means I won't hear about a flexible blonde from a third party.'

'What I don't understand,' said Ruby, looking into her glass of whisky, as if all the secrets of life were there, 'is why we go on believing that most people tell the truth, when in fact hardly anyone ever does.'

'We can dream,' said Sadie, starting to laugh. 'We can close our eyes and dream a little dream.'

Later Sadie said she wanted to go up and have a bath. 'I know where my room is,' she said, without thinking, and Maude felt like a visitor in someone else's house and for a moment she wanted to kill Sadie for not telling her right at the beginning, before it all got so complicated.

Ruby and Maude were left sitting at the table, in a small pool of silence. Then Ruby smiled her good familiar smile, and said, 'Can we walk round the block, even though it is dark now?'

'Yes,' said Maude. 'We can.' She realised that she wanted to get out of the house. She had only been alone with Ruby once before, the time when they talked about Sadie's mother dying – the mother Maude now knew was Claudette – but she felt some gentle ease with her. She wanted to tell Ruby all her secrets and ask all her questions.

'If we stay close to the house,' Maude said, 'there is enough light.'

There was a short path that led round the house, and the lights fell out on to the gravel like a balm. The moon was full and they could see the black shadows of the mountains sketched against the thick navy blue sky. The air was cold and clean and had the secret feeling that it took on at night. They walked slowly in step, finding their way, their shoes sounding in small contained snaps on the gravel.

'Don't be cross with Sadie,' said Ruby. 'She believed that she was doing it all for the greater good. She has always been like that, even before her mother died. She always wanted to save the world with her bare hands.'

'Yes,' said Maude. 'I can see that. It's a shock, that's all. I hate the idea of people knowing something I don't. Perhaps I am afraid of being made a fool.'

Ruby stopped walking and looked at Maude in the dim light.

'Will you tell me,' she said, 'what it was that happened to you?'

Maude told her, in short hard sentences. She didn't hesitate. She told the story, and it was only the third time she had told it, and she didn't feel much as she was telling it; a curious sense of distance fell on her, as if she were talking about someone else.

Ruby sucked in her breath and let it out in a sigh. 'My God,' she said. 'Ah. That's a thing to happen.'

She took Maude's arm, that small physical reassurance saying as much as words ever could, and Maude found her eyes filling with tears, that dried again in the night wind.

'All our hearts that get busted and broken,' said Ruby. 'Everyone gets that, everyone I ever met. But this is something else altogether. No wonder you and Alexander . . . I mean, there couldn't be anyone else, for either of you.'

'Yes,' said Maude. They started walking again, behind the back of the house. Through the kitchen window they could see gleaming amber light shedding its promise of warmth and comfort out into the still night. 'That's how it seems,' she said. 'I thought I would live alone for ever, and then there was someone who could understand, like no one else.

'I get frightened and bent out of shape sometimes,' she said, 'because I read so many books during those ten years, and they all say the same thing. They say you have to save yourself. I get scared because I think that he saved me, really, and that seems wrong.'

'You are saving him too,' said Ruby. 'Of course you are. It's just men don't show it in the same way, the need they have for getting saved. There's the insidious idea that women are the needy ones and men are like oak, independent and mighty, planted in the earth. But everyone looks after men, they get wives and mothers and wives who act like mothers; they get their laundry done and their food cooked and someone who will let them cry in the still watches of the night. That's what women are taught to do. So it seems that men are more independent, because their desires are getting tended to all the time. They're not brought up to do the same for women, and their women have to ask for it, and then they get called needy, which doesn't strike me as fair.'

Maude stopped and considered. She had never thought about it that way. 'Well,' she said, 'maybe you are right.'

'Of course I'm right,' said Ruby. 'I'm smoking hot at theory. Practice, on the other hand, is my weak suit.'

'What about Sadie?' said Maude. 'She always seems as if she has all the answers.'

'Her mother checked out,' said Ruby. 'Long before she died. She wasn't there and she didn't care. She was running around and being beautiful and getting her picture in the paper. Alexander did what he could, but it never filled that space. So that's why there was the most commitment-phobic man in the world, and that's why there is Dean now. I hope that this one will work. I do hope that.'

'And you,' said Maude. 'What about you?'

'Life,' said Ruby, 'isn't just about being in a pair. That's not the only thing that works. There are enough shitty arrangements for us to know that's the case, enough cases of cruelty and deceit and desperation. You have to know why you are doing it, and you have to know it is a choice, rather than a blinding need. You're right, you can't save someone, but you can have mutual resuscitation, if you're lucky. I got hurt too badly, that was all, and I need some time to get over that. My dad died, and he left me that place in the Talgarth Road, and I sat there for months feeling bereft, and then there was the man who cheated and lied. What an old cliché that was, I remember thinking, as I was crying in the night, why he couldn't have been more original? So all the old scar tissue broke open and bled over the floor, and I'm just waiting, for the moment, gathering my resources, and that's all right.'

They were round the corner of the house now, walking back to the front door. They walked easily in time, and Maude thought, a fast thought that ran through her head before she could make much sense of it, that this walk was as important to her as what had happened with Dent. Afterwards she thought it was because she had resigned herself to the role of the outsider, the outcast, never having a talent for intimacy, even before the ugly accident that marked her for ever as other. She thought that there are many different kinds of love, and all of them are vital, for us to mend our broken hearts.

Ruby said, as if she knew some of this, 'You will be all right, with Alexander. You will be all right, because you both got so smashed up, and now you can make that better. And me, I'm just waiting, until my bruised heart gets bold again, and then who knows?'

'Who knows?' said Maude. She thought of the women in her life: she thought of Sadie and she thought of this walk with Ruby and she thought of Violet, and it seemed as if they were in a magic circle and nothing could come and touch them.

It was a fleeting thought, but when she went inside the awkward terrors of the afternoon came back to her, and she walked upstairs and wondered why it is that we go on yearning for simplicity when everything is always so complicated.

Dent came in later when she was lying in the bath. The sky was black outside her window; she hadn't bothered to close the shutters and it was like a hole in the room.

'What are you doing?' he said.

'Thinking,' Maude said.

'I'm sorry,' he said. 'She asked me not to tell you. She wanted it to be a surprise.'

'It's a conspiracy,' said Maude. She knew this was not true, but it felt a bit like that. There was a joke in her voice, but she wasn't sure it was a joke.

'It's not Watergate,' Dent said. He sat on the side of the bath and looked down at her long naked body.

'Why do you call her Cal?' Maude said abruptly.

'It's her real name,' he said. 'Her real name is Callisto. It was a stupid name, really, Claudette was reading Ovid at the time and it was the seventies. She changed it to Sadie, which was her middle name, because she didn't want the press to swoop on her. She wanted to be her own woman, not just the daughter of someone with a lurid past.'

'Yes,' said Maude. 'I see that.'

Dent looked at her and smiled. His eyes slanted when he smiled, his eyebrows arched and his mouth curved upwards into his cheekbones and usually Maude only had to see that to feel weak and grateful.

'Can I come in with you?' he said.

'No,' said Maude, lying immobile in the water. 'I'm thinking and there's only room for one.'

Dent stayed sitting and looking at her.

'What were you doing with Dean in the shed?' she said.

'Talking,' Dent said. 'Catching up.'

That was so unlike him that Maude knew it was not quite true. Dent had never caught up with anyone in his life, she knew him well enough to know that. She thought he had never done that, even before the accident.

'Was Richard there?' she said.

'Well, yes,' said Dent. 'He was.'

'So the three of you talked,' said Maude. 'For four hours.'

'We had a glass of beer,' said Dent.

'And what did you talk about?' said Maude. 'All three of you, with your glass of beer, in the shed? For four hours.'

'I don't know,' said Dent. 'Things. All sorts of things. You know.'

'I don't,' said Maude. 'I don't know at all.'

The water was thin and cooling around her body and she didn't want to move.

'So what did *you* talk about?' Dent said, trying a small counter-attack. 'You three women, all afternoon?'

'Secrets and lies,' said Maude, and she got up in one fast movement so the water fell off her body with a crash, and the stillness of the bath was shattered, and Dent leant back with surprise.

'And *we* had whisky to drink,' she said, walking into the bedroom and shutting the door behind her.

16

The first evening, Maude found it hard to relax. She felt furious with herself that she couldn't. Dent and Sadie cooked the goose; they roasted it until the skin was dark shining brown and made boiled potatoes and red cabbage to go with it and it was a fine dinner. It was Christmas Eve and Maude felt like a spectre at the feast.

I don't know why, I don't know why, she said over and over in her head. I wish, she thought, they could have told me the truth. She smiled and nodded and watched the evening unfold in front of her like a film with the sound turned down.

It was also something to do with the fact that the others had all been here first. Dent wasn't quite such a recluse; less and less, as she knew more of him. There was Richard, had always been Richard, from the beginning; there was Mickey, and Violet and William; there was Nora, with her memories of Paris. And Ruby and Dean had been coming here for Christmas every year.

Maude felt as if she had her face pressed up against the window-pane, looking in on the merry folks with their table of plenty. She sat at the end of the table and drank a glass of good red wine and despised herself.

And also, she thought, perhaps in some bizarre way she was jealous of Dent; she thought she was there first with Sadie too. Sadie had been the forerunner after all; Sadie had been Maude's first forbidden taste of feeling like the chosen. Now she watched Sadie with Dent, and saw that they knew all about each other, had secrets and memories going back twenty-seven years and Maude felt that she counted for nothing.

'Say something, Maude,' said Sadie. 'Tell me how you liked the goose.'

'The goose was fine,' said Maude, and she painted a smile on her face so glossy and bright that she hoped no one would see the cracks.

Maybe, she thought later, lying in the dark, with Dent asleep beside her, it's Christmas too. She had always hated Christmas, ever since she was a child. Her parents ignored Christmas partly because they felt it was a cynical commercial marketing exercise, partly because as good rational humanists they had no deity, and partly because they couldn't be bothered with all the work it entailed. So where other children got Santa Claus and mince pies and plum pudding and crackers to pull, Maude got another ordinary day; a flat quiet day like Sunday, all the shops shut and no traffic on the streets. It always felt to her as if some terrible catastrophe had happened and at any moment the radio was going to crackle into life with H.G. Wells announcements, like the *War of the Worlds*, which her father had given her to read for her eighth birthday. Ever since, she had been haunted with the end of the world, and Christmas Day always felt like the apocalypse to her.

After the accident it was worse; she imagined this would be the day that the mother would miss her dead child most. So she added to the post-apocalyptic feeling the weighty burden of her guilt and had herself a merry little Christmas, all alone with a ham sandwich in her dark basement room.

Now, for the first time, she had some inkling of what it might be like to deck the halls with boughs of holly, and instead of feeling glad and pleased, she felt stilted and empty, because Sadie had arrived with her secret and her joke, and Maude felt as if she was the only one who didn't get it.

On the morning of Christmas Day, Maude woke early. She saw Dent sleeping beside her and she woke him up and held on to him and put his hand between her legs so she smiled with it. He kissed her and she felt the familiar sliding feeling, as if she were rolling over the side of a cliff, and for a while she didn't care what day it was.

Afterwards he looked at her for a long time and stroked her hair with his hand and she stared back into his eyes as if the whole world was there and nothing else mattered. He leant over and smiled and kissed her eyelids and said Happy Christmas and Maude smiled back and thought perhaps the apocalypse wouldn't happen that day after all.

She gave Dent an old copy of *The Waste Land* that she had found in a second-hand shop in the back streets of Elgin. He rubbed his hands over the faded cloth cover and the foxed pages, and he read the inscription and he blinked a little and then he said, 'Thank you, that's the nicest present I've ever had.'

He gave her a ring.

'It's not a hint,' he said. 'It's not to do with marriage or signing anything. It's pretty, that's all, and it made me think of you.'

It was a small square-cut amethyst and it fitted perfectly on Maude's third finger.

'You are not to be trusted,' she said.

'I want you branded,' he said, his voice flat with irony, 'so no other men get any ideas of messing with you.'

'*Messing*,' said Maude, rolling over in bed and kissing his shoulder-blade. 'What kind of company have you been keeping?'

For a moment at breakfast she felt trapped and self-conscious again, when she walked in with her tousled hair and her sleepy eyes and found Ruby and Sadie sitting round the table and talking about shoes.

'We're not really talking about shoes,' said Sadie. 'We're talking about the state of western morality with specific reference to heels.'

'Happy Christmas,' said Maude.

'Where's my stocking?' said Sadie. 'I still believe in fairies.'

'Where's the snow, is what I want to know,' said Ruby, looking out on the imperturbable day. It was a clear sere morning, the sun filtering through the windows, the mountains hazy and blue in the distance. 'It's Christmas, it's Scotland, where are the blizzards and icicles?' Ruby said, laughing to herself. 'I want my money back.'

'It never snows at Christmas,' said Sadie. 'You know that.'

'It snows in November and March,' said Maude, thinking of Violet at breakfast in another house, in another time. 'There are old men up here who will tell you that they remember the days when they got snowed in every year, October to April, regular as clockwork.'

'Global warming,' said Sadie, darkly. She looked at the table. 'Is this teak from a sustainable source?'

Dent and Dean came down soon after, and Dent made

some eggs, and they sat round the table and ate them and talked about nothing in particular. Maude let the feeling of strangeness and dislocation and being found out settle and fall away from her; she still got a frisson of it, if Sadie turned her head and looked at her too fast, too searching; she wanted to hide her eyes and look away. But Sadie was in love herself; Maude saw that now, for the first time. When Dean walked into the room, Sadie stopped talking and missed a beat and smiled a goofy smile all over her face and then had to say, 'What? What was I saying?'

Dean sat right next to her, and Maude could tell that their legs were touching under the table and she saw that Sadie knew all about this, that in some ways they were in the same boat.

Ruby ate her way through four pieces of toast with Marmite and smiled beatifically at them all, knowing perfectly well what everyone had been doing.

'I feel like the Mother sodding Superior,' she said conversationally. 'Which is not an effect I ever aimed for.'

After breakfast everyone got dressed and came back downstairs and they opened presents and Dent got out a bottle of champagne and then he and Dean went into the kitchen and made the lunch.

'I can't cook,' said Maude. 'I lived alone for so long I just ate out of tins and now I feel ashamed of it, as if I'm betraying my biological imperative.'

'It's a Jewish thing,' said Sadie. 'Or an Italian thing. It's a food thing. When you are in love, you want to feed them, you want to make them perfect little morsels of things they won't get anywhere else, so you are imprinted on their sense memory.'

'Is that it?' said Ruby. 'Is that really what it is?'

'Yes,' said Sadie, 'that's what it is. I don't know, who knows what it is? It's as good an explanation as any. It's the kind of theory I like.'

'Are you in love with Dean?' said Maude, thinking these were treacherous waters, but perhaps better to dive in instead of the slow torture of one inch at a time. They were going to have to talk about love sooner or later – why not on Christmas Day, with the lights glittering on the tree, and Sadie's father in the kitchen, cooking up the turkey?

'Yes, I am,' said Sadie. 'This one is different in so many ways I can't count on two hands. With the most commitment-phobic man in the world it was all tension and fear and bravado and stretching disbelief until it snapped. This is easy, like falling into a feather bed. This is like a homecoming.'

Maude dropped her eyes and remembered what Dent had said about coming home.

'It's quite common,' said Ruby.

'I thought it was quite particular,' said Sadie.

'It happens all the time,' said Ruby. 'You are friends and friends and friends and it's uncomplicated as the hand in front of your face and then one day everything shifts like plate tectonics and all your clothes fall off.'

'Oh, I see,' said Sadie. 'Is that how it happened?'

'Yes,' said Ruby. 'It was obvious to me. Of course it was. It was evident to me.'

'She likes to know best,' said Sadie to Maude.

They drank champagne and the day was clear outside but they still had all the lights on so that they were sitting in a blaze of radiance. The fire was snapping in the grate and there was a distant smell of peat in the room and from the kitchen they could hear Dean and Dent laughing.

'I do love him,' said Sadie. 'But who knows where it will all end?'

Maude thought for a moment she was going to ask about Dent. Please don't say it, Maude thought. Not yet, I don't have the words yet, now everything is changed. Give me a little more time, to know how to frame it.

The door opened and Mickey and Violet and William walked in and the house was full of people and it was Christmas and there wasn't time.

'Happy Yuletide,' Violet said, coming straight over to Maude and kissing her on both cheeks, as if they had been celebrating this festival for years together, up here in the far north. 'I brought you Christmas roses and dried lavender.'

She held out the flowers wrapped in a long cone of out-of-date newsprint, the headlines for October wilting around the treacherous green stems. The lavender she had sewn into flimsy muslin bags, as delicate as moths' wings, and for some reason Maude found herself absurdly moved. No one had ever sewn anything for her before.

'Thank you,' she said, looking down at her gifts. 'Thank you. They're perfect.'

'They're for your pillow,' said Violet, smiling so that her opaque eyes were drawn in black lines against her square face; she smiled right at Maude as if there was no one else in the room, as if nothing else mattered but this offering of presents. 'They are so you can sleep in the night. I can never sleep. I never learnt how to sleep.'

Maude looked at her in surprise and pleasure; she

remembered the sense of complicity that had hit her like an arrow when she first met Violet in that low red room over the mountains.

William and Mickey stamped their boots as if there was snow on them although the day was perfectly fine and said hello to Ruby and Sadie, and Ruby looked rather speculatively at Mickey and Mickey looked right back, and Maude thought that it was one of those days where anything might happen because it was Christmas and she was in a strange house and nothing was as it seemed.

'The men are in the kitchen, gossiping and stuffing that bird,' said Sadie to William and Mickey. 'You had better go and help them out. I'm going for more champagne,' she said, as if it were a mission of life and death.

Maude thought: Should I be doing that? She had no idea what it would be like to be in charge in a house, to be the hostess. Her mother had never done that. People came to the house all the time, there was never a time when it was empty; but it was never in a formal way – people came in like refugees, passing through from foreign countries, stranded in London with no money and nowhere to go. They made their way to the dark narrow house near Russell Square and sometimes they stayed for weeks and Maude would run into them on the stairs and they would pat her on the head and say something in no language she had ever heard.

Some women, Maude understood, knew how to keep a house, how to entertain guests, how to bring gracious living into the twenty-first century. But she was all at sea, having no models to ape, so she let Sadie mix up champagne and orange juice in a jug and hand it round and tell everyone where to go.

How did Sadie know that while she didn't? Maude wondered. Had Claudette been the last of the great hostesses, had she had a literary salon, where the shining stars of the cultural set sat around draped over long sofas talking about what was wrong with the world? Had Sadie learnt all this from her beautiful mother?

Maude realised with a jolting shock why she was jealous: it was not that Sadie and Dent had a relationship that she would never truly know; it was not that. They were daughter and father after all, how could you be jealous of that? Maude knew people were, because jealousy has nothing rational about it, and nothing controllable either; once it has got you in its inflexible green jaws, there's not much you can do except keep very still and hope it will get bored and drop you back in the murky water where it found you. You can't talk yourself down off the ceiling with jealousy because words don't mean much to it. But it was not that Maude minded, she saw now, as she watched Sadie pour the drinks and throw a log on the fire and sit back down in her seat, so clearly at home here, because this was her father's house: it was not that.

It was that Sadie was a relic of her mother. Sadie was Claudette, half of her was, and she looked so much like her, not with the blind beauty but with all of Claudette's dark Celtic colouring, the white skin and the black hair and the dark gleaming eyes, and although her mother was dead, it was she that Maude felt jealous of now, in some twisted way she didn't fully understand, and how much more irrational could you get than that, being jealous of a dead woman?

'Tell me about your life,' said Violet, coming to sit down next to Maude.

Maude brought her mind back into the room; she noticed that Violet had put her red hair up on her head with a vermilion ribbon threaded through it and that it looked fine like that. She was wearing a patterned green dress that was pinched in at the bodice and looked as if it came from a second-hand clothing store in Greenwich Village. Maude smiled, because she liked the way Violet chose her clothes, as if every day was fancy dress. Maude envied it a little, because you had to have a certain ease with yourself to be able to wear things like that, and she knew she didn't have that kind of ease, not yet, and perhaps she never would. She wondered what it would be like to have that; she wondered if it was so much part of you that you didn't even notice it was there, self-assurance as natural and involuntary as breathing. She wondered how you came by it and how you kept it; she wondered what it would take for it to disintegrate into nothing more than a memory. She wondered if you were born with it, or whether you learnt it, like most things, the hard way.

They ate lunch at two. The table was covered with a linen cloth and laid with silver knives and forks, heavy and venerable with age, and dressed with green branches of holly. The turkey was perfectly cooked, the flesh tender and fragrant from the herbs it was stuffed with. There were two kinds of stuffing, one with chestnuts and sage and one with sausagemeat and oregano; there were potatoes roasted in goose fat and flavoured with garlic and rosemary, and tiny Brussels sprouts hardly bigger than broad beans, and bread sauce perfumed with cloves and bay leaves, and a dish of green peas with mint and butter, and parsnips baked in olive oil, and a celeriac mash sprinkled with nutmeg. Maude thought she had never seen food like it in all her life. She had never even dreamt food like it.

She looked up the table at Dent. He was laughing at something that Ruby had said, and she wondered who this man was, who knew how to make all this food.

As she looked around, she noticed that there was a seat extra, an empty space at the table. She was wondering whose it was, who was missing, and then the door opened and Richard Hunter walked in. Dent looked up from the bottle he was opening and said, Oh, come in, Richard, come in and sit down, and Maude felt something fall in her stomach as if she had a sickness there.

But lunch was fine. Everyone laughed and talked and drank and ate, and even the silent Richard seemed to speak and smile and act as if he went out to lunch usually, and Maude forgot the knot in her stomach and thought, This is Christmas, this is not something to fear. She turned to William, who was sitting beside her. She smiled at him and he told her a story about the ospreys he was watching near Boat of Garten and how he thought they would mate this year. He said he hoped they would, because there were only 150 pairs in the whole of Britain and they were beautiful birds to see, and she thought, This is all right, this is real life, this is Christmas. She thought: One day, when the weather is fine, I shall drive up to Speyside and take a look at those rare birds.

The pudding was brought in drenched in brandy and set alight, and when everyone got theirs they found silver charms and fifty-pence pieces. 'Just like when we were children,' said Violet, laughing. 'I'm going to keep this charm for ever and it will keep me safe.' It was a St Christopher, the patron saint of travellers, and Violet said that was appropriate. As she said it William threw an urgent frightened look at her before he could stop himself, and although he recovered himself quickly and went back to his normal cheerful expression, Maude saw it and knew, just as if she needed reminding, that nothing was ever as it seemed on the surface.

Dent raised his glass to everyone and to Christmas and to all this food, and everyone raised their glasses with him, and then he said, 'And I want to make a toast to Maude, because she's changed everything.' Maude felt hit with shyness and ducked her head away. She thought how curious it was, because he was not the kind of man to make toasts. She wondered if he had drunk too much wine, but then she looked up and saw his face, and she realised that he had done it because he wanted to prove something to her, by saying that in front of all these people, by saying it in front of the daughter he hadn't told her about.

Sadie was smiling as if she was pleased and Maude thought that it would be all right between them. But then she looked across the table and she saw Richard Hunter's face and it was as if it was hewn in stone and she thought: It's Christmas and it's the season of goodwill and everyone round this table wishes me well, but this man wishes I were dead.

It was a fast thought and it ran through her mind like smoke and afterwards she thought she was being fanciful, that there was something in Richard Hunter that struck the wrong chord in her, that was all. He was just a man without many social graces. She was perhaps jealous of him in the same way she was of Claudette, in that pinching irrational way, because he was here first, and she loved Dent so much she wanted to know all of him, to have all of him, for there to have been no one else first, no one who might know him better than she did. It was childish, and she knew she would have to get through it and be balanced and rational and stop thinking such wild thoughts because they didn't do a person any good.

But she thought of that look Richard wore on Christmas Day, much later, and she wondered.

Everybody left on Boxing Day, packing up and getting into cars and driving off in different directions, and Maude stood in the wide front room and said, Goodbye, goodbye, come back, come again soon. They kissed her, and thanked her, and told her how lovely it all was, and she laughed at herself, because only three months ago she had been living in her twilight world and could barely conduct herself with Mr Seth. But now she wondered if it would always be like this. Would there be people coming to the house now, Christmas parties and weekend visits? Perhaps in the summer they would go on expeditions and take picnics up into the mountains and find some crystal burn to sit by and eat chicken sandwiches and hard-boiled eggs. It seemed strange but it seemed possible.

When the house was empty again, it didn't feel deflated to Maude, as houses can after a party. It felt calm and clean and ordered, as if it belonged to her, and she thought that was the first time she had ever felt that way about it. It was as if, by leaving it, all those people had given the house to her.

She built up the fire and cut slices of poppy-seed cake that Dent had made the week before and sat on the red sofa and looked out of the high windows at the blue afternoon. There was no sound at all, not even the calling of the birds in the woods, and she felt tired and peaceful and glad to be alone.

Dent came in later and found her sitting in the twilight. He sat beside her and drew her head on to his shoulder and said, 'Was that all right?'

'Yes,' she said. 'In parts it was strange, but I think it was all right.'

'I think so too,' he said.

'I didn't know you could cook like that,' Maude said. She took his hand in hers and smoothed the back of it, as if it were a tablecloth that needed the wrinkles running out of it. She smoothed it and smoothed it until it was done.

'Nora taught me to cook,' said Dent. 'She had a flat in Paris when I was there and she cooked all day long. She sat at her table and read Elizabeth David, she would fill the kitchen with food, she would do one thing this way, and then another way to see if that was better, and sometimes at midnight she had so much food there she would have to go down to the Closerie des Lilas and bring some of the drunks home to eat it for her, so she could start again in the morning.'

'There,' said Maude, lifting her head. 'That's a story. I need more like that.'

'What do you mean?' said Dent, although Maude thought he knew exactly what she meant.

'I mean,' she said patiently, seeing that for some reason he needed it to be named, etched in black and white, 'that you *are* all your stories. You are the sum of your stories, and I need to know them. I want you to tell me one story every day, every day I want to know one secret.'

Dent was silent for a while and Maude laid her head against his arm and watched the light die around them and then he said, 'All right, I can do that,' and she nodded as if that was all settled.

17

When Sadie was back in London, she sent Maude e-mails just like before, as if everything was the same, as if everything that needed to be said was said. She was back at work and thinking about a new project and she was in love with Dean and even that seemed as if it had been going on for ever.

Maude was a slower study: it took her longer to adjust to sudden swerves in direction. Sometimes now she looked at Dent and saw something of Sadie in him, the way he used his hands, or a private smile he wore when he was thinking about something else. It twisted something in Maude and she wasn't sure what it was. She hated the idea of having been deceived, even if the intention was entirely benign.

She wasn't sure where she got this tic from, this hatred of secrets and lies. Her mother had not spent much time with her before she died, but the one thing Maude remembered was her devotion to the truth. One time there was a scandal about a colleague of her mother's faking a source and being stripped of prizes and letters after her name and her chair at one of the venerable old universities; for weeks afterwards the people who gathered in Maude's parents' house could talk about nothing else.

'How could she?' they said, in a harmony of disapproval. 'What was she thinking of?'

The disgraced professor came to the house late one night and Maude's mother refused to see her. Maude opened her bedroom door a crack to listen and heard raised voices in the stairwell. Her father was saying, 'She's come all this way, you should at least hear what she has to say,' and Maude's mother said, in a low, furious voice, 'I know everything I need to know, she told a lie and she has to live with that and I don't want to have a single thing to do with it, that's all.'

Maude's father went down the stairs and Maude could hear his voice, indistinct and muted, and then a woman's voice, higher, strained. After a few minutes the front door slammed, and all the time Maude's mother stood on the stairs and listened.

'Go to bed, Maude,' she said, although she had not looked up to Maude's open door and Maude had made no noise. 'Go to bed and go to sleep and dream the dreams of the just, which is more than some people can do,' and Maude knew from her voice that she was really angry, more angry than Maude had ever heard her.

Maude shut her door and sat in the dark and thought that she should never tell a lie if that was what happened to you afterwards.

'Do one thing for me,' said Maude, that night, just before she fell asleep, in the still suspended time between wake and sleep, when you are not sure what you are saying or who you are or whether you make any sense at all. 'Just one thing, whatever happens, because it's the one thing I can't take. Don't ever tell me a lie. Tell me all your secrets. Tell me every single one of your secrets so that we never have to be surprised about anything ever again.'

Dent didn't say anything. He kissed the back of her neck and pulled his arms closer around her and she went to sleep thinking that there would be no slamming doors in the middle of the night and no one standing on the stairs, listening to the fragmented sound of someone else's shame.

The spring came late that year, even for Scotland. The cold went on and on and there were low flat skies and the trees stayed bare longer than Maude would have thought possible. The Christmas they had spent faded like an old photograph and time seemed suspended, as if minutes and hours had taken on some new aspect, some other dimension that no one had discovered yet. Maude felt that summer would never come, that she would never grow any older, that she was trapped in the amber of some mysterious limbo and she would never come out the other side. She thought sometimes that it had something to do with her being so far away from anything she knew. She thought sometimes it was that she was back in the Antarctic world with her old explorer and she was blinded by the light.

She had two worlds: the white imaginary world that she went into in her work, and the world she lived in, that had only her and Dent in it, and this curious stalled weather, as if someone had stopped the clocks and turned off the outside world and sealed it, with them inside.

She thought that in some ways she liked it, but she knew it wouldn't last and she was afraid of what would come afterwards. She wanted to be able to see into the future and she couldn't and it frustrated her.

'That's what women want,' said Dent. 'Everyone

wants to know what women want. Freud couldn't work out what women want. I think they want to be able to see the future, to have their own internal crystal balls. Women think about the future much more than men do.'

'Is that true?' said Maude. 'Is that why only women are fortune-tellers?'

'Yes,' said Dent, starting to laugh. 'Yes, yes. That must be exactly why.'

'Why don't you want to know what will happen?' said Maude.

'Because you can't do anything about it, most of the time, so why have to worry about it until you get there?' said Dent.

'But you could have more certainty,' said Maude, 'if you knew. Some things anyway, not all things, but some.'

'I don't think so,' said Dent. 'I think you can only have certainty by inventing your own possible futures and aiming at them like a bull's-eye on a dartboard, so you have tunnel vision.'

'Is that really what you think?' said Maude.

'That's really what I think.'

'I'm not sure,' said Maude. 'I'm not sure what I think. I'm not sure that you are right.'

Dent laughed again. 'Maybe I'm not sure either,' he said.

Later, Maude thought of that, and she wondered whether if she had been able to see into the future it would have made any difference at all to anything.

Then, one day in early May, without any warning, spring started. It was as if overnight the world changed, everything shifting on its axis. One day, there was the low white sky and the bare black trees and the stark dun of the mountains and the dead stalks of the daffodils giving up the ghost and the fragile uncertain shimmer of white blossom; the next, Maude woke up to find the sky blue and the sun shining hot and yellow, and the world was green. The trees had come into leaf almost miraculously, putting out shoots of such vivid stinging greenness that Maude couldn't believe such a colour existed.

'Look,' she said, getting out of bed and walking across the room in her bare feet and throwing open the window so that the air came in new and gentle against her face. 'Look what happened while we were sleeping.'

Dent went into his study as usual, but Maude was too excited. She took the morning off and went walking in the woods, breathing in the smell of life and green and earth and growing things; remembering what it was like. It seemed so long ago that the country had felt like this, she realised that she had come to believe that it would sleep for ever. Now it was awake. Birds were singing and animals were moving about in the woods; the oyster-catchers had come slanting in from the coast and were building their nests down by the river, and the gulls were banking and gliding low over the fields beyond the water, making raucous cries like drunken sailors on shore leave.

The wood was a dark and mysterious place and when Maude had first come she was too frightened to walk there by herself. The floor was thick with brown pine needles and packed dirt and the trees were ranged so closely together that the light could barely penetrate, except in odd lone shafts. It was full of strange noises, sounds that she couldn't identify as anything she had ever heard before, either animal or human.

Now, it didn't frighten her any more. She felt somehow that was symbolic of something, but she was not sure quite what.

If she walked up the hill, all the way to the top, she would come out into a small clearing and get a view out over three ranges of mountains, falling away behind each other in dipping blue ridges, like the sea. On some days, if the light was right and the sky was a certain colour and the clouds were moving into high formations, she could not tell where the mountains ended and the sky began. But today she would be able to tell because the sky was unmarked altogether; a sheer, soaring arc of unbroken blue.

She got to the top just after ten o'clock and the sun was high in the sky. As she looked out over the endless vista of mountain and sky she could see the early morning mist still hovering in the valley. She smiled with childish delight because it was more beautiful than anything she had ever seen before. She knew that it meant the end of this still time, this frozen winter, and that things would change, as they always did in the heat, and she felt excited by that, not apprehensive. She realised that she wasn't frightened of change as she used to be, that in some way being with Dent was making her brave.

Just then, looking out over that mysterious and impossible view, she felt invincible, as if she could do anything, as if all the dark things in the world could have no more terrors for her. She felt that the country in some way was on her side, that the mountains wouldn't let her down. She felt as if she could fly.

I must tell Dent this feeling, she thought; she knew that he would understand.

Later she walked down to the river, and it was gentler down there, not the wild grandeur of the higher view, but still and calm and green and burnished in the sun. The water was clear like polished glass and if Maude stood very still and watched hard she could see the shadows of small brown fish moving over the dappled stones. She remembered Nora looking at the black river at Mickey's house and talking about the water clearing in the spring. She felt happy as she remembered it, it gave her a nebulous feeling of belonging, of building some history, of having times that she could look back on.

She turned and looked up at the house, and it was glowing in the sun, the stones catching the light and dancing with it; she felt that if a building could smile, this one would.

I'm growing soft and sentimental, she thought, the sun is making my brain hazy. But she didn't care, because she felt childish with hope and possibility, and that was something she hadn't done since her parents died. It was like being given a present on a day when it's not Christmas or your birthday or any occasion, but just because. She felt like running and turning cartwheels and whooping with exuberance but she didn't; she stood looking at the house where she lived with Dent and she kept all that feeling inside her, so that it built in her stomach until she thought she might take off with it.

I am happy, she thought, that's what this is. I am happy because the sun is shining and in that house, behind the third window from the left, the man I love is writing and he doesn't know that I am watching his window and thinking about him and that my heart is filled with him so that I am smiling like a fool.

She laughed to herself and she turned away from the house and looked out to the hills again and she felt hungry. She wondered if it was too early for lunch. She was thinking about bread and cheese and unsalted butter and thin ham and sharp green gherkins when Richard Hunter came up beside her, so silently that he might have been walking on stockinged feet.

Maude was taken by surprise and it took her a moment to rearrange her face from dismay to welcome. She never wanted Richard Hunter to see how much she didn't like him so she put on her good face when she knew he was around, but this time he was too quick and he must have seen something, because he gave her a nasty smile and said, 'Where's Al?' and Maude smiled falsely back and said, 'He's writing.'

Afterwards, she was to remember the smallest details: the faint sound of the burn, a sudden wind that moved across her face, the call of lambs from a distant pasture, a pair of swallows flinging over the meadow.

'He's not writing,' said Richard.

'Yes,' said Maude. 'Yes, he's in his study. I took the morning off.'

'He doesn't write,' said Richard. 'He doesn't write those books. He hasn't written a single word since his wife died.'

'I don't understand what you mean,' said Maude. 'Of course he does. There are four novels since then, I've read them.'

'The novels exist,' said Richard Hunter, 'but he didn't write them.'

Maude wanted to say like a child: Oh *yeah*, so who *did* then?

'Who did?' she said, in a normal voice.

'I did,' said Richard Hunter.

The world stopped and everything spilled off it and Maude felt as if she were hanging in mid-air, with nothing under her feet.

She had no doubt that he was telling the truth.

'Well,' she said, in a voice that was not her own. 'Well done.'

She turned and walked up to the house and even though the sun was still shining as bright as it had a few moments ago, before she knew this new thing, this horrible knowledge that she didn't want, it was as if the house was in black shadow, as if there was an ugly cloud that had come out of nowhere and blotted out the light.

Maude walked straight into Dent's study. She hadn't been there before; he had never invited her and she had never asked. She had enough respect for this place, his private place, because she thought it was where he did his work, and she certainly had respect for that. Everyone needs their secret place, she thought, where they cannot be invaded.

Dent was sitting at a big black lacquered desk looking out of the window. There was a book closed in front of him, face down, so that Maude could not see the title. There were sheaves of paper on top of a silver filing cabinet and a pot with pens in it but no other signs of any object that could be used for actually writing anything.

'Richard told me what your secret really is,' she said, and it came out ugly and accusatory and dramatic, like something out of a cheap daytime soap. She was ashamed of it the moment it came out of her mouth, but she was so angry and singed and betrayed that only a very small part of her cared.

'Yes,' said Dent. He didn't seem surprised. It was as if he was waiting for her, as if he had been sitting there all this time, with his closed book on his shining black desk, staring out of the window, waiting for her to arrive with the truth.

'Is that all?' said Maude.

'What do you want me to say?' he said. He didn't quite look at her, he couldn't meet her eye. Maude felt as if she was watching everything she knew and loved and believed in disintegrate in front of her eyes. He looked smaller to her suddenly, diminished.

'You lied to me,' said Maude. 'You lied and evaded and you let me believe that was all your own work and you never said anything.'

'I didn't know how to say it,' said Dent. He shifted in his seat and he still couldn't look at her. She could see his profile etched against the light that came in from the square window in front of him, that straight profile that she loved so well, that she had thought she knew so well.

'I was waiting,' he said, in a flat voice. 'I was waiting until there was a right time. I wanted to give myself a moment when you didn't know; I wanted to make sure we were on strong enough ground before you knew. I'm sorry, it was cowardly of me.'

He was so calm, thought Maude, it was as if he was reading the words off an autocue. She almost looked around to see where the idiot boards were hidden.

'No,' she said. 'That doesn't cut it. Don't you understand? You've ruined everything. It's smashed and spoilt and there's no point to any of it.'

'It's just a thing,' he said, in the same preternaturally calm voice. 'It's just words on a page.'

'That's another fat lie,' said Maude. She wanted to grab his face suddenly, to take it between her hands and turn it so that he had to look at her. She felt everything that she had believed in, all that fragile new belief, shatter inside her. 'That's the fattest lie of all. It's everything. It's what you are. It's what I thought you were, and now there's nothing.'

'I'm still the same person,' said Dent, as if he had rehearsed this somewhere. 'Don't conflate the work and the man.'

'Did you write that in one of your scholarly monographs?' said Maude. She could hear a repulsive sneer in her voice and she couldn't stop herself because she was so hurt and she wanted to hurt him; she wanted to hurl every ugly sharp thing she had in her arsenal at him and watch him bleed all over the floor. But he was calm and still and it was as if she was looking at him through a plate of glass. She wanted to shatter it and throw the shards at him but she couldn't find the weak spot, and the glass held.

'There's no point to this,' said Maude. She thought the tragedy was that when she really needed him to understand her he left her marooned on swampy ground, past the point of rescue. She felt as abandoned as a child waiting for an absent parent who will never return.

'I'm going now,' she said, because she didn't know what else to say or what else to do. This is the end, she thought – she could see it clear and sharp, the credits rolling in a darkened cinema – The End.

'Don't go,' he said.

He did look at her now for the first time and she could see that his eyes were filled with something; shame or hurt or fear, she didn't know which. She wondered afterwards if he had reached out then, if he had walked across the small space between them and physically held her, stopped her going, whether she would have stayed. She gave him a moment, to see if there was any more, but there wasn't; he turned away and looked out of the window again.

'I would like it if you would stay,' he said, and Maude remembered him saying those words before. She remembered how they had made her heart loose its moorings and fly up into the ether, but now her heart was like a stone in her chest and she couldn't imagine that it would ever be light again. Now words were not enough: they were small and pitiful and didn't seem to mean anything.

'I'm going,' she said.

She waited for a moment, everything falling within her, all the lightness she had grown used to hitting the ground with the small sound of broken promise.

'Goodbye,' she said. She walked out of the room and up the stairs and she put her things into her overnight bag, just the ones she had come with, leaving everything else, all the things they had bought together, and there was so little it only took five minutes, and she came down the stairs and the house was empty.

She walked out of the front door, leaving it wide open behind her, and she got into her car and drove steadily down the drive. She turned left for the main road, and ten miles later she took the right turn which brought her over the mountains and down on to the Edinburgh road, and then she set for the south, through Carlisle and Kendal and Liverpool and Manchester and Birmingham and Oxford and Thame until she was back in the Talgarth Road, where she had started.

18

It's strange how easily you can go back to an old life; everything remembered and known and familiar, the shock of it dulling as fast as water drying on glass.

The flat was dark and empty when Maude let herself in. She realised as she stood in the dim silence that it was Sunday, the same day of the week that she had left it. There were no lights on and no sound at all, not even the rumble of the trains.

Sadie wasn't there. She had mailed Maude two days before (two days: it might as well have been a lifetime) saying that she was going abroad for a job, that she would be away for a few weeks. 'I am going to double-lock everything and leave the lights on a timer and Ruby will check on the place,' she wrote, and Maude, who was learning optimism, wrote back blithely that she should leave all the doors open and let Gerald and his pack of compadres come in and make themselves at home.

She was glad Sadie was away: she didn't want to have to explain. She didn't want to speak to anyone. She wanted to hug her secret to her, her smashed heart; she wanted to carry the broken pieces close to her chest and not answer any awkward questions.

Hearts might get mended once, she thought, but no one gets any second chances. Why did she know that? She knew it though, it was the only certainty she felt she had. She planted her feet on it carefully, as if to stray off that one known path would lead to quicksand and perdition.

There was no food in the place; Sadie had cleaned everything out before she went. The flat looked like a show home, gleaming and silent and empty.

Maude went round to Mr Seth, who looked at her with his solemn eyes and blinked and gave no sign that he had noticed she had been away for so long.

'Hello, Missy,' he said slowly. 'Come to buy sun cream? Because that ozone layer is *fucked*. You have malignant melanomas all over your pretty head before you can say global warming. I gave Gerald a hat, but he sold it for dope.'

Nothing has changed, thought Maude. It's all the same. The last few months have been a mirage; it happened to some other woman, it didn't happen to me. But the dates on the papers had changed. It wasn't the Indian summer of September any more; it was real summer this time, June, slanting rain and low skies, the kind of flat summer you got in the south. Looking at those dates, lined up in neat, irrevocable rows, Maude knew that everything had happened to her, there was no ducking that.

She bought food without thinking about it, anything she saw on the shelves: chickpeas and cumin and fat green gherkins in brine and thin Spanish ham and eggs from a farm near Penzance and black-eyed peas and bunches of coriander tied with string; she bought small tomatoes and shallots and the kind of long pale mauve aubergines that you saw in the East. She never cooked, but now she was buying food, she didn't know why. She bought bottles of ginger ale and Angostura bitters and thin bars of black chocolate from Guatemala.

'Stocking up, Missy,' said Mr Seth, nodding in gloomy approval, 'in case that asteroid hits. The suits in White-hall don't dare say a word, but they know it's coming.'

The shop smelt, as it always had, of saffron and garam masala and limes and some unidentifiable dusty urban smell; not a London smell, a hotter city, Madras or further east. Maude had never been to the East, but she knew it would smell like this. She hoped it would smell like this. A small buried part of her was almost glad to be home.

She got back and arranged the food on her shelves and sat down and made a cup of coffee. She gave it her entire concentration: measuring out the grounds, damp and black like loam, screwing the dull silver pot together, setting it on the stove to cook, laying out a single china cup – not hers – a delicate china cup from some foreign place, something that Sadie must have bought, a pale blue cup, thin as paper, with a delicate gilt line running around the rim. Maude had never owned a cup and saucer in her life.

When the coffee was done she poured it out into this beautiful alien cup, watching the steam rise off the surface, letting the familiar hot bitter smell get into her. She sat at her clean kitchen table, in her silent flat, with her tins and boxes of food on their neat shelves, and she looked at the perfect china cup that was not hers, and she opened her mouth as if to speak and a terrible tearing noise came out and everything shattered.

No no no, she thought; then she heard herself saying it, out into the room: No, please no.

There was a panic in her, the old voices shouting instructions: Don't cry don't cry don't let go; you got through once before, you can do this again. Don't let yourself disintegrate here in the kitchen because who will clear up the mess, who will come and put the pieces back together again?

She looked down and realised that she was holding on to her gut, as if to stop something opening up, something spilling out. But she couldn't hold it, it hurt too much, like that kind of stomach ache which makes you cry and yell because the pain is so shockingly bad that the only way to ride it is to call out. The panic grew in her and she didn't know where to go or where to put it. She got down from the table and stumbled into the corner of the room and sat down on her haunches, but that wasn't it, that wasn't right. She moved out in a crab-like walk, bent over, to the bathroom: she needed something hard and safe, to shelter her. The bath was white and solid and she leant against the side of it, feeling it cold and reassuring; she put her flank against it and knelt on the floor, crouched low over her knees, and she rocked herself back and forth, and the tears spilled out of her eyes on to the black linoleum floor so she could see them splash into little glittering pools, and she was shouting so loudly that she was glad when the trains started up to cover the noise.

What happens when you go back to a life that you thought was dead? You breathe animation back into it, day by day, inflating again the known routines, walking the same worn paths.

As if the last few months hadn't happened at all, Maude slid back into the shallow trough of her old habits. After that shocking moment in the bathroom, she turned back to her past life as if she had never been away.

Ruby came down one evening and said, 'I saw the light and thought it was burglars,' and Maude said, 'No, it's just me.'

Ruby stood on the step, undecided. She was wearing her hair pulled back from her face and she had dark red lipstick on her mouth and her eyes were tired.

'Do I come in?' she said, and Maude wondered for a moment whether there was something wrong because Ruby wasn't usually so tentative; the familiarity that had grown in them on that distant Christmas walk seemed to count for nothing now. Then she thought, There's nothing wrong with her, it's just that she can see there's something wrong with me.

For a moment she wanted to break the walls down: she wanted to hold on to Ruby's arm, hard and fast; she wanted to pull her into the kitchen and tell her the whole sordid story.

'No,' said Maude, and her voice was brittle and forbidding. 'Don't come in. I'm on my own now, I'm taking some time on my own.

'It's not anything to mind about,' she said, lying easily and carelessly, she who had always held such a regard for the truth. 'It's nothing at all.'

Ruby might as well have held up a flashing sign saying I KNOW THAT'S NOT RIGHT, but she seemed to understand that sometimes we need to tell lies and sometimes we need to get them accepted, even though everyone knows they are so paper thin that they could put their fist right through them and not even hear the sound of the tear.

'All right,' she said. 'I'm upstairs. I'm working at home now. I got a show and I gave up the day job and Pearl and Dean moved out so it's just me.'

Maude knew without being told that Ruby meant: there is comfort up there, there is a place where you can be private and quiet and bring your secrets and you won't be scorned or laughed at or ridiculed. There is a room where you can be heard.

It was a fine offer, and Maude knew she couldn't take it. She was living in a house of cards again, and she knew that if she moved one ace of spades the whole thing would come tumbling down and there would be only ruins.

She went through the motions, efficiently; slick and practised, she went back to her silent life.

She wrote her book. She had lunch with her editor. She paid her bills and saw to the business end. She bought the paper and a bottle of water every day from Mr Seth, and she started to cook in the evenings. She learnt about spices and sauces, she taught herself what to do with garlic and ginger and groundnut oil and tamarind seeds. For some reason, she taught herself the cooking of the East; she made thin sour soups with enough bird's eye chilli in them to blow your head off. She ate them slowly, tears of pain rolling down her cheeks.

In the night, when she couldn't sleep, she remembered being with Dent so vividly it was as if he was there with her in the room and she had to rock herself violently back and forth to rub the memory out of her body. She could remember the taste of him and the density of his skin and how it smelt of the sea; she remembered how she used to lay her nose against the smooth part of his upper arm and breathe in the smell of him, and how intoxicated she had been by it. She remembered how his face looked in sleep and how she sometimes woke to find him lying beside her, touching her side with his strong hand. She remembered how he moved when he was performing small everyday tasks; cutting up ham for a sandwich, making a pot of coffee on the stove. She remembered the black smell of it and how it tasted burnt and exotic on her tongue and how it was the taste she associated with him. She remembered sometimes having to look away from him because she was so filled up with love that she didn't know what to do with it.

At night, when she couldn't sleep, she was assailed by these memories; they came at her hard and unrelenting as a swarm of bees, and sometimes she literally lifted up her hand to swat them away, as if they were actual, out there in the dark above her head.

Like an athlete who trains herself to hit the pain barrier harder every day, until she becomes immune to it, until pain walks beside her like an old dog, Maude learnt again to live with it. Between gritted teeth, she told herself she could do this, she could do this. She had done this before.

In the twisted and deformed logic that had never entirely gone away, she told herself that this was fitting and proper and what she deserved. The first voice, back in fine fettle, as if it had been limbering up while she had been away, told her that of course this was what she deserved, that the very idea that she could get herself loved and get herself healed was far-fetched and preposterous.

So she lay in her bed each night, swatting away the memories, trying to smash them as one might annihilate a whining mosquito, and telling herself that there was no going back.

*　　*　　*

Sadie came back late one night in October.

She had been away for three months, driving round the small trash towns of the southern states of America, with her camera crew and her native wit, and in the end it was this piece of work that was to make her name and put her into the big league, but she didn't know this then.

Maude heard the door and looked up with a small sharp movement of her head. She had been waiting for the door to go for the last three weeks; she had been waiting for it, subliminally, ever since she had got back. She would have thought that such a long time would have given her an idea of what to say, but now the key was scraping in the lock the words flew out of her head and left only a blank fog of space and she had no idea how she would explain what she was doing there. This was Sadie, she thought; this was her friend. But she knew it wouldn't feel like that.

Sadie turned on the light and said, 'What are you doing, sitting here in the dark?'

Then she took a beat and the world seemed to catch up with her, and she said, 'What are you doing here at all?'

'Sit down,' said Maude, standing up. 'Sit down and I'll get you a beer because you look beat and you've been away for a long time, and then I'll tell you.'

She got two beers out of the fridge. They were some American brand that Sadie had left behind, with a brown glass bottle and a hectic label and Maude, who never drank beer, felt glad at the sight of them. This is what people did when they had a big talk, they drank a beer and smoked a cigarette and looked straight into each other's eyes and told the truth.

Sadie sat down abruptly at the Formica table. Her face was white and thin with tiredness and there was something in her eyes that happens to people when they have seen things that perhaps they don't want to see.

She took the beer and shook a cigarette out of a flimsy paper packet and lit one up and sucked in the smoke and narrowed her eyes through it. 'I can't give up,' she said. 'I want to give up but I can't.'

'What happened?' she said, after a moment. 'I'm still on Texas time, so I don't understand anything too sharply just now.'

Maude wanted to run away. She didn't want to tell this part; she didn't want to talk about it. She had that feeling that children have, or rather that adults have and think of as childish: a furious desire that none of this had happened, not Dent, not the afternoon in north London, not her parents dying, not any of it. I wish I had never been born, that was what adolescents said: I didn't ask to be born. Maude wanted to wipe it all out with a sponge and then there would just be a blank space and instead of the weight in her stomach there would be air and freedom.

She remembered, watching the thought fly through her head like a bird at sundown, a line from a film she saw once: For some people, said one of the characters, a beaten-up jaded cynic of a character, who turns out in the end to have a heart of gold (*of course, of course*), it's not a question of why to kill yourself, but why not.

'I found out about the books,' said Maude.

Sadie started to say something, as if she didn't know what books, but then her eyes sharpened and her brain clicked in, like a rivet into a groove, and whatever she was going to say stopped before it got anywhere.

'Oh,' she said. 'Oh. I see.'

'Richard Hunter told me,' said Maude. She was using a low, even voice, a rational voice, as if by doing that she could keep everything calm and ordered. 'Richard Hunter told me that he wrote Dent's last four books, so I left.'

'Alexander never told you,' said Sadie.

Maude suddenly thought of something. 'You knew all the time?' she said.

Sadie looked back at her. 'Yes,' she said. She shrugged up her shoulders and put her head on one side. 'Yes. I knew.'

'Why didn't you say anything to me?' said Maude, and now the rational voice was breaking up, rocks were showing through, and it was getting ugly.

'Not my tale to tell,' said Sadie. She shook her head. 'No. That wasn't my story. I couldn't tell you that.'

Maude suddenly felt vicious and irrational. 'All those things you never told me,' she said. 'Ever since the first time you came into this flat and saw the books by your father. All those lies by omission. I thought you were my friend. You were the first friend I ever had.'

She knew she was sounding maudlin and self-pitying now; she despised herself for it. She realised, sitting across the table from this bright tired woman (she was so real, Sadie, she was so defined, so *existent*), that it was a double betrayal. Sadie was the forerunner, she was the first intimate, she paved the way for Dent, but all the time she had been conniving and hiding the truth.

'I don't see it like that,' said Sadie. 'This is not some objective fact, this is what you are making of it. I'm sorry if you feel that way. I didn't mean for you to feel that way.'

'But I do feel it,' said Maude. 'And now it's worse than before. It's worse than if none of this ever happened. I got a glimpse of something, of life, of moving out of exile, and then it was all snatched away.'

'No,' said Sadie. 'That's not true. It's not exactly as you dreamt it, that's all. That's what life is, that happens all the time. You can't blame anyone else for that.'

Maude wanted to shout: *Yes I can, Yes I can.*

'I still don't understand why you are here,' Sadie said.

'You don't understand anything,' said Maude.

'Well,' said Sadie, and now she was the one keeping her voice low and even, and there was a strain in it, as if it was an effort not to shout, 'why don't you explain it to me?'

'I couldn't stay,' said Maude. 'I couldn't. Lying is the thing I can't deal with. I said to him, Tell me all your secrets and he said, Yes, I can do that. I said, Do one thing for me, don't ever tell me anything but the truth. All that time he had lied to me, let me believe that he was what I thought he was, and it was a sham.'

'Not exactly,' said Sadie. 'Perhaps he was afraid of telling you, perhaps he wanted to but he couldn't.'

'I am tired,' said Maude. 'I'm tired of being in the dark. Everything is ruined and broken because no one told me the truth. So I left, and I'm not going back, and that's all.'

'You're breaking your own heart,' said Sadie. There was a new hard note in her voice that Maude had not heard before. 'You don't have to do that. Life will break your heart, all on its own, you don't have to help it along.'

'It's not me doing this,' said Maude. 'If you love someone and trust them and show yourself to them, naked and vulnerable, and you discover they have lied to you about something so fundamental, then the contract is smashed. You know about that.'

'Where did you learn all these rules?' said Sadie. 'Who taught you this?'

'I worked it out,' said Maude.

'You're a fool,' said Sadie. Her voice was harsh and unguarded, and Maude could see she was really angry. 'You're a fool and you're being stupid and self-indulgent, because it's not just your heart you're responsible for. Alexander loved you in a way he's never loved anyone in his life, not even my mother. He made one small human mistake and you're punishing him for that because you're the one who's so scared of life that you were looking for the merest excuse to run away. Well, now you have found it, and you've run, and I hope you're satisfied.'

Maude stared in surprise. 'I'm not satisfied,' she said. 'I'm in agony.'

'Only you can do anything about that,' said Sadie. 'Go back and take the chance you've been given at life and let him explain; it's not finished, you just decided that, in some fit of terror or self-righteousness or whatever this is. He didn't do a bad thing; you are making him pay as if he went out and hired strange women for sex or sold drugs on a street corner or did something truly terrible and cruel. I don't understand,' she said, 'how someone who has known suffering like you clearly have could be so righteously judgemental. I thought it was suffering that was supposed to make people tolerant and empathetic. Well, it hasn't worked in your case.'

Maude took these words like blows to the body, like fists falling into her soft flesh.

'You should go now,' she said. What she wanted to say was, Get out, get the fuck out and leave me alone and never come back. She wanted to say, I hate you, I hate you, because you were my friend and you lied and now it's all smashed and broken and there's nothing left.

'I'll go,' said Sadie. 'Dean moved out. He lives in

Kensal Rise now. I'll go and stay with him.' She looked in her bag and got out a cheque book and wrote in it. 'Here's the money for the rent,' she said.

She stood up and stared down at Maude. 'You were given a chance for happiness,' she said. 'I don't know what it was that made you withdraw from the world and you never saw fit to tell me, but I can see enough to know that you never thought happiness would happen to you, and then it did. You saw that there was a possibility that you could get those fragments of your heart that you carried around with you like a burnt offering mended, and not everyone gets that chance. But I think maybe after all those years you had grown to like being one of the twilight people, and when you saw an excuse to go back to that closed world you inhabited you took it as fast as you could, without giving anyone a chance to explain. You can blame me all you want because I don't care, but don't you dare blame Alexander, because he is a good and honourable man and you know that is the truth.'

She walked out of the kitchen and down the dim green hall and out of the front door. It closed behind her with a snap, and a dispassionate part of Maude's mind thought, What a grand final speech, what a fine exit – as if none of this was really happening, as if they were at the theatre and at any moment the curtain would come down and the applause would start with the sound of rain falling on asphalt.

In the long drab weeks that came after that, she thought about what Sadie had said. She knew in some ways that Sadie was right: that she was not being fair, that she was making more of this than she should. She knew that Dent was a good man who had loved her well. He hadn't fucked other women and called it nothing; he hadn't cheated on her and laughed at her gullibility.

But each time she started to feel rational about it, think that she could go back and start again, something in her veered away, like a shying horse. He lied, he lied: she heard it in her head like a taunting chorus. She loved him and believed in him and offered herself to him; he lied about the most central thing in his life; how could she ever trust him again, after that? It was as if the contract she had made with him, with herself, was so new and fragile that all it took was one blow to shatter it irrevocably, and she couldn't see a way to mend it.

She wondered, in the dark lonely hours, when her work was done, when she sat in her room with the lights out, as the twilight slanted through her Venetian blinds and cast the room in thin monochrome – she wondered whether, if she were another kind of person, she might be able to see a way through. She wondered if there was something in her that had always been broken, that the accident had just come along and made a visible, a *plausible*, reason for something that would always have been the case. Perhaps she was born to be a recluse, one of those people who can't quite manage usual human relationships, who spend their lives apart, standing to one side, able only to watch while other people go about the business of living in the real world.

She looked back into the past, which stretched behind her like a narrow corridor; she saw her inability to make friends, to have a boyfriend, to be part of the gang. She wondered if she was like those people who have Tourette's syndrome, their brain missing some crucial link, so they walk down supermarket aisles shouting fuck fuck

fuck bugger shit fuck, startling all the good shoppers. She wondered if it was like that for her, some synapse not connected, the wiring not quite right, so that she could never fully engage in the world. She wondered whether that was just an excuse, because she was scared to death, and at least, in this dark silent basement, she knew how everything worked and there were no surprises.

October went past, and November, and she tried not to think about this time last year. But she remembered it all, until she wished that she had a switch in her head so she could turn it off like a television and just have a blank screen, instead of all this taunting remembering.

She wondered if Dent would come and fight for her. She felt sunk in hopelessness, out of ideas, but there was a haunting thought that he might do it; he might fight. She thought if he came to her door, if he begged and pleaded, then perhaps she could get it back, be brave enough to start again. But there was nothing from him. She found herself watching the telephone and listening for the postman in the morning; but the phone never rang, and the post brought only brown envelopes and junk mail.

He doesn't care, she thought. If he really cared, if he really wanted me back, he would wade in and fight. If he doesn't fight, she thought, he wasn't worth it; it would never have worked.

Then she hated him, for not coming for her.

The weather changed and the leaves turned brown and finally black, and fell from the trees. Maude tried not to think about the wild autumn she had spent in Scotland, when she was happy. As it grew colder, and she got out her woollen jerseys and her winter coat, she tried not to think about the night she and Dent had spent together with Mickey and William and Violet and how everyone said, Oh, you are with Alexander.

She tried not to remember standing in the snow with Nora and talking about Paris.

She tried as hard as she could, but she remembered everything as if it were yesterday, and she didn't know if she could bear it.

There was work: work was what would pull her through. Work was the thing, after all, that lasted. Love was a mirage, some outdated notion of redemption. No one believed in love any more, not these days, not with the soaring divorce rates.

She finished the polar explorer. She put all her heart and her thwarted passion and her fury into it, and there was something of her younger self in it, something of the way she had written about Rita Lane, all those years ago.

The publishers were pleased, and the explorer wrote her a restrained and elegant letter, thanking her, and although it was barely a page of short English sentences, it gave her frozen heart a small glow, just for a moment, as if some ray of sun had broken through the frost.

She went to lunch with Joan Bellow, as if everything was normal. She sat and ate food and talked sense and took another commission, for more money.

'I want work,' she said. 'I'll do this one and I'd like to go straight on to something after that.'

'You deserve a holiday,' said Joan. 'Why don't you go away somewhere?'

'I need to work,' said Maude. 'Work is what I want just now. So give me anything you have.'

*　　*　　*

Mr Seth said that globalisation was gathering pace so fast that soon the whole world would be covered in fast-food outlets and flashing neon signs and there would be no wild places left and in twenty years no one would remember what real food tasted like.

'We will all eat poison and die of tumours that they don't have a name for,' he said, in gloomy satisfaction. 'The only person who is fighting it is one farmer in France and he is nearly dead with age and despair.'

In the bookshop, the old spinster remained silent and impassive, and Maude thought it wouldn't be long before she herself was just like that. She wondered, with bitter irony, whether she should offer to take over the lease when the bookshop woman reached retirement age.

Sadie kept away, as if everything that there was to say had been said. Maude had wondered if Sadie would fight for her, in the way she hoped Dent might. When nothing happened, no call or visit, Maude thought that it showed their fledgling friendship was of no importance to Sadie, that she had shrugged it off her shoulders and moved on, forgetting that anyone called Maude had ever existed.

Some days Maude felt that she *had* never existed, as if the pathetic attempt at life she had made was being erased from the record, like in science-fiction films about parallel universes and time warps. She imagined that people were looking through her in the street, seeing only a space where there should have been a human being.

19

Christmas came on, inexorable. Maude tried to pretend that there was nothing happening. But even Mr Seth had the shop smelling of cloves and oranges, and a cluster of red paper stars with small lights inside glowed over his head as he doled out newspapers and the latest information on the end of the world.

Maude felt as if there was an elastic band holding her head together and she wondered when it was going to snap.

Two days before Christmas, there was a loud banging at her door. The afternoon was dark as pitch, as if someone had forgotten to turn on the street lamps, and when Maude opened the door and saw three dim figures singing 'The Holly and the Ivy' she thought that they were drunken strangers, playing games in the street.

Then Sadie said, 'Now you have to invite us in for cake and cherry brandy,' and even though Maude was tight back in her isolation bubble, hermetically sealed from anything that anyone might call living, she found herself laughing with a shock as intense as if someone had thrown cold water over her. She couldn't help it. Sadie had always been able to do that to her, right from the start.

Sadie was wearing a red Father Christmas hat edged

with white fur, and behind her were Ruby and Dean. Sadie dragged off the preposterous hat and pulled Maude towards her and held on to her for a moment. 'I'm sorry,' she said into Maude's ear. 'I am sorry. I am.'

Then she stood back and she was Sadie again, the fearless laughing woman who had so impressed Maude the first time they met, and she said: 'Come on then, break open the bubbly.'

'I didn't know how else to apologise,' she said a while later, when they were sitting in Maude's front room with glasses of whisky because that was all Maude had. 'After I said all those terrible things. I was so angry I didn't know what I was saying, and then I didn't know how to repair it. It was Dean who came up with the idea. It was Dean who said I should apologise, he said that there was never anyone so kind to him as you when his heart was broken and it wasn't for me to go judging people all over the shop. He said that I should remember about Nick Carraway's father, who said when you get to judging people just remember not everyone has the same advantages that you do.'

Dean watched Sadie as she said this; she was talking fast, as if she wasn't used to finding herself in this position and wasn't sure how it was done. Maude saw him watching and knew without any shadow of doubt that he loved Sadie more than he would ever love anyone else. She remembered how Dent used to look at her like that and she had to close her eyes for a moment, to stop herself growing giddy with it and falling off her chair on to the floor and making a scene.

'Everyone gets too cross with everyone,' said Dean. 'Everyone is always going off about something, bruised pride or mistaken pique, and I think life is too short, and we're none of us angels, and you can call me old-fash-ioned.'

'We can,' said Ruby, her face falling into a smile. 'But we won't.'

For a while, Maude remembered what it was like, when she had caught a glimpse of life again, after all those years of silence. It was so alluring, tempting her: but the voices were back with her now, yelling in her head, telling her that what had happened had happened for a reason and this time there was no going back.

She suddenly realised that something was missing; something was different. 'Where's Pearl?' she said.

'She got a job in Tasmania and never came home,' said Dean. 'We'll find her on our doorstep in three years' time with a laughing husband and four brown babies. It's the kind of thing she does.'

Maude wondered what it would be like to have that facility.

They left after midnight, rather drunk.

'I can't tell you to do anything,' said Sadie, 'because it is your life and none of my business, but if you ever decide that you are not going to lock yourself away for ever, if you ever think about changing your mind and going back, you are going to have to do it. He won't. I know that much. He has more pride than anyone I ever met and he won't know how. If you want your life to change you have to do it; it's your destiny and you have to want it and act on it. So don't sit there wishing, if you are wishing, and I know I shouldn't have said even that much, so now shoot me.'

'It's all right,' said Maude. 'You can say anything,

because you came round and stood on my step and sang carols and no one ever did that for me before.'

'Well, you see,' said Sadie, although she never said what there was to see. She kissed Maude on both cheeks, said, 'Don't be a stranger,' linked arms with Dean on one side and Ruby on the other and walked steadily up the steps and into the street. Maude went back inside and sat all night in the kitchen watching the light change because she couldn't sleep at all.

She couldn't sleep the night after that, and the one after that. She couldn't sleep on Christmas Eve or Christmas night or the night of Boxing Day. She walked around the flat in a half-light trance, not knowing what was actual and what was not. When you are that tired, you can't think about anything, you just have to concentrate on the small trudging motions of getting your body through the day. Maude wondered whether her subconscious was being very clever, forcing her to stay awake so she couldn't think about what Sadie had said.

On one of the long nights, when she couldn't sleep, couldn't even bear the comfort of her bed because it reminded her too poignantly of lying close and still with Dent, she sat in her dark room and watched the television, staring mindlessly at the screen, barely taking in the flickering pictures that came and went.

An old film came on and it was the one in which Rita Lane made her comeback, all those years ago. The young director who had called her up and given her a part had become rather famous, always running around at the Oscars and picking up prizes at Cannes, and they were doing a retrospective. It was a raw and urgent film, shot in bright singing colours, the kind of film that you can only make when you are young and dauntless and you have not one single thing to lose.

Maude watched Rita and remembered the days when they had sat together in the dusty aquamarine room in Hans Crescent; she remembered Rita's defiance and spirit. She wondered where Rita was now. Perhaps she had gone to live in a palace in Bel Air, now she was a success again, now she was fêted and sought after, now she had been reinstated as a grand old dame of the silver screen.

All that was before her, in this picture; this was back in the days when she had reached the end of the line. Her character was flat broke and busted, a busted flush, and Rita played it straight and without any flashy eye-catching tricks and it broke your heart to watch her. 'No one said it was going to be easy,' she said, diving into another bottle and watching herself sink or swim. 'No one said it was going to be a hay-ride. But you can make it into a carnival, some nights, if the light is coming from the right direction.'

Three days after Christmas Maude called a taxi and drove to the street in north London where the mother of the child she had killed lived.

Maude didn't know if she would still be there, it was eleven years ago now, and no one ever seemed to live in the same place for any length of time any more. But she went anyway, because she knew that she should have done this years before, and now it seemed as if she was facing a blank wall, and it was time to see if there was a way round, or whether she just had to go back the way she had come. It was time, she knew, to do something, to take action, because she had been sitting in her room for too long.

She was still stunned from misery and bafflement and lack of sleep. She got into the taxi and gave the address before she could think better of it.

The taxi driver was short and middle-aged and silent. Maude watched his round bald head in front of her; she was glad that he didn't want to talk.

They drove through the empty streets and everything was quiet and still, as London always was over the Christmas holiday, as if someone had paused the city for a moment, turned down the volume. The trees were bare against a dun sky and there was no one on the pavements and no sign that anything remarkable had ever happened here.

They turned into a small terraced street, neat red-brick houses with white painted lintels and window boxes with some brave winter-flowering roses. It was a quiet re-spectable street, where people lived good expected lives.

Maude paid off the cab and knocked on the door and wondered if there would be anyone at home; the mother opened the door without hesitation. Maude recognised her instantly, even though it was eleven years. Mrs Patricia Burns, just the same as she had been in the dull courtroom, except now her eyes were not wild and swollen with crying and fury. She was neat and pretty, and something else, Maude thought: contained some-how, clearly delineated. Her brown hair was pulled back from her face, and there was colour in her cheeks, as if she was healthy and contented.

It took her a moment. She frowned and opened her mouth to say something and then stopped and looked again, and said, 'Oh, my goodness.'

'I'm sorry,' said Maude, pushing the words out fast before she lost her nerve. 'I'm sorry to turn up like this, but I very much wanted to talk to you. Is that all right? I can go away if you would rather. Do you remember who I am?'

Patricia Burns nodded. For a fleeting moment she looked distressed, and then she smiled and said, 'Of course, come in.'

The house was as neat and shining as she was. It was warm and the walls were painted white and there were pictures everywhere and yellow lamps lighting up the raw day.

'Come into the kitchen,' said Patricia Burns. 'Come and sit and I'll make us a cup of tea. You came at a good time, the rest of the family have gone to the park, so it's just me here. It's Maude, isn't it?'

Maude nodded miserably, wishing it wasn't, wishing it was anyone else.

'Sit down,' said Patricia Burns, holding out a chair round the kitchen table. 'I'm Pat. Well, you probably remember.'

She made the tea, in a celadon green pot that looked as if it came from China. She set the tea things down on the table, milk in a delicate jug and sugar in a blue bowl and cups and saucers, and then she sat down opposite Maude and looked at her.

It was eleven years and she was the same but she was also completely different. The wild grief that Maude remembered so well was gone, but it was more than that. She looked as if she had made a pact with life, seen that it was not all it had promised, and shaken hands, sealed the bargain, and never gone back on it.

Maude thought she shouldn't have come. She had had

no sleep for the last week and she felt an incipient madness in her, growing like a sickness. She remembered that the Japanese had used sleep deprivation as a favourite torture, the quickest way to break down brave and resourceful men and get them to spill all their secrets.

Mrs Patricia Burns looked at Maude and then she said the most unexpected thing.

'Oh, duck,' she said, and Maude shook her head in surprise at the endearment, 'you look terrible. What happened to you?'

No no, thought Maude, this is supposed to be the other way round. The terrible thing happened to *you*, and I did it.

'I came here,' said Maude. She stopped, not knowing how to say it. What was the point, all these years later? Why had she never come before? Why had she been such a filthy coward, hiding in her room all that time, when she should have been here, making amends? 'I came,' she said, 'because I wanted to say . . . to say . . . I wanted to tell you how very sorry I am. I'm so very, very sorry. I wanted to tell you that.'

It was just words, she thought, and they didn't count for very much. They didn't count for anything at all. She thought that Patricia Burns had every right to turn her out into the street, to hound her out of town.

'You poor thing,' said Patricia Burns, slowly. She gave Maude a smile of blinding sympathy. Maude had to turn her head away. 'Is that why you look like this, after all these years? You've been carrying that with you, all this time, and now you look as if you have two black eyes from worry and shoulders with all the care of the world on them.'

Later, Maude wondered that she should speak this

way; she realised that the picture she had carried in her head for so long of an embittered, ruined, inarticulate woman was like a myth, something that perhaps had never existed.

'It was such a long time ago,' said Patricia Burns. 'And you have to move on with life, otherwise it is gone and you have only regrets.'

'How do you do that?' said Maude. 'I did this terrible thing to you, and you are offering me tea.'

Patricia Burns smiled. Maude saw then that there was still sadness in her face, and perhaps there always would be. But there were other things as well, there was room for other things.

'It was terrible,' said Patricia. 'Oh, it was terrible, and I don't forget it. I never forget David, I think of him every day. But it wasn't your fault.'

'Yes,' said Maude. 'Yes, it was. It was my fault.'

'It was an accident,' said Patricia. 'That is what it was. Everyone wants someone to blame, when the worst thing happens. I wanted to blame you, once, I wanted very much to blame you. Then I blamed myself. I was so young, and I was unsettled in those days, I didn't look out for him as much as I should have done. I was arguing with his father and that took up all my time. And then I realised that blaming everyone wasn't going to bring him back. All I knew was that he was gone and I could sit and hate the world or I could get up and go on.'

'No,' said Maude, and the word was shaken out of her with a horrible sharp sound. She stopped and shook her head and tried again. 'I mean,' she said. 'It's never that simple.'

'Oh, but it is simple,' said Patricia Burns. 'Yes, yes, it is.

It is also the hardest thing you ever have to do. It's not complicated, but it is hard.'

'I don't understand,' said Maude. She meant – not just this, but everything. Patricia Burns seemed to see that. She leant across the table and put her hand over Maude's. Her hand was warm and strong and dry and Maude felt it and wanted to cry.

'You can live,' Patricia said. Her clear straight eyes looked right at Maude, as if she minded. 'Just because one person dies doesn't mean everyone has to. It's not an eye for an eye.'

'Because then the whole world is blind,' said Maude, and she thought of Dent and wondered if that was what she was doing now: blinding the world.

'Yes,' said Patricia. 'Sometimes the worst thing happens, the worst thing you can ever imagine. I think that losing a child is one of the worst things, perhaps the worst thing that you can ever face. You don't think you will ever recover from it; you think you will have to drag your broken body around like a deformed thing for the rest of your life. But you can do it, you can put the pieces back together, if you try hard enough. I have a family now, I have two more children and I am still with David's father, and we don't fight any more because we discovered that you can only get through something like that if you have love, so that's what we held on to, like a life raft.'

'You can't be so sane,' said Maude, in a kind of wonder. She felt humbled; she felt ashamed, because she hadn't managed to find that kind of reason herself. 'No one is that rational and strong.'

'It doesn't feel like that,' said Patricia, smiling a little. 'It was a choice, that's all, live or die. There will always

be a small part of me that is missing, it's like a – like a—'
She stopped and patted her hand against her heart and
smiled again her good smile. 'It's like a gap inside; but it's
not fatal. It's a space, and I learnt to carry that within me,
and that's bearable.'

She sat back in her chair and looked at Maude with her
clear eyes. There were small lines of pain around them,
but there were laughter lines also, and lines from looking
into the light: lines from other things.

'You are young still,' she said. 'What are you, in your
thirties? All that life you have in front of you. You should
go out and not waste that. Because otherwise there are
two deaths instead of only one. Oh, duck,' she said, 'go
out and make something of your life, because if you don't
then it's all too much waste, and what good does that
ever do?'

After she left, and took the bus home, Maude thought
that all those years in the shrink's office, not so far from
this ordinary street, much the same things had been said
to her and she couldn't hear them and they didn't make
any sense. After she heard Patricia Burns say them,
Maude felt as if she had been trying to unlock a padlock
with the wrong key, so that the mechanism jammed and
snarled up, and now someone had given her the right
key, and she could feel it slide into the lock, the teeth
catching smooth and sure and the tumblers falling open
like silk.

After she left, looking back over her shoulder so she
could see Patricia Burns standing in the doorway with
her hand raised in goodbye, like a final salute, after she
walked away past the tidy red houses with their square
windows and their lovingly tended boxes full of growing

plants, she wondered what she was going to do, now the lock had fallen open and there was no excuse any more.

When she got home, she felt that she had been away for weeks, on a long journey, to a country where she didn't know the customs or the language; she felt the small shock of adjustment you get when you come back home after a long time abroad. It was as if some great burden had been lifted off her, and for the first time in a week she got into her hard square bed and slept for twelve hours without waking.

When she woke it was another day and she wasn't sure what time it was. She sat up and looked at her clock and it was just after eight and she knew she had to get up and get back into the world. She knew also, in some uncertain way, that everything had changed one more time and she wasn't sure what to do about that.

She got up and brushed her teeth and dressed and ate a piece of toast and then there was just the day, waiting for her.

She didn't know quite what to do with it and she felt restless and uncertain. She thought this should feel cinematic and monumental, but there was a gap now, something unknown that needed to be bridged, and it would take her time to get used to it.

She sat for a long time in the still dim light of her basement room; the world rolled away and came back to her, fragments of the past moving through her mind like oil on water. She saw, as clearly as if someone had opened her life in front of her like a map, that she had always hidden, trapped by fear – of what? – her own inadequacy, the sense she had of being insubstantial, invisible, not having the right stuff. She had never questioned the life she chose after the accident: she thought now that it was all of a piece. Why didn't I fight? she thought. She saw now that her fury with Dent for not fighting for her was really fury at herself, because she had never once fought for her own life.

I have to learn to do that, she thought, otherwise nothing is worth anything. I have to get out and fight.

This idea was so new and vast that it pinned her to her seat, and she stayed sitting in her dark room for five hours, still and trapped as the light died around her.

I have to go back, she thought. I have to get into my car and go and give it another shot. Maybe it won't work and maybe it is too late, but I have to give it a chance. But she also knew that she needed a moment, a pause, to turn herself round.

It's Thursday, she thought. It's a Thursday in the middle of winter and I shall go on Sunday, because Sunday was the day I went before and Sunday was the day I came back; Sunday is the time to do it.

She felt light with relief and decision when she came to the end of this thinking. I need a rest, she thought; I need a rest from all these voices in my head. She looked at her watch, ticking away the seconds of her life. It was after five; it was five past five on a Thursday afternoon in January and all the lights were on.

She walked up to the bookshop. She would buy a book. She would buy a book and go home with it and make a pot of coffee on the stove and drink it and read the book and after that she would sleep and then she would wake up and it would be another day, it would be her new life with her new resolution in it, and it wouldn't feel so strange.

The bookshop woman was smiling when Maude walked into the shop. Maude had to look twice, in case it was a trick of the light. The bookshop woman, who had never said more to Maude than, That will be twelve pounds, and Thank you, and Here is your change, looked straight at her and said: 'There is a new book by Alexander Dent just in and you should buy it because it's the most moving thing I've ever read in my life.'

The book was called *All The Lonely People*. It had a black and white photograph on the cover of a woman's face in silhouette and inside the dedication read: To Maude.

It was only a hundred and fifty pages long, and it was unlike anything Dent had ever done. It was unlike his early work and it was nothing like the four books that Richard Hunter had written for him. Maude knew, reading it, knowing Dent as she did, that it was his work, because it was like hearing him speak, when he talked to her in the closed darkness of the bedroom they had shared together. It was the night talk, that he saved only for her.

It read like a prose poem. It was, in one hundred and fifty dense, lyrical pages, a declaration of love.

Maude read it fast and everything fell away from her like a veil and she felt very simple and very certain and as if nothing that had come before mattered. She felt shriven and new, as if the old skin had come off and left something clean and strong underneath.

It was as if this had come along on the very day that she had made her resolve to go back and find him, like a sign; another small shooting star of fate, telling her that she was right, that she could do this. She remembered what Sadie said and what Patricia Burns said and she knew they were right. She remembered how Sadie said that Dent had more pride than anyone she had ever known.

Maude had thought he would never fight for her and now he had in the only way he knew. It was as if this was confirmation that she had to do the last part, as if it had made her resolution real; but there was still a small remnant of the old life, a distant echo of the old voices, muted now, as if they were walking away down a long track, but still just audible, that was frightened. She knew that if she did this, there were no more excuses; there was no more hiding and no more running.

She thought: I can stay here and be frightened and end up silent and bitter with only regrets for company; or I can fight.

At that moment the telephone rang. It was a shocking sound in the silent room, shattering the quiet like a fire alarm. Maude thought it must be Dent and she picked up the receiver in delight and pressed it to her ear.

'Turn on the television,' said Ruby. 'BBC 2.'

'I don't,' said Maude, confused.

'Just turn it on,' said Ruby.

Maude turned on the television, and there was a blue studio and a long desk and a contained female presenter who covered the arts for the BBC. She was called Paula Stein and she was famous for her perfect hair and ruthless intellect. Sitting opposite her, dressed in a black suit and a white shirt, was Dent.

Maude caught her breath, seeing his familiar loved face, flattened by the studio lights. She had no idea what was going on. Paula Stein was starting with some preamble, and there was a banging at the door, and it was Ruby and Sadie.

'Have you got it on?' said Sadie.

'Yes,' said Maude, and they walked fast back into the room and sat down and Maude clicked at the remote to turn up the sound, and Dent said: 'Yes, it is true that the last four books were not my work.'

Maude felt the breath pulled out of her.

'Jesus God,' said Sadie. 'They're going to crucify him.'

Paula Stein leant in, her face pitiless and hard.

'So you mean to say that the books that came out under your name were not actually written by you?'

'Yes,' said Dent. 'That is what I am saying.'

'You have,' said Paula Stein, 'been defrauding the reading public.'

'That bitch,' said Sadie. 'I bet she never gets laid.'

Dent said: 'You could say that. I have no excuse for it at all. There is a complicated set of circumstances, but I make no special pleading.'

Paula Stein, clearly used to yards of special pleading, looked slightly discomposed. 'Who did write them?' she said.

'I can't tell you that,' said Dent. 'My own privacy is my business, but I can't invade that of someone else.'

'Is this why you refused the Booker three years ago?' said Paula Stein.

'Yes,' said Dent.

'And do you think that there is any explanation for this that might make any sense at all?' said Paula Stein. 'This is unprecedented.'

'Oh, she's enjoying this,' said Sadie. 'Look at her face. She's loving it.'

Dent said: 'I can tell you what happened, but then it is

301

up to people to decide what they want to think. I can't tell them that.'

'So could you tell us what happened?' said Paula Stein. Dent took a deep breath.

Oh, God, thought Maude; this is the hardest thing for him, of all people, the man who guards himself so jealously from the world.

'After my wife died,' Dent said, 'I found I was unable to write. It had been the central thing in my life and I couldn't do it any more. I met a man who had also been a victim, if you like, of circumstance. He was a writer, but he was obsessively private and alarmed by the idea of exposing himself to the world. He knew my books very well, and he wrote in the same vein. We talked a great deal, and he showed me his work, and in the end he asked me, since I couldn't write any more, if he could put his work out under the umbrella of my name. It sounds grotesque and fraudulent, saying it now, but there were many reasons why it made sense at the time. When your world is turned upside down, the fantastic makes more sense than the probable. I was living with a deep guilt about what happened to my wife, and I felt that in some way I could help this man, by offering him something he wanted, so I said yes.'

Paula Stein seemed taken aback. 'So you are saying it was an act of philanthropy?' she said.

'I wouldn't put it as grandly as that,' said Dent. 'It was an offering, that was all.'

'And why would you want to reveal this now,' said Paula Stein, 'when you are notorious for never talking to the press?'

'Something happened,' said Dent, and then he faltered and Maude found herself clenching her fists so hard that her nails dug into her palms and she looked down to see what the pain was. Dent got himself back and took a breath and started again. 'Things changed,' he said. 'There were . . . circumstances. I started writing again. I wanted to get the slate cleaned.'

'Even though you must know that this might be the end of your career?' said Paula Stein.

'I have to take that risk,' said Dent.

'And this new book,' said Paula Stein, brandishing it at him like a protest, 'is all your own work?'

'That is all my own work,' said Dent. He paused, and then he said: 'I'm not asking for anything, I'm not making any excuses. I think that people must judge the last four books on their own merits, and decide if they have intrinsic value as works of art in their own right, regardless of who wrote them. If anything good can come of this, then it might be that people realise how much they invest in a name, rather than the words on the page. Perhaps it might make people think about fame and branding and expectation. But I don't say that will be the case, and I don't say that it lets me in any way off the hook. I am culpable, and I must take what is coming to me.'

The steam went out of Paula Stein then, she deflated like a pricked balloon, turned fast to the camera and said: 'That's all now from our Edinburgh studio; we go back to Stanley in London.'

She turned back to Dent and said: 'Alexander Dent, thank you. Can I ask, before we go, what you are going to do now?'

Dent smiled for the first time, a tired translucent smile. 'I'm going home,' he said.

Maude and Ruby and Sadie watched in silence as the

programme shifted back to a panel of metropolitan talking heads. All the food groups were represented. The maverick talking head was roaring with laughter and saying it was the most post-modern thing imaginable and that it would set the insular literary establishment on its ear and bloody good thing too. The purist head was white and righteous with indignation and held forth about the good old days of Shakespeare, when a man knew where he stood in the world of letters, until he remembered that there were slight question marks about Bacon and the Earl of Oxford and trailed off into bluster. The liberal talking head perched uncomfortably on the fence and saw both sides. The anchor made a provocative point about best-selling writers whose editors were rumoured to do more than a little work with the red pencil, then abruptly changed the subject, as if his producer was yelling into his earpiece about possible litigation. Everyone used the word integrity more than once.

'Oh,' said Sadie. 'Think what the papers will do.'

Ruby started to laugh. 'No, no,' she said. 'He will survive it. People will read this new book and realise it is the real thing and next week there will be another scandal.'

'They never forget,' said Sadie darkly. 'They are like packs of mean old elephants gathered round a waterhole.'

'It's my fault,' said Maude.

'No,' said Sadie. 'It's not your fault.'

'He didn't have to do this,' said Maude. 'I was going to go back anyway; I was thinking about it all afternoon. Then I went and found the book in the shop and it was like a sign, and I was going to go back.'

Sadie leant over and took her hand, and said: 'Maybe

he didn't do it just for you. Maybe he needed to tell the truth too. Perhaps he was in a Dr Faustus pact with Richard Hunter, who knows. Perhaps he knew that if he ever started writing again, Richard had the whip hand over him, and might blackmail him with the secret. Now it's out and it's told, and there is no more power in it. That's what telling the truth does.'

Maude thought of how she had felt when she told her secret to Dent and later to Ruby, and she knew that what Sadie said was true.

'Yes,' she said. 'Yes, you're right. You are.'

Sadie looked at her again, and there were twenty different messages in her eyes and she said: 'Are you going to tell me the truth?'

Maude looked over at Ruby and said, 'You didn't tell her?'

Ruby shook her head. 'Not my remit,' she said. 'It's your story.'

Maude told Sadie. She told her everything, right up to the part about going back to see Patricia Burns, and when it was finished Sadie smiled at her and said, 'There you are, you see, you are both free now, and that's worth more than anything. Not that it may ever be easy or plain sailing, but the way is clear.'

Ruby and Sadie didn't ask any more questions then, as if enough had been said, and after a while they stood up and left. They parted from Maude easily, without declaration or meaning, although they all knew that something significant had happened between them.

After they had gone, Maude sat in her room and let the events of the day settle about her. She could hardly remember that morning, it seemed so long ago. She sat in the darkness, so familiar to her, so known and remembered, and she thought about everything that had happened, and she knew that she could not wait until Sunday, that she didn't need any more time, that she didn't need anything else at all.

She packed up a bag and went out into the street. The night was dark and empty, the traffic moving in a glittering stream along the Talgarth Road, the street lamps gleaming like beacons over the slick pavements. It was just before nine. She got into her car and drove out to the west.

She remembered the road, even in the dark, and for long stretches it was just her, with no other car in sight. She felt as if her headlights were cleaving the night apart, as one might open up a story book. She felt as if the looming shadows of the country were not there at all until the lights of her car conjured them into existence.

She played the sad songs she liked best all the way, eight hours of sad songs, but she didn't feel sad. She felt something that she didn't have a word for.

When she swung off the road on to the long stony track that led to Dent's house it was five in the morning. The sky was black and pitch and studded with stars. She had forgotten about the stars.

She opened the front door, which was never locked, and when she walked in she saw Dent sitting on the red sofa. Her body was still humming from the road and her head was light with it and she wondered for a moment if she were seeing ghosts.

Then he said: 'I couldn't sleep.'

She stood in the doorway, looking at him, and she said, 'I couldn't sleep either.'

His face was thin and seamed with tiredness and his eyes were dark in their sockets and she knew that she had never loved anything in her life like she loved him. She felt still and calm with it, as if a stone had fallen into a deep pool. She felt certain and she knew that this time she would never go south again.

She said, 'I couldn't sleep so I drove instead.'

He looked at her and for a moment they were both still, like statues in the dim light.

'I read your book,' she said. 'I read it. You must have written it very fast.'

'I wrote it fast,' he said, 'and I bullied them to publish it fast, because I was lost without you and I didn't know how else to ask you to come back.'

'I'm sorry,' Maude said.

'No, I am sorry,' said Dent. 'I should have told you and I didn't know how because I felt ashamed. I didn't want you to think less of me and I didn't want to lose you.'

'We don't have to talk about this now,' said Maude. 'We can talk about it later. We can talk about it tomorrow or next week or next year or not at all.'

Dent started to smile; a light came into his eyes as if he hadn't been sure that this was really happening but now he had proof.

'Yes,' he said. 'Whenever you like.'

'It was a beautiful book,' Maude said. 'None of the rest of it matters now. It was the most beautiful book I ever read.'

'I wrote it for you,' Dent said.

Maude walked across the room and sat down beside him on the scarlet sofa and he put his hand out so that she could lean against his shoulder and feel his arm close around her. She put her hand up to his cheek and drew his face against hers and she smelt the smell of him, of salt and water and the sea, and she turned her head and kissed him and he kissed her back and this time it was as if she was coming home.

'I wrote it because of you,' he said.

They didn't say anything else. They sat on the sofa, silent, breathing in time, in the last small hours of the night, waiting for the dawn to break.